Maybury Place

KEITHA SMITH

Other books by Keitha Smith

The Bell Curve

The Tender Conflict

The Journey

Non-fiction work :

Mothering Heights
by Keitha Smith & Susan Brereton

PUBLISHED BY JUDSON PRESS

Maybury Place

Maybury Place

Copyright © 2014 by Keitha Smith

First Printed : September 2014

Published by : Blue Sky Creative Ltd

Book layout and cover designed by Paul Smith

A catalogue record for this book is available from the National Library of New Zealand.

ISBN : 978-0-473-29427-4

In memory of my
fabulous father, Ross, and
my incomparable in-laws,
Rita and Arthur,
all sadly missed.

*"For what do we live, but
to make sport for our neighbours,
and laugh at them in our turn?"*

- Mr. Bennet, Pride and Prejudice

CHAPTER ONE

As the three o'clock newsreader told Joan Davis about the current disasters of the day an insistent peeping cut across the announcer's report. The piercing sound made Joan forget the problems of the world's economy and its implication on the price of housing. As her head swiveled toward the window a second sound joined the first: the throbbing of a large engine.

"Well, Jess," Joan said as she whisked the dozing cat off her lap, "what do you suppose is happening?"

Jess, aggrieved at being ousted from her comfortable position, was not about to take any notice of matters outside.

Joan, on the other hand, could not suppress her interest. She pushed aside the film of her net curtains. Sure enough, there, in the middle of Maybury Place, a large truck reversed down the length of the small street. Joan watched as a strapping young man waved to the driver to continue on his present course.

"'Elite Removals'," Joan read out. "'All care *and* responsibility.' I suppose they must be moving furniture into Number Seven. But where are the new owners?"

Joan could see the young man yell something to the driver above the noise of the engine.

"Monday seems a funny day to be moving in, doesn't it?" Joan said, glancing over at Jess as though expecting an answer.

Getting not so much as the stir of a whisker, Joan made an impatient sound.

"What am I talking to you for?" she asked, and headed straight for the phone.

At Number Six, Maybury Place, Lisa McLean sat on the couch in the lounge with her feet up on the coffee table. She'd been attempting to work on her cross-stitch all afternoon, threads and patterns draped over every available space, the work itself balanced precariously on her ever-expanding stomach. Progress had been hampered by the telephone that now rang again, for the fifth time in two hours.

Lisa rolled her eyes, set the work aside, and heaved herself to a standing position. She went across to the low table under the window and snatched up the receiver.

"Hello?"

"Lisa? It's Joan here. From across the road."

"Of course," Lisa said, knowing full well who Joan was. "How are you?"

"Fine, thank you. Yourself? Everything all right with the baby?"

Lisa looked down at her stomach. "The little tyrant is already keeping me up at night, but apart from that all seems to be going well, especially now I've finished work."

"I hope I didn't wake you," Joan said.

Lisa stifled a sigh. "No, don't worry."

"It's just that I wondered if you'd seen what was going on outside."

Lisa peered out into Maybury Place. From the spot in the lounge where she stood she could get a reasonable view of the street over the top of a scattering of camellia bushes and the hedge in the front garden.

"It's a moving van," Joan said, her voice full of childlike enthusiasm. "It seems we are to have new residents at Number Seven at last."

"I suppose it had to happen at some point," Lisa said. "After all it must be at least two months since the Marshalls sold and moved away."

"Try three. It was well before Christmas when they left."

"I suppose I should have remembered," Lisa said, eyeing her stomach again. At the moment her whole life seemed to be measured by the passing of days. Each week was ticked off and accounted for as though she was some sort of time bomb waiting to explode. She'd reached the point where time had taken its own dimension, with the weeks both crawling by and yet disappearing like morning mist.

Joan said, "Never mind, dear. It isn't as though you haven't got other things on your mind. How long to go now?"

"Seven weeks."

"Not long at all. I guess the new neighbors will be settled by then."

"I should imagine so," Lisa said.

She watched the removal men wrestle with a solid wooden bookcase, its cumbersome weight making it difficult to maneuver. She felt sorry for the man who had to walk backward with it, even though he managed it with practiced ease.

"Any sign of the owners?" Joan asked.

"None. Perhaps they're still cleaning up at their last house."

As if on cue a small green sports car sped up the street, braked, edged around the removal van and shot down the driveway to pull up in front of the small shed at the back of the property.

"What can you see?" Joan asked. "The truck is blocking my view."

Lisa looked. Her vision of the car was on the verge of being obscured by the growing row of young lacebarks planted to divide the house at Number Seven from the neighbors at Number Eight. A few moments later the occupant emerged from the car and went to speak with the removal men.

"It's a woman," Lisa reported.

"What does she look like? Does she look nice?"

Lisa watched as the woman talked with the two men. Her hands moved with nervous energy as her gestures accompanied her instructions.

"It's hard to say. She's wearing dark glasses, and her head is covered by some sort of scarf."

"A scarf? It's a bit warm for a scarf, wouldn't you say? Is she Muslim do you think?"

"I don't think it's that sort of scarf. She looks very elegant. Kind of like a movie star."

"A movie star? What would a movie star be doing buying a house in our street?"

"I don't know," Lisa said. She was beginning to lose the will to live. "She's probably nothing of the sort. In any case I can't really tell what she looks like."

"On account of the glasses and scarf? Well who knows? Maybe she's got something to hide."

"Oh, there's someone else," Lisa said, watching a second figure join the woman. "It's a boy."

"A boy?" Joan was agog. "What kind of a boy?"

"Just a boy. Quite normal looking."

"How old?"

"I'm not terribly good at children's ages. About seven or eight?"

The boy stood close to the woman in a way that suggested deep familiarity. He had jet-black hair, and wore on his face an expression of evident boredom. As if to emphasize this he kicked at a few tiny stones on the driveway, scuffing his shoes back and forth.

Suddenly, the interview between the woman and the two men was over. In an attempt at maternal protection the woman draped her arm over the stiff shoulders of the boy as she led him off toward the house.

"Now what's happening?"

"They're going inside."

"Oh."

"Nothing more to report, I'm afraid," Lisa said.

"No sign of anyone else? A husband?"

"No. Just the movers."

"Oh well. I suppose we'll see more of them in due course. It all seems a bit mysterious to me. I can't help wondering about the delay. It seems so odd that a person would buy a house and wait all that time to move in."

"I suppose it does," Lisa agreed, winding the telephone cord around her fingers. "Who knows? Maybe you'll soon find out about that too."

"Maybe. When will Roger be home?"

"Five, five-thirty. Somewhere around there."

And the first thing she intended to say to him when he walked through the door was that she would go out tomorrow and buy them a cordless phone.

"I'm hungry," Matthew said to his mother.

His mother appeared not to have heard him. She had her attention fixed on wrestling his baby sister's legs back into her outfit, her mouth set in a grim, determined line.

"I'm hungry," Matthew said again. He said it louder this time, over the noise of the crying baby.

"Yes, yes," his mother said. "I'm afraid that until I've finished changing Rose's diaper, you're going to have to wait."

Matthew sagged. He'd heard that one before. It seemed like Rose was always doing something that needed his mother's attention. She'd either made a disgusting smell, or had thrown up, was wailing with hunger or was just plain old grumpy.

"Come on then, Rose darling," his mother said, lifting the still screaming bundle into her arms. "Let Mummy just wash her hands and then you can have your feed."

"What about me?" Matthew asked, trailing into the bathroom in her wake.

His mother laughed. "You're a bit old for a feed," she said.

Matthew recoiled. "No, I mean I want something to eat."

Not to be outdone, Rose's wailing went up another decibel.

"In a minute Matthew."

"But Mum!"

"In a minute, I said," his mother snapped. Then she softened. "I won't be long, I promise. What say I put a DVD on for you while I go and feed Rose? She'll be going for a sleep after that and then I can get you some afternoon tea."

"S'pose."

"Good boy."

Matthew followed his mother into the lounge where she clicked a disc out of its box with her free hand, then posted it into the player. All the while Rose continued her howling.

"Back in minute," said his mother, passing him the remote.

Matthew hoisted himself up onto the couch and got ready for the program.

"Not *Barney*!"

Matthew's disappointment was immense. Didn't his mother realize that boys of four and a half did not watch *Barney* any longer? Nobody he knew at kindergarten watched such babyish stuff.

He tried to make the program more interesting by hanging upside down but that seemed to make him feel hungrier. He longed to change the disc, to put on something more interesting, but his dad would be furious if he knew Matthew had been playing with the DVD player. Better yet would be if he could watch something really cool, like *Ben 10*, but that wasn't allowed either.

Matthew became aware of a commotion outside. When he went over to the window he saw, at the end of the street, an enormous truck. Beside the truck stood a man who was shouting to someone else that Matthew couldn't see.

Temptation overwhelmed Matthew. He wanted a closer look at the action. The more Matthew thought about it, the more it seemed to him that there was no harm in going out for a better view. Besides, if he only went for a minute or two he could be back before his mother realized he'd been gone.

"I'm going," he announced to Barney.

He let himself out of the back door. The warm afternoon sun shone on his face, so he ran back inside to find his hat, figuring that he probably shouldn't break too many rules all at once. He then collected the shiny red trike that he'd been given for Christmas, and set off down the driveway.

Matthew paused by the letterbox and surveyed the short length of Maybury Place. None of the neighbors seemed to be around. Nobody to tell him off apart from the two men, but they were so busy Matthew thought they might not notice him. He set off toward them, pedaling with unhurried circles.

This was a journey Matthew had undertaken many times since Christmas, although always with his mother or father. He liked the street where he lived and could say with pride, "My name is Matthew Fleming and I live at Number One, Maybury Place." He'd learnt this just in case he got lost, and he knew his telephone number too. He knew that there were only eight houses in his street, and he knew who lived in most of them.

He cycled past Mrs. Davis' house at Number Three and thought perhaps that he could see her looking out at the truck, but he couldn't be sure. Matthew was a little frightened of Mrs. Davis, who had about her a musty smell. His grandmother had the same smell too, but while his grandmother made him laugh to the point where his stomach ached, Mrs. Davis didn't appear to have much experience with humor at all.

"Hello there, dear," she would always say. "Being a good boy, I hope?"

Next door, at Number Five, lived Mr. Milne. He was about the same age as Matthew's father and worked from home. His house was two storied and when Matthew looked up he could see the top of Mr. Milne's head as he bent over his big desk by the front window. He seemed a very quiet man to Matthew. Nice, but quiet.

The only other house on their side of the road was Number Seven. The Marshalls had lived there and Matthew had played several times with their little girl Anna, but they had moved away leaving Matthew the only child in the street apart from Rose. And Matthew figured you could hardly count her since she was only six months old.

Across the road and directly opposite Matthew's house lived Mr. Price. If Matthew was frightened of Mrs. Davis, he was terrified of Mr. Price. He looked as though he was about a hundred, his face covered in lines. Although he always winked at Matthew and gave him a smile, he seemed very scary.

"He fought in the war," Matthew's father had told him in a whispered tone.

Matthew didn't know what war was, but the fact that Mr. Price had fought anyone at all was enough for him.

Beside Mr. Price lived a lady called Karen. She lived at Number Four. Matthew liked Karen. She cut his hair at the place where she worked and would talk to Matthew as though he knew much more than he did. Then, at the end of the visit, she would always have a lollipop handy and knew how to give it to Matthew in such a way that he had it in his mouth before his mother could object.

Karen seemed to spend a lot of time with Lisa and Roger at Number Six. Matthew knew that Lisa was going to have a baby. She seemed happy about this but Matthew couldn't help feeling sorry for her if Rose was any indication of babies.

Last of all lived a man and lady Matthew didn't know very well. He'd hardly seen the man, who was always coming and going in his white van. He'd seen the lady, Mrs. Haskell, more often. She sometimes talked to his mother in the street. Matthew recognized her because she wore a silver necklace that had a little man dangling on a cross.

Matthew neared Number Seven.

"Better keep back there, sonny," one of the men said.

Matthew looked up at him in awe. To Matthew's astonishment the man was carrying not one box, but three at a time.

A few minutes passed and the other man returned to the truck for another load. "Hi there, mate. What are you doing here? Where's your mum?"

Speechless, Matthew managed to point down the road toward his house.

"Right then," the man said. "Be careful, won't you?"

Matthew was about to turn back and head for home when he became aware of another figure lurking behind a bush in the front yard of Number Seven. It was a boy, quite a bit older than Matthew. The boy stood very still and wore an expression on his face that Matthew found hard to read.

Matthew decided to risk waving. The boy waved back then beckoned him over. Matthew waited until the two men were out of sight then pedaled for all he was worth past the truck and into the driveway, over to where the boy stood.

"What's your name?" the boy asked.

"Matthew," he said, taking off his hat.

The boy raised his eyebrows. He looked at Matthew for a few moments then simply said, "I'm Thomas."

The sixth interruption of the afternoon came in the form of a knock at the door.

"Surprise!" said Karen.

Lisa smiled at her friend, pleased to see her open, cheeky face. Today she wore jeans and a simple white midriff top, and wore her tawny hair piled up on top of her head. Lisa envied the way Karen could make her hair do anything she asked of it. Lisa's own blonde locks were fine and had a mind of their own. She couldn't help feeling wistful about the way Karen could show her tummy in public. Those days were long gone for Lisa.

"Surprise indeed. I didn't expect to see you after work."

Karen's green eyes danced with merriment. "Well, seeing as I've obviously missed a fair amount of excitement this afternoon I thought I'd call in for an update on proceedings."

"You'd better come in." Lisa led the way into the lounge. "How about a drink?"

"I wouldn't say no. In fact I wouldn't say no to a nice glass of wine or something, but it'd hardly be fair to partake while my best friend stays firmly on the wagon now, would it?"

Lisa laughed. "Needs must I'm afraid. Orange juice all right? Or how about a nice cold water?"

"What the heck, I'll go all out. Water would be fantastic."

"Try to find somewhere to sit," Lisa called over her shoulder as she headed for the kitchen.

"Hell's bells," came Karen's voice along the hall. "What happened in here? It looks as though you invited all of the neighborhood cats in to help you with your cross-stitch."

Lisa reappeared, grimacing as she handed over the water. "I don't know how it happened," she said. "All of a sudden everything just seemed to get itself into a tangle. One too many phone calls, I think."

"What, every well-meaning soul in the world calling you up to see if you're all right?"

Lisa nodded.

"At the very least you should be grateful people take an interest in you," Karen said. "Look at me. There I am day in and day out, cutting the same people's hair, and do any of them ever ask me how I am? No they don't. The second they sit in that chair something seems to come over them, and before I even say, 'Will it just be a tidy up today, Mrs. Robinson?' I'm half way through the latest installment of their life stories. And believe me, some of them are not half as interesting as people seem to think."

"Poor you."

"Then to top it all off I had Mrs. Dexter in today."

"The one who gets depressed?"

"I don't know what you'd call it. Let's just say she makes me depressed. Somebody told me she'd once stuck her head in the oven, and do you know what happened?"

"I shudder to think."

A small smile crept slowly across Karen's face. "She came out with a bad case of sunburn. It seems nobody ever told her it was supposed to be a gas oven."

Lisa looked at Karen. "I do hope you're joking," she said.

Karen laughed out loud. "Of course I am. And now you can tell me how wicked I am to joke about such a thing."

"Well you are," Lisa chided.

"I know, I know. However, I didn't come here to be told off."

"Not that you'd pay any attention."

"You're right, I wouldn't. No, I came to find out all about our new neighbors. I just saw her driving in as I arrived home and I felt sure you'd know all about it already."

"A lady in a green car?"

"Green? No, this car was red."

"Red? The car that came this afternoon was green, driven by a woman who wore dark glasses and had her head swathed in a silk scarf."

Karen raised her eyebrows. "The woman I saw was blonde. A great unruly mop of blonde hair, the color straight out of a bottle. Slim. Good figure. Rather short skirt and lots of cleavage."

Lisa shook her head. "That doesn't sound anything like the woman I saw. Did she have a boy with her?"

"Nope. No sprogs."

"Definitely sounds like somebody different."

Karen gave Lisa a questioning glance. "Sounds as though you got a good look at all the action."

Lisa buried her head in her hands and groaned. "You've got no idea," she said.

"Why? What happened?"

Lisa lifted her head. "I didn't even hear the truck arrive although how I missed it I don't know. I was sitting right here. Joan phoned with the news.

Before I knew it she had me looking out the window and giving her a blow-by-blow description of what I could see."

"What with you being closer to the action?"

Lisa nodded. She put her head momentarily in her hands again. "Oh God, I've been off work two weeks and I'm already turning into a busybody. How did that happen?"

Karen laughed. "You'll have to blame it on peer pressure."

"Please. The day I start to get as interfering as some of the women in this street is the day you can shoot me. Anyway, you could hardly call me a peer of Joan's. She must be nearly seventy. Even the description of us being neighbors is an exaggeration. She's simply someone that lives across the road."

"Someone who likes to take an excessive amount of interest in what's going on around her, you mean."

Lisa made an expansive gesture. "I think she's lonely."

"You're too soft," Karen said, "and Joan knows it. You'd never catch her calling me up to swap gossip."

"Maybe. But it seems to me a small thing to pay a little attention to a lonely woman."

"Small but potentially dangerous. Once you start these things who knows where they'll end?"

"Don't be ridiculous. She's perfectly harmless. The way you're talking she'll turn out to be some sort of elderly psycho."

Karen laughed. "You never know."

"Karen," Lisa said firmly, "Joan has been our neighbor for over three years. She hasn't lived there much less time than we have. I think we'd know by now if she was unhinged."

Karen laughed again. "I love winding you up," she said with a wicked grin.

Lisa shook her head. "You are incorrigible." She paused then said, "Anyway, I can't help thinking that we might be like her one day, all alone with few friends and long boring days to fill."

"We? Me maybe, but not you."

"Why you and not me?"

"Just look at you," Karen said. "You've got a lovely husband, a baby on the way and stacks of people calling you up to ask how you are. I, on the other hand, have reached the ripe old age of thirty-four without even managing to land a husband. The way I'm going there'll be nobody to call me up when I'm old and blue."

"I'll call."

"Of course you will," Karen agreed. "That's why you'll have plenty of family and friends around you until your dying day, and the only person I'll have left to call me is you."

Lisa went to open her mouth to reply when the telephone burst into life once again.

"There," Karen said with a sigh. "I rest my case."

Sandra Fleming woke with a start.

She'd gone from being comatose to wide awake in a fraction of a second without having any idea of what had disturbed her from her slumber. Her eyes darted around the room as she orientated herself before she looked down beside her. There Rose lay sleeping, her little chest rising and falling gently, her bud mouth ajar and askew.

Sandra sat up with care so as not to wake Rose and looked at the bedside clock. To her astonishment she saw it was four thirty. Good God, she had been asleep for over an hour.

Matthew. She'd left the poor boy to watch television, meaning to be but a few minutes when exhaustion had gotten the better of her. Why hadn't he come and woken her? Why, she wondered, was the house filled with such unnatural quiet?

Sandra edged off the bed then surrounded Rose with a barrier of pillows as a precaution, even though obstinate Rose hated rolling. She made her way down the hall and into the lounge, fully expecting to see Matthew asleep on the couch in front of the television.

The couch sat bare; the television hissed static.

She headed for the kitchen. No sign of him. No sign of remnants of afternoon tea either.

Her heart leapt as she raced to his bedroom and flung open the door. No Matthew. Just the bed with the *Thomas the Tank Engine* duvet showing vague signs of a depression of where Matthew had sat this morning while Sandra had put his shoes on before kindergarten. Those same shoes were now lying with Matthew's kindy bag on the floor of the wardrobe. The only evidence of activity was a scattering of Lego in one corner where some marvelous creation had been started, then abandoned.

Sandra tore down the hallway, tears beginning to well. She half expected to see Matthew lying in the middle of the bathroom floor surrounded by empty pill bottles, even though she knew full well all that sort of thing was inaccessible to small searching fingers. The room was empty. Relief and fear mingled for the briefest of moments.

"Matthew!" she yelled.

She waited, but no reply came.

"Matthew!" she called again.

No response.

"Oh, God," Sandra said, her voice a mere whisper. "Where are you?"

"Hello?"

"Lisa, it's Sandra."

"Sandra, what's wrong? You sound terrible."

"It's Matthew," Sandra sobbed. "You haven't seen him this afternoon, have you?"

"No. Why?"

"I don't know where he is. I fell asleep. I didn't mean to. When I woke up he was gone."

"Gone? As in missing?"

"He's not anywhere. I've checked."

"All the rooms? The cupboards? Under the beds?"

"Yes."

"What about outside? He's not in the garage, or up a tree?"

"I've looked everywhere. He's vanished," Sandra said, breaking down. "Oh, Lisa, where could he be?"

CHAPTER TWO

"What was that all about?" Karen asked.

Lisa replaced the telephone receiver and flopped into the nearest chair.

"It was Sandra Fleming. Matthew's disappeared."

"So I gathered. How? When?"

"Sandra said she fell asleep by accident. When she woke up he was gone."

Karen raised her brows. "Ho, ho, there goes her Mother-of-the-Year award."

"I'm not sure this is the time to be making jokes."

Karen held her hands up to defend herself. "You do have to admit she comes across as being a bit holier-than-thou. It's out of character for her to have made a mistake. She gives me the impression that most books on parenting have been written solely on her advice."

Lisa gathered up some of her cross-stitch threads and smoothed them across what was left of her lap. "I'm sure she didn't mean to fall asleep. She said she didn't. And you have to admit that Rose doesn't seem to be the easiest baby. Every time you see her she's howling. Not to mention the fact that Sandra's got two children to look after, not just one."

Karen looked at Lisa as if to say, "How hard could it be?" but softened. "I suppose you're right. I can't say I'd relish looking after a new baby."

"Whatever the rights and wrongs of the situation, or whose fault it is, Matthew is still missing. We have to think what we can do to help."

"You told her to call Joan."

"Joan was looking out of the window just like I was. She would've had a much better view of what was going on down the length of the whole street, whereas I was focused on what was happening at Number Seven."

"But where would he have been going?"

"I don't know."

"The poor blighter probably just wanted some breathing space."

Lisa frowned with disapproval.

"Okay, okay. Maybe he was going to see someone?"

"Maybe," said Lisa. "Sandra's parents live somewhere nearby, so perhaps he decided to go and visit them."

"Surely he wouldn't know the way?"

"He might. I haven't a clue as to what children of four know and what they don't. Anyway, I assume Sandra's parents would call if he turned up there out of the blue."

"What about Ian's parents?" Karen asked.

"To be honest, I don't know," Lisa said. "I don't really know much about Ian at all."

"Where else could Matthew have gone?"

"Kindergarten? The shops? To see one of his little friends?"

"God, he could be anywhere."

"Precisely. And Sandra can't go looking for him herself. Not without taking Rose. You have to admit that isn't an ideal situation."

"So you think we should go?"

"Yes. We could take your car and drive around a bit, see if we can spot him."

Karen considered this then began to look resigned to her fate. "It's a plan I suppose."

"Right," Lisa said, heaving herself to her feet. "I'll phone Sandra and tell her what we're going to do, and write a quick note for Roger just in case he comes home while we're out. We don't want there to be two searches for missing persons going on, do we?"

"Write me a note to tell me what?" a voice said from the behind them.

They turned to see Roger leaning in the doorway, hands shoved in his pockets, tie loosened, and his dark hair falling casually over his forehead. His handsome, boyish face was filled with speculation.

Lisa, relieved beyond measure, sighed and said, "Thank goodness you're home."

Sandra wore a track in the carpet. She clutched at her chest in a vain attempt to slow her heart's staccato beat. Her brain had become an empty pit. Panic washed over her, paralyzing her into indecision. She needed to *do* something but could not decide what that might be. She'd made herself hoarse yelling Matthew's name out of the back door. Three quarters of an hour had passed since she realized he'd gone. Still no sign of him.

Her breath came in shallow, irregular snatches but this fact barely registered as she paced from room to room. She kept expecting to discover Matthew somewhere, just sitting there, the same way a lost possession can appear in a place a person has checked five times.

So hopeless did the situation appear that Sandra's imagination started to fill the void left by her scattered thoughts. Every pictured scenario ended with her clothed in black, distraught and wracked with guilt for the rest of her life. The only small comfort lay in the fact that Rose continued her peaceful slumber. Sandra didn't think she could trust herself to carry Rose around without mishap right now.

Having done the circuit of the house and garden yet again, Sandra returned to the living room and the telephone. She snatched up the receiver and, for what felt like the thousandth time, dialed Ian's number.

"Hi. This is Ian Fleming. I can't take your call right now, but your business is important to me, so please, leave your name and number after the tone, and I'll call you back as soon as I can."

"What," yelled Sandra into the telephone, "is the point of having a cell phone if you've always got it switched off?"

She crashed the receiver down then snatched it up again.

Joan's line was still engaged. Who on earth could she possibly be talking to for half an hour? How could she be so oblivious and uncaring when right next door Sandra's world threatened to fall apart?

She tried her parents again, but the phone went unanswered. She tried Ian's work again. They still had no idea where he was, no idea when he'd be back, no way of contacting him if he wasn't answering his cell.

She slammed the receiver down again, tears rolling down her cheeks. Where was everyone in her time of need? Why would no one help her?

Worse still came the thought that while she might be desperate for help, she did have resources she had at her disposal even if they were proving of little use. What about poor Matthew? He could be anywhere, need anything, and probably didn't have a soul to help him. It made Sandra feel physically sick to think of her poor boy, without her, lost and alone. She wasn't there to help him and he could be in danger.

"Oh God," she cried. "Would somebody please do something?"

Then, as if she had been heard, the phone began to ring.

As Roger helped Lisa into the car he said, "I wouldn't be too long. There's no point in driving aimlessly around if you can't find him."

Lisa nodded. "We'll just drive to the kindergarten, down some of the side roads around here, then go down to the local shops and wander around a bit and see if we can see him."

"There's the playground, too," Karen said.

Roger closed the door and bent down to talk to Lisa and Karen through the window. "I think if you can't see him after that, come straight back. If he's still missing, I'm afraid it'll be time to call the police. They'll no doubt have a strategy for searching."

Lisa shuddered. "Don't even say it."

"Hopefully it won't come to that. Meanwhile, make sure you don't over-do it yourself. You are supposed to be resting, remember?"

He looked with concern at his wife. She had soft features that at times gave her a vulnerable appearance. It brought out in Roger a fierce protectiveness. He could feel it now as he regarded her caring blue eyes, whose sparkle gave Roger the impression that at any moment she might start to cry. Then, as if to dispel this notion, she smiled and tossed her blonde hair back in a carefree gesture. Roger reached through the open window and touched her hand.

"Don't worry, boss," Karen said, her face lit up with her trademark cheeky grin. "I'll look after her."

"See that you do. I'd better get over to Sandra's since she'll be wondering where I've got to."

Roger straightened and waved as the car pulled away from the curb. He watched as it disappeared then turned on his heel and walked across the road.

Sandra answered the door holding Rose, who was shoving her fingers into her mother's ear and gurgling with interest. Sandra, Roger thought, looked like death warmed up.

"Thank you for coming," she said, opening the door to let him in. He saw no sign of the usual self-assurance on Sandra's face. Under the circumstances it came as no surprise to see that she'd been crying but he was taken aback that the exertion of it had left her shackled by a strange listlessness. The boy had been gone less than two hours but Sandra already appeared to have given up hope.

Roger followed Sandra down the length of the hall, his footfalls echoing as his shoes struck the polished wooden floor. He had never been inside the Flemings' home but everything looked as immaculate as he would have expected. All the surfaces were polished and clean, all the possessions orderly and practical. No sign of anything amiss.

Sandra led him into the front sitting room and gestured for him to take a seat. He perched himself on the edge of the nearest available sofa. Looking at Sandra, he had no idea what the poor woman must be going through, no idea at all how to navigate such unfamiliar waters. Her face, most often covered in an expression of fervent intensity, was pinched and drawn, a look not helped by the fact that she had her bushy black hair pulled with some severity into a ponytail.

Sandra too, sat down, balancing Rose on her knee. She picked up a rattle off the nearby coffee table and gave it to the baby. Rose seemed delighted and put it straight in her mouth.

"Thank you for coming," Sandra said again.

Roger smiled. With a conviction he did not feel he said, "Try not to worry. I'm sure that wherever Matthew is, he's probably quite safe."

"Do you think so?"

Roger nodded, unable to compound the lie with more useless platitudes.

"The thing is," he said, "we need to decide what to do for the best."

This time it was Sandra who nodded.

"As Lisa said on the telephone, she and Karen are going to drive around just in case he decided to go for a bit of a walk. You know what boys are like, full of adventure and the pioneering spirit."

"Not Matthew," Sandra said, shaking her head in disbelief.

Roger said, "Don't forget that I was a small, not particularly intrepid boy once myself. I got into my fair share of scrapes and lived to tell the tale."

Sandra's face fell with the thought that some boys don't live to tell the tale. Roger kicked himself.

"Anyway," he said, "did you manage to get hold of Joan? Did she see anything?"

"Her line was busy," Sandra said, "so I couldn't ask her. I wanted to go next door and knock but Rose was still asleep and I didn't want to leave her on her own."

"Very wise," Roger said. "Perhaps that's where I should start? Why don't I go over to Joan's and see what she knows. If she doesn't know anything I'm going to suggest that she and I canvas the other neighbors. Maybe they'll have seen something."

"What about me?" Sandra asked. "What should I do?"

"I think you should stay here. Matthew might come back of his own accord, in which case he'd be upset to find no one home. I assume you've called Ian?"

Sandra's face clouded. "Nobody knows where he is either. I've left messages at his work and on his cell, but other than that I can't reach him."

"I'm sure he will call soon. When he does he'll be very worried if he can't reach you and find out what's happening. Maybe you should call your parents and have them come over and help."

"They don't appear to be home."

"Keep trying," Roger said. He stood up. "I'd better get going. I won't be very long."

"I can't thank you enough," Sandra said.

"Nonsense. What are neighbors for? Try not to worry and I'll be back soon."

"I thought I heard shouting," Joan said to Roger, "but I didn't think anything of it. Matthew quite often likes to play out in the back garden, and it's not unusual to hear Sandra calling for him."

"You never saw him this afternoon?"

Joan shook her head. "Of course it's fair to say that I was watching out of the window for quite some time this afternoon." She leaned forward. "We've got new neighbors, you know."

"Lisa told me. She said she never saw Matthew either."

"It's a bad business. How long has the little chap been missing?"

Roger glanced at his watch. "Sandra's not sure. A little less than two hours."

Joan sucked in her breath. "That long?"

"I'm afraid so. Anyway, I told Sandra that if you hadn't seen him, we'd go and check it out with the other neighbors. Fancy helping?"

"Naturally."

"I thought the best plan of attack would be for us to work along our own sides of the street. It won't take long. Karen and Lisa are out driving around in case they can spot him. That leaves Gordon Price and the Haskells on my side of the road. Then, on this side you'll only need to ask Geoff Milne if he saw anything."

"Right," Joan agreed. "What about the new neighbors?"

"I imagine they'd have been too busy to notice anything but I guess you never know. Do you mind asking them?"

"Not a bit," Joan said, her face lighting up.

Roger couldn't help suppressing a smile. In spite of the seriousness of the situation he'd just made Joan Davis' day.

The weatherboard house at Number Two was painted a light shade of sky blue. It sat in sharp contrast to other houses in the street which, for the most part, were painted white with smart trims or, like Roger's own, stained a woody brown.

Gordon's house had remained unchanged since at least the 60's. It had sparse gardens and a neat expanse of lawn and a vegetable patch in the back yard. It was a mercy to see no sign of the classic garden sculpture of a seal balancing a ball on its nose nestled in a rock garden. Nor was there a single multi-colored model butterfly in sight.

Roger went to the front door and rang the cobweb-covered bell. It made no audible sound, leaving him unsure whether the contraption even worked. He waited and waited, but the door remained unanswered.

Noticing open windows, Roger decided to try around the back and discovered Gordon busy unearthing potatoes in his vegetable garden. Since Gordon had to be well on his way to ninety Roger did not want to be responsible for frightening him into his grave. He coughed as he approached. Gordon's gaze lifted.

Roger couldn't help likening Gordon to a barrel with legs. He was short and stocky and even at his considerable age had powerful looking shoulders that indicated he'd been a man of some strength. During the course of his lifetime huge changes had come to pass but Roger suspected that very little of the world's advancements had altered Gordon's life in any material way. Despite the passage of time, Gordon's eyes were clear and his gaze steady. He still retained an impressive crop of hair on his head, even if it was now grey. He lifted his chin in greeting, but remained predictably mute.

"How are you?" Roger asked.

"Can't complain," Gordon growled, wiping a grimy hand across his tanned, leathery brow. "And even if I did no one would listen."

"I sometimes feel the same way," Roger said with a grin.

Gordon's eyes narrowed in a way that suggested Roger had no cause to have grievances that needed airing.

"Your missus had her baby?"

"Not yet. Still seven weeks to go."

"She's not following this modern notion of working until she nearly has the baby at her desk?"

Roger smiled. "No. She might have, but she's had a lot of trouble with her blood pressure. She was told to pack it in or risk going to hospital."

"Right nasty, is that," Gordon said. "My Martha had terrible blood pressure when she was alive. Used to drive her crazy."

Roger longed to say, "That wouldn't have helped her blood pressure," but he knew Gordon wouldn't appreciate his attempt at humor. Instead he said, "It's been a bit of a worrying time all right, but she seems much better now."

Gordon nodded and turned his attention back to his potatoes. His sinewed arms worked the spade, turning over the loamy soil with ease. Roger could see the dark outline of a tattoo on Gordon's upper arm, partially covered by his rolled up shirtsleeve. With age his skin had sagged so that the patterns and words embedded there were now obscured by wrinkles.

"I suppose you've come for something," Gordon said, finished with the pleasantries.

Roger smiled again. No one who knew Gordon expected too much in the way of idle chatter.

"I've come because Matthew Fleming is missing."

Gordon looked up at this and stopped working. "The little lad from across the road?"

"That's right."

Gordon leaned on his spade looking thoughtful.

"Been gone long?"

"A couple of hours at most."

Gordon pursed his lips. "He'll come home when he's good and ready."

"He is only four."

"So? I've seen the way his mother mollycoddles him, always at him about something or another. He probably just wanted some peace and quiet."

"Still, four is pretty young. It's a dangerous world out there these days."

Gordon drew himself up to his full stature, puffing out his barrel chest. "And it wasn't in my day? Didn't we have both Gerry and the Japs knocking at our door?"

Roger knew better than to go down that track and put up his hands to pacify the old man.

"Of course you did, Gordon," Roger said.

"Yes, well, it's something that ought not be forgotten. Anyway, you can go now. I have to get on with this before dark."

"So you haven't seen Matthew?"

"Course not," Gordon snorted. "Would've said, wouldn't I?"

"Well, thanks for your time," Roger said, and as he walked away he could hear Gordon muttering under his breath, doubtless about the state the world and the ingratitude of youth.

"You're just going to have to wait for your dinner, madam," Joan said, as Jess tried to make her point by weaving herself in and out of Joan's legs. "There are more important things afoot than the state of your stomach."

Jess let out a meow of protest.

Joan turned her attention back to the mirror and continued to work her way through the process of tidying up her face with powder. Every year it seemed to get harder and harder to do justice to the job, and although she managed the application of make-up with a skill that came as second nature, the results were ever more disappointing.

She then turned her attention to her hair. Once it had been her crowning glory, soft, blonde and easy to twist into various styles. Now it was grey and thinning but she still wore it long, especially for her age. For convenience sake, however, she usually kept it contained within the confines of a neat bun.

"That poor little boy is lost and not a soul knows where he is," Joan said before putting the finishing touches on her lips.

"There," she said to herself. "All ready to face the fray."

Joan let herself out of the front door and paused on the doorstep. Maybury Place was swathed in late afternoon sunlight, and in Joan's opinion looked quite charming. She had only lived in the street for three and a half years, but they'd turned out to be some of the happiest of her life.

It wasn't an affluent street. No one had a swimming pool or a Jacuzzi, and no one had a garage with internal access. The street wasn't tree-lined, but the houses were all well maintained and the gardens cared for with pride. It would never win any "Street of the Year" award, but the people were pleasant to one another and all on speaking terms. Quite simply, Joan was at home there.

She made her way down the front path, out through the gate, and headed next door to Number Five. It was the newest house in the street, all angles and pitched roofing, and had been built shortly after Number Seven, some time in the mid 80's. Both of these houses were the only double storied dwellings in the street.

Geoff Milne owned the house at Number Five. He lived alone in a quiet way, his natural reticence not making him a great aficionado of conversation. In spite of this Joan always found him to be a good neighbor, pleasant if not a little aloof for her tastes.

As Joan turned into the driveway at Number Five she saw Geoff let himself out of the front door. He turned to lock the door behind him, struggling as he balanced a set of files under his chin and a long plastic tube and a satchel under his left arm.

As he regained his balance and headed for his car, he spotted Joan.

He gave her a brief smile. He was a tall man but his reserved demeanor and serious disposition prevented him from being what Joan would call commanding. He was not classically handsome, but nor was his face weak. He had about him a quiet confidence and a direct way of looking at a person that brooked rebuke. His dark hair was thick and curly, his eyes brown and questioning.

"Hello, Geoff," Joan said as she neared, her smile warm.

"Joan. You are well?"

"Pretty well. It's certainly been an interesting day."

"Oh?"

"You must have seen the new neighbors moving in. Unless you weren't working at home today?"

"No, I was in," Geoff said. "And, yes, I did notice the moving van."

"A mother and son, I understand?"

"I'm afraid I wouldn't know."

His voice betrayed his lack of interest in the subject so Joan asked, "Are you going out?"

"Yes. I've got a meeting with some clients." He looked briefly at his watch. "In about ten minutes."

Joan glanced at her own watch. It was 5.15pm. She shook her head. "You're certainly expected to keep some pretty irregular hours these days, aren't you?"

"It's a commercial reality in my line of work. It's very competitive out there and unless you're willing to work in with your clients' busy schedules, they'll go and find someone more accommodating."

"You're finding work hard to come by?"

"Not at all. I've been lucky enough to get a few big projects of late." He waved the tube at Joan. "And the house that I've been commissioned to design for these people is very sizeable."

"I don't know how you do it. I couldn't be an architect if you paid me."

"Well, people do pay me," Geoff said, "and if I want to keep that up, I'll have to get going, I'm afraid."

"Oh, of course," Joan said. "I didn't mean to hold you up. It's just that I need to talk to you about a matter of some importance."

Geoff raised his brows. "Can't it wait?"

Joan shook her head. "It's Matthew Fleming. You know, the little boy that lives at Number One. He's gone missing."

"Missing?"

"I'm afraid so. No one has seen him for hours. I don't suppose you saw him at all this afternoon?"

Geoff frowned. "No I didn't. It's true that I was working at my drawing board by the window, but I was pretty busy trying to get this stuff finished." He shook the tube again. "My work took up all my attention."

"Oh," said Joan. It seemed incomprehensible to her that one wouldn't at least take some interest in all that activity in the street. "Well, I'd better let you get to your meeting."

"Sorry," Geoff said. "If it wasn't for that, I'd help you look."

"Don't worry," Joan told him.

As he headed for his big four-wheel drive parked in the garage at the end of the driveway, Geoff paused. Over his shoulder he said, "Good luck."

At Number Eight, Maureen said. "Oh no. Sandra must be frantic."

"She is," said Roger. "I think having to look after Rose is all that's keeping her from falling apart."

"Poor thing. What an ordeal."

"With a bit of luck he'll turn up soon, and then all the panic will be over."

"Children can be such a worry," Maureen mused. "When my two were little they were always getting into scrapes. Especially Shaun." She shook her head. "Always Shaun. Oh, what a boy."

She stood in the doorway fingering her crucifix as she recalled past memories.

Maureen Haskell was a thin, nervous woman. If Gordon could be compared to a barrel then Maureen was akin to an old sofa, sat upon and a little frayed around the edges, careworn but somehow still functional. Today she wore a floral dress of thin material, perhaps purchased fifteen years ago, into which she seemed to have shrunk. It swam on her and made her thin arms and legs look skeletal. But while the rest of her had faded with the passage of time, her red hair remained vibrant, and together with her green eyes, betrayed her distant Irish ancestry.

"You never saw him?" Roger asked.

"Matthew? No, I'm sorry. I've been out all afternoon." She looked over her shoulder at a small collection of plastic supermarket bags clustered together just inside the door.

"What about Brian? He comes and goes during the day, doesn't he?"

Maureen's expression changed fleetingly. "Brian? He might have come home some time during the afternoon, but whether he would have noticed Matthew is another thing."

"I see. Is there any way of finding out?"

"Well," Maureen said, "I could have a look at his appointment book and see if it gives any indication of where he might have been. Hold on."

Maureen disappeared into the house, leaving Roger waiting at the door. He had lived beside the Haskells for four years, during which time he had never once crossed the threshold. Brian had been over to their house a couple of times when he came to install the security system Roger had bought, but never since. Brian was the sort of man you glimpsed in passing rather than stopped to talk with. Although a short, slight man, he made up for his lack of stature, as far as Roger could tell, with an astonishing temper.

Glancing around, Roger saw that the furniture all seemed to be in pretty much the same condition as Maureen herself. Although everything was neat and tidy, there was an air about the place that suggested neither of the Haskells were particularly interested in hearth and home.

Maureen returned bearing a green, leather-bound book in her hands.

"It says here that he was supposed to be wiring up over at those houses in Butler Road. You know, the new terraced ones?"

Roger nodded.

"It's a big job. Lighting, sockets, phones, security. I'd imagine that unless there was a real emergency he would've stayed there all day."

"Perhaps you could ask him when he comes home."

"Oh, he won't be home for ages," Maureen said. "Monday night he usually goes out with some of his other electrician buddies."

Roger said, "I guess I'll leave you to it then. Sorry to bother you."

"Wait!" Maureen said as Roger went to leave. She took a quick look at the pile of shopping, considered for a moment, then said, "If you don't mind, I think I'll come with you."

Joan looked up at the facade of Number Seven. It already looked different, as though with taking in new residents it had also taken on a new lease of life. To Joan there was something sad about an empty house. The fact that the property was no longer neglected seemed reason in itself for Joan to welcome the new residents to Maybury Place.

Emboldened with such sentiments, Joan approached and knocked on the door. She waited with uncharacteristic patience, a ready smile fixed on her face, but no reply came. She knocked again, and waited.

Just as she went to knock for the third time the door opened the smallest fraction. Joan attempted to peer through, convinced she could see the silhouette of the dark haired woman.

"Yes?"

Joan increased her smile and said, "Welcome to Maybury Place."

"Sorry?" came the voice through the thin slit of doorway.

Joan, undeterred, said, "Welcome to Maybury Place,"

No response. When Joan neither said any more nor made a move to leave, the woman said, "Did you want something?"

This took Joan aback. Never in all her years had she heard such ingratitude to a warm welcome.

"I...I..," she spluttered then, pulling herself together and drawing herself up, she said, "I wondered if, while you were moving in this afternoon, you hadn't seen a small boy, four years old, sandy hair?"

Suddenly behind the door there was a commotion and the door slammed shut. Straining to hear to what was going on, Joan overheard the voice of a second woman berating the first. It sounded as though they were having an argument, the subject of which being that the first woman should not have opened the door. Joan couldn't imagine why ever not.

Since she still had no reply to her question, and couldn't very well leave the subject until another day, Joan hammered on the door.

Inside the house, Joan could hear the voices fading as they withdrew into the recess of the house. As she teetered on the verge of giving up the door flung open. Joan was greeted by the sight of a tall woman looming over the top of her. Straight ahead lay the sight of an ample cleavage, and so Joan moved her eyes up to behold a striking woman, heavily made up, late thirties in age, her face framed with a wealth of frizzy fly-away blonde hair. Joan swallowed.

"What do you want?" the woman demanded. "Can't you see we're very busy?"

Joan was beginning to be affronted. "As I was asking your...er...friend, I wanted to know if you'd seen a small boy this afternoon while you were moving in."

"Boy? What boy?"

"His name's Matthew Fleming. He lives on the corner, at Number One. He's been missing for a good part of the afternoon, and he's only four years old."

The woman shook her head. "I wasn't here," she said, her tone cold. She then shouted over her shoulder, "Thomas!"

A few moments passed and a boy with a petulant expression appeared. He leered at them both. It struck Joan that he looked as though he needed a good spanking.

"Thomas, this woman says there's a boy missing, and that we might have seen him this afternoon."

The boy looked sulky, but said nothing.

"Well?" the woman demanded. "Did you see him?"

"No," Thomas spat out. "I never saw anyone. Not all afternoon."

"That's it then," the woman said to Joan. "We saw nothing. So, if you don't mind, we're very busy."

And with that she shut the door in Joan's face.

When Roger returned to Number One, with Maureen Haskell trailing in his wake, Sandra snatched open the door. She clung on to baby Rose like a lifeline. Worry and fatigue strained her face, yet she still had a hopeful look in her eyes, even though it was quite clear Matthew was not with them. All Roger could do was to shake his head.

Sandra's face fell.

"You'd better come in," she said,

"I'm so sorry," Maureen said to Sandra as they entered the lounge. "Is there anything I can do for you? Take Rose? Make cups of tea?"

Sandra shook her head as she deposited Rose on a play mat on the floor and gave her a couple of toys. "There doesn't seem any point, does there?" she said to no one in particular.

"Perhaps Joan will have had more success?" Roger said. "Or Karen and Lisa? By now they must have covered a fair amount of ground."

A heavy sigh seemed to well up inside Sandra. It came out as might a lament: slow, sad and bereft of hope.

"Have you managed to get hold of Ian?" Roger asked.

"Yes and no," Sandra said. "His receptionist phoned to say that they were able to track him down and that he was heading straight home. Apparently his cell phone's broken so he couldn't call himself."

As she spoke they heard a car pull up outside and their heads shot up in anticipation. Maureen looked out the window. "It's not Ian. It's Lisa and Karen."

"Is Matthew with them?" Sandra asked.

"Not that I can see. I'm terribly sorry."

"I'll go and let them in," Roger said, seeing Sandra sitting still, staring into space.

"No luck?" Roger asked as he opened the door.

"No," Lisa said, following him back down the hall and into the lounge. "Hi, Sandra."

"Hi. Thanks for going to look."

"No problem. I'm sorry we weren't successful."

"And no one had seen him?"

Karen shook her head. "We went everywhere. There was no sign of him at the shops or the supermarket. The teachers were still at kindergarten and he hadn't been back there."

"What about the park? Did you check the park?"

"Yes," Lisa told her. "There were a couple of mothers there with a bunch of children. One of them told me they'd been there for the best part of the afternoon, making the most of the weather while it lasts. She said they'd been the only ones there the whole time. She said they certainly would have noticed a boy by himself."

"I'm not sure he would know the way on his own," Sandra said, her voice barely audible.

Everyone fell silent. The small gathering had begun to run out of fresh ideas and sympathetic comments.

The sound of another car punctuated the silence. This one, however, pulled into the driveway.

"Ian's home," Maureen said.

Sandra catapulted to her feet and rushed out of the room.

"Poor thing," Karen said. "She looks wretched."

"The whole thing is making me feel sick," Lisa said, scooping up Rose who had begun to grizzle. "I just can't even begin to imagine how bad she must be feeling."

"You aren't overdoing it?" Roger asked her. "Maybe you should go home and rest if you're getting too tired."

Lisa shook her head. "I couldn't. It's just too worrying. Besides, I don't feel too bad. More heartsick than physically sick."

Maureen said, "Where can he be?"

"If we knew that, we all wouldn't be here," Karen replied.

Silence fell yet again. Only Rose made the odd gurgle. The minutes ticked by. Then, at length, Sandra and Ian joined the gathering.

Roger, used to seeing an Ian Fleming whose boldness touched on arrogance, could not believe the look on the man's face. He had turned an unsettling shade of grey, his face curiously immobile, as though shock had rendered his facial expressions inoperative.

"Thank you all," he managed to say. "It means a lot to us, you pitching in like this."

"Don't worry," said Roger. "I'm only sorry we weren't able to find any trace of him."

"There's still Joan," Karen said. "Maybe she'll succeed where the rest of us have not."

Sandra and Ian both slumped into chairs to continue their vigil. Rose, seeing her father, began to make mewling noises that, on being unanswered, turned into a full-scale howl. Lisa passed her over and the noise stopped. Rose grinned at him and tried to stick her pudgy fist into her father's mouth. He could barely muster up a smile in response.

During the ensuing silence Karen examined her fingernails, Lisa sat back in quiet contemplation and Maureen squirmed uneasily in her chair, her gaze darting around. Roger felt disempowered. He wanted to do something but could think of nothing other than calling the police. That idea had yet to be mooted by anyone other than himself.

Then Joan came back. While Maureen went to answer the door it seemed as though everyone else in the room held their breath. As soon as she came into the room it was evident by the expression on her face that she too had failed.

"No luck, I'm afraid," she said. "Geoff Milne had his eyes glued to the drawing board all afternoon, and the new people at Number Seven wouldn't give you the time of day if you asked for it."

The odd eyebrow shot up at this comment.

"What new people?" Ian asked.

"We finally have new residents," Joan told him. "They moved in this afternoon and seem to be a funny bunch. Something decidedly odd about them, if you ask me."

Sandra broke down in tears. Lisa, sitting beside her, put an arm around her.

Ian stood up. "That's it then," he said. "You've obviously all done your best, but it will be starting to get dark soon. We've got no choice but to phone the police."

CHAPTER THREE

The police arrived not long after six o'clock, a male and female officer, their presence filling the already crowded room to capacity.

The male officer was middle aged and had a look about him that suggested he'd seen it all. The woman was young, perhaps not long past her training. She was solid and seemed to have no problem wearing her heavy Kevlar vest. She had a petulant expression and seemed eager to make up for her lack of years by an astonishing display of confidence.

They sat down in the last two available chairs. Although they introduced themselves no one absorbed these details.

"So you say the last time you saw Matthew was at approximately three fifteen?" the man asked.

Sandra nodded. "I left Matthew watching a DVD while I went to feed his sister and settle her to sleep."

"Only you fell asleep yourself?" the woman asked, her tone sharp.

Tears trickled down Sandra's cheeks. She nodded.

"And you woke up at what time?"

"Half past four."

"At which point you did what?" the man asked.

Sandra sniffed. "I realized at once what I'd done and went straight away to look for Matthew. I thought he'd be where I left him."

"You didn't think to call us then?" the woman asked in such a way that suggested this might be something only an imbecile would overlook.

"No. I thought...I thought...I suppose I thought he wouldn't have gone too far. He's a good boy and he knows not to go anywhere without me."

"Of course not," said Joan, passing Sandra a tissue and glaring at the woman.

"Do you have a recent photograph of Matthew?"

"The most recent ones are still on the camera," Ian said. "I could download them if necessary. Otherwise there are some I printed off from about two months before Christmas."

"Could I see them?"

Ian went out of the room and soon returned.

The policeman flicked through the photos and selected one. "This is Matthew?"

Ian and Sandra nodded, the very sight of their boy bringing fresh tears to Sandra's eyes.

"And do you know what he was wearing today?"

"Navy blue shorts, green polo top with a navy blue collar," Sandra said without hesitation.

"Are you sure?"

She nodded. "I dressed him myself this morning."

"So you know of no place Matthew might have gone?"

"The only place I could think of was my parents' house," Sandra replied. "We've been enough times that he might have tried to make his own way there."

"And you've checked with them?"

"They were out for most of the afternoon. I only managed to get hold of them while we were waiting for you to arrive. They said there's no sign of him having been there at all, let alone being there now."

"And your parents, sir?" the man asked.

"They live a bit further away." Ian's voice was like that of an automaton. "Matthew doesn't get to go there as much as he does to Sandra's parents. I doubt he would know the way."

"Nowhere else he might have wanted to go? No toys at the toy shop he's been pestering you to buy? No particular place he's always asking to be taken?"

"None," Sandra said.

"Was there any reason you can think of that Matthew might have wanted to leave?"

"Such as?" Ian asked, not liking where this line of questioning was going.

"No arguments or disputes between you and the boy?"

"No!" Sandra said.

"Come now," the woman said. "Surely you have to tell Matthew off from time to time? Did anything like that happen this afternoon? Something that could have caused him to run away?"

"He hasn't run away," Sandra shouted. "He's just missing."

Ian put a comforting arm around Sandra's shoulders. She turned to bury her face in his embrace.

"Try not to get upset, Mrs. Fleming," the man said. "It's important we ask these questions to determine the sequence of events."

Sandra looked up at him, her eyes wide. "How could I not get upset? My baby is missing."

"I know," he said. "And we're here to do all we can to find him. So, if you could just answer the question please."

Sandra sighed. "Nothing happened," she said. "He wanted some afternoon tea and I asked him to wait. I put on a DVD and left him to watch it. I was only going to be a few minutes."

"Might he have gone off in search of food?"

"I checked the kitchen. He didn't seem to have helped himself. He knows he's not supposed to."

"Right. So, if there was nothing that happened this afternoon to make Matthew leave the house, is anything else going on to make him feel unhappy?"

"Like what?" Ian asked, his tone becoming sharper by the minute. He was conscious of being watched by so many pairs of eyes.

"Any marital or financial problems that might be affecting the boy?"

Both Ian and Sandra shook their heads, appalled at the suggestion.

"Everything's fine," Ian said. "Or at least it was until this happened."

"What about pre-school or day care or even baby-sitters? Nobody else that might have upset Matthew?"

"He's at kindergarten," Sandra said. "Five mornings a week. He loves it and seems to get on with everyone. His teachers haven't said anything about there being any trouble. Besides," she added, "I know my son. If he was upset about something it would have been written all over his face."

Maureen said, "At four they can't hide anything from you, can they?"

Sandra managed a small smile of gratitude for Maureen. "I don't think they can," she said.

"So," the man said, "the next question has to be about what was going on in the street this afternoon." He looked around the room. "Does the street participate in the Neighborhood Watch scheme?"

Everyone shook their heads.

"And I gather that you've already gone house to house asking about Matthew's whereabouts?

Roger said, "We thought someone might have seen something."

"We drove about a bit too," Karen said.

"So you obviously know some or all of your neighbors?"

"We all know everyone," Lisa said, "at least to say hello to."

"Except the new neighbors," Joan said with a disapproving sniff.

"You have new neighbors?" the woman asked.

"Yes," said Joan. "They moved in just this afternoon. Into Number Seven. And they aren't very neighborly, let me tell you."

"What time was this?"

"The moving van arrived at three o'clock," Joan said. "Didn't it, Lisa?"

The man ignored Lisa's nod, but asked, "And you are?"

"Joan Davis. I live next door at Number Three."

"And am I to gather that you watched the proceedings?"

"I did," Joan said with pride. "Lisa and I both did."

Lisa cringed.

"But neither of you saw Matthew? Didn't see him go outside for a closer look?"

Both women shook their heads.

"In that case, I don't suppose either of you saw the name of firm of movers?"

"I did," said Joan again.

"And?"

"I'm thinking." Everyone waited while Joan racked her brains. "It was something short and efficient sounding."

"Lisa, is it?"

She nodded. "I'm sorry," she said. "I never noticed."

"Elite," Joan said. "I'm sure it was Elite. And it said something on the side of the truck about how careful they were."

The male officer nodded to his counterpart and she removed herself from the room.

"You think they might know something?" Sandra asked, a new hope in her voice.

"Hard to say," the man said. "It might take some time to locate anyone who will know since it's out of hours."

"Maybe we should make some tea," Lisa suggested, elbowing Karen.

"Right you are," Karen said.

The waiting dragged on. Lisa and Karen distributed drinks to all. A number of stilted conversations were started and abandoned before the woman came back into the room.

"I managed to get hold of the company owner who had stayed back to do the books," she said. "He gave me the name of the truck driver and his sidekick, and although the driver wasn't home, his helper was."

Everyone looked expectant.

"He said he definitely saw Matthew this afternoon. They both did. He was riding his trike around on the footpath by the truck, watching as they unloaded. He said he asked the boy where his mother was and that he pointed toward this house."

"What time was that?" the man asked.

"He couldn't be sure. He thought it was about quarter to four, four o'clock. They were gone just before four thirty he reckoned."

"And did he see where Matthew went?"

"Well that's just it. He said that he and the driver had to carry a big chest of drawers inside, too heavy for one person. When they went inside Matthew was there on the footpath. When they came back he was gone. The man said he assumed the boy had got bored and gone home."

Sandra rushed from the room, and was back within moments.

"His trike is gone," she said breathless from rushing. "I didn't think to check before."

"Right," said the man. "Well that's at least one positive sighting." To Ian and Sandra he said, "We'll go and check it out and come back soon."

"What do you reckon then, Dave?" the woman asked her partner as they walked away from the Flemings' house.

He shrugged his burly shoulders.

"Don't know. Always hard to say in these cases. They seem legitimate enough."

"So you don't think it's suspicious she took so long to call us?"

Dave raised his eyebrows. "To give her time to bury the boy in the back yard? Come off it."

"How can you be so sure?"

"I've seen this kind of thing before. There's a certain type of woman who thinks they'll be able to solve all of their own problems. I'd say our Mrs. Fleming is just that kind of person."

"Ah, but what problem did she have to solve?"

"Helen, I think you'd be suspicious of the Pope himself," Dave said as they neared Number Seven.

"Of course I would. Where there's money and power there's always trouble, not to mention all their other goings on."

Dave laughed. "Okay, bad example. In this instance I think we've got a case of a little boy with an insatiable curiosity who, seeing an opportunity to leave the gilded cage, let temptation get the better of him."

"Where do you think he is, then?" Helen asked as they paused outside Number Seven and looked up at the house from the footpath.

Dave shrugged again. "He's got to be somewhere. Did you ask the moving guy if there was any chance the boy could have crept inside the van?"

"Yup. He said the truck was totally empty when they'd finished and that there was no place to hide."

"He couldn't have climbed inside some of the furniture and been carried inside, could he?"

"I thought of that too. The guy reckoned they'd definitely have noticed if something was heavier than it was meant to be. And then there's the matter of the trike. The boy would have had to find somewhere to put it, since neither man recalled seeing it abandoned on the footpath."

"Right. Perhaps that's where we need to start. Why don't you go and knock on the door and see what you can get out of these new residents that they didn't want to tell that old biddy. I'll have a snoop around the grounds to see if I can see any sign of the bike."

Dave watched Helen go up the path and knock on the door. After a few moments it opened, answered by a blonde bombshell.

"Crickey," he said under his breath.

He could see Helen gesticulating in her particular fashion then look over her shoulder in his direction. The striking woman followed her gaze. He nodded and she gave a faint acknowledgement his presence, enough for him to be certain she understood the score. He then turned on his heel and began looking around the yard.

Sunset approached, casting elongated shadows across the ground. Fall would soon be upon them. Dave made his way around to the back of the property, walking down beside the house at Number Five. It formed a corridor mostly of lawn, with little place for anything to be concealed. Behind the house the same green grass and open spaces. The previous owners had not been inspired gardeners.

In the back corner, beside what Dave assumed was Number Eight, sat a small shed. In need of some remedial assistance, it looked both disused and overused at the same time. A grimy window faced the house but the fading light rendered it opaque.

Dave checked the front of the shed. It wasn't locked, but someone had shoved a thick twig through the hole where a lock might be placed. Recently, he surmised, since the end of the twig was shattered and showed traces of life where it had once joined the rest of some bush. It had the effect of acting like a lock and although it would keep no one out, it might keep someone in.

Dave withdrew the twig and opened the door. A smell of potting mix, rusty tools and dereliction assailed his nostrils. He put his head inside the door and there, cowering in the corner behind a red trike, was a small boy. Matthew Fleming.

The boy took one look at Dave and screamed for all he was worth.

The group waited in near silence. Sandra's parents had arrived to join the vigil, unable to bear the thought of their daughter suffering, their grandson lost. Sandra's mother bore Rose off to give her a bath, as much to keep busy as to help. A series of distant squeals of delight and howls of protest floated down the hallway as the process of washing got underway.

Maureen kept darting nervous glances out of the window and fidgeting with her dress. No one knew whether she kept a look out for the police or for her husband. Every so often someone would think of some encouraging thing to say, or would ask a question hoping to trigger a thought of where to look next. At one point Roger asked Ian and Sandra if they wouldn't rather the whole group left them alone. Ian declined. In truth nobody wanted to go without hearing any substantial news, and Ian and Sandra seemed grateful for the support.

Their patience was soon rewarded. By the time Diane re-emerged with a fresh smelling Rose the police were already on their way back with Matthew. Maureen spotted them coming down the road.

"Here they come!" she shouted. "They've got him!"

Everyone rushed over to the window.

Lisa could scarcely remember a more welcomed sight than that of the big, burly police officer bearing young Matthew down the road. The woman officer carried Matthew's trike in one hand and his hat in the other.

Sandra screamed Matthew's name with relief and rushed to the front door. The neighbors watched as Matthew peeled his arms from around the policeman's neck and threw himself at his mother. Sandra could be seen holding Matthew as though she would never let him go. She buried her face in his little shoulder and poured out a fresh torrent of tears. Ian was seconds behind, enclosing his wife and child within the protection of his arms.

"Thank goodness," Joan said as they watched the tableau through the window.

Maureen agreed. "It seems like a miracle."

"He looks in one piece," Karen said.

"Thank goodness," Joan said again. "I just wonder where he's been, where they found him."

"We're about to find out," Roger said, as both the police officers and the family made a move to come inside.

Everyone resumed their seats but this time the faces of the people in the room were transformed, the atmosphere changed to one of relief and happiness. Matthew, overwhelmed to find so many people encamped in his lounge, clung tightly to his mother and buried his head in her shoulder.

"Where did you find him?" Joan asked, her curiosity getting the better of her.

"In the shed behind Number Seven," the policeman said.

"Where?" Ian said, his voice incredulous.

"There's a little shed at the side of the property," Maureen said. "It's between our house and theirs."

"And he was in there, you say?" Joan asked. "Doing what, may I ask?"

"It looks as though someone shut him in there with his trike. The door had been barred from the outside."

Sandra's shock was palpable. "He'd been shut in there?"

The policeman nodded.

"But who would do such a thing?" Ian demanded.

The policeman sighed. "That is something we're yet to ascertain. The residents of the property claim not to have seen him even though the removal men placed him directly outside at the time. And," he said, "I'm afraid we haven't been able to get anything out of Matthew either. It took all my powers of persuasion to get him to come out of the shed at all."

Sandra hugged Matthew tight. "It's all right darling," she said. "You're safe now."

She shifted him around on her knee so that the group could see his grimy tear-stained face, his dusty, crumpled clothes.

"Darling, do you think you could tell these nice police officers what happened to you?" Sandra asked.

Matthew said nothing.

"It would be very helpful if you could," his father added. "You could show everyone what a brave boy you are."

Matthew pursed his lips. "He shut me in," he said.

"Who, darling?"

"That boy."

"Which boy?"

"Thomas."

"Why did he do that, darling?"

"He said he had a great game we could play. That he had a really fun trick to show me in the shed."

"So you went to see?"

Matthew nodded. "He pushed me."

"Into the shed?"

Matthew nodded again. "I couldn't get out," he added, his bottom lip starting to tremble.

"Hush," his mother soothed, hugging him tighter. "It's all right. Mummy's here." She looked up at the police officer. "So what is to be done?"

He frowned. "It's a difficult situation."

"In what way?" Ian asked. "It seems quite clear to me. Surely there is something you can charge the boy with."

"Such as?"

"You're the policeman. What about kidnapping for a start?"

"The trouble is there is we only Matthew's have word. It might have been a harmless prank."

"Harmless?" Karen said.

"Isn't Matthew's word enough?" Joan asked.

"Not really."

"Well, there'd be finger prints, surely?"

"Yes, but again, this Thomas lives there. You'd expect to find his finger prints there."

"He's only been there five minutes."

"That doesn't really matter, I'm afraid."

"So you'll do nothing?"

"Not nothing," the policeman assured. "We'll go back and talk to them again, see if Thomas has anything more to say for himself, put the frighteners on him a bit. But he denied all knowledge of having ever seen Matthew. Even when we found him in the shed the boy still denied it." He stood up. "The important thing now is to look after Matthew. He seems fine but you may want to have a doctor check him over just to be on the safe side."

Sandra looked down at Matthew. "How do you feel Matthew? Are you all right?"

Matthew looked back up at this mother, and said, "I'm hungry."

Hard on the heels of the departure of the police, the main party made a move to leave.

"Thanks everyone," Ian said.

"I don't know what I would have done without you all," Sandra said.

"Think nothing of it," said Roger. "I'm sure you would have done the same for us had the roles been reversed."

"Still, it meant a lot to us both to have you here," Ian said.

As they left, Sandra went inside to Matthew. Only Joan lingered on the doorstep.

"Are you sure there isn't anything you want me to do?" she asked Ian. "Maybe I could make you some more tea while you tend to Matthew? Or mind Rose if you want to take Matthew to the doctor?"

"Thanks Joan, but I think we'll be okay. Sandra's parents will stay a while. I'm sure if we need to take Matthew down to the emergency place, they'll stay behind with Rose."

"Right then," Joan said. "I must say I think you're very calm. I don't think I'd be so even-tempered if my boy had just been terrorized by some neighborhood bully."

"To be honest, right now calm is the last thing I feel. When things have settled down, I think I might just have to pay a visit to our new neighbors."

"Hmph," Joan snorted as she turned to leave. "Good luck. Believe me, you'll need it."

Ian found the family in the kitchen, his wife and his parents-in-law hovering around Matthew as he spooned great helpings of baked beans with astonishing speed into his mouth. For once all admonitions toward good manners and warnings about his digestive system were forgotten.

"I still don't understand what made you go out there in the first place,"

Sandra was saying to Matthew.

"I wanted to look at the truck," he said without looking up.

"But you know not to go anywhere without me," she said. "Or to at least ask me first before even going outside."

"You were busy with Rose," Matthew said, his voice a whisper.

"Yes, but..."

"Just leave it, Sandra," Ian said. "Plenty of time for recriminations later."

Sandra looked up at him, seemed about to say something, but changed her mind.

Ian said, "Let's just be thankful for now that he's safe and sound, eh?" She nodded.

"What a scallywag," Sandra's father said, ruffling his namesake's hair.

Ian said to him, "If you don't mind holding on here for a bit longer I think I might pay our new residents a visit. Joan thinks I'll be wasting my time, but I'm going anyway."

"Do you think that's wise?" Diane asked.

"What will you say to them?" Sandra said.

Ian shrugged. "To be honest I don't know. I suppose at the very least I'd like to hear what they have to say. From the sounds of it I suppose an apology is too much to hope for."

"You don't intend to argue with them?" Matt asked.

Ian shrugged. "I can't just stand around and do nothing, whatever the police say. There must be an explanation. I'll be damned if I go without one."

Sandra frowned. "Couldn't you just leave it? For tonight at least?"

Ian's expression was tight. "No, I could not."

He headed for the back door, the same one through which Matthew had left hours earlier. "I won't be long," he said, and before anyone could object, he was out the door and off up the drive.

Dusk had given way to night. Although the sound of traffic on the main road floated on the breeze, and the odd bird called out in the trees, the air was tranquil. The police patrol car had gone, and everyone had returned home. Lights shone from the neighboring properties as they all went about their business.

At Number Seven all the ground floor curtains were still open. Every light in the house appeared to have been switched on, throwing pools of light onto the front lawn. Ian looked up at the house before going to knock on the door. In reality he had no idea what he was going to say, but that hardly seemed relevant.

A statuesque blonde woman answered the door.

"Yes?" she said, standing there, hands on hips, a gesture which seemed to draw attention to her ample chest.

Ian straightened. "I'm Ian Fleming, from Number One."

"God, not another neighbor," the woman said under her breath. "Don't you people have your own lives to live?"

Ian was outraged. "Excuse me, but until you came along we seemed to be managing that just fine. It was your son who locked my boy in your shed."

"He is not my son," the woman said. "And as we all told the police, none of us even saw your precious boy. If you can't keep a proper eye on your children you can hardly expect us to do it for you."

Ian's jaw dropped. "Well somebody shut him in there. The police told us that the door had been barred from the outside. Furthermore, Matthew said that a boy called Thomas shut him in. Although he might not be your son, I understand that he does live here?"

"Yes he does, but Thomas said he didn't do it. Why would he?"

"Perhaps if you can't answer that, his parents might be able to," Ian said, his tone short. "Are they in?"

"That's none of your business."

"So just who are you then?"

"That's none of your business either."

"I think you owe me the decency of giving me your name," Ian said. "Or the name of the boy's parents?"

The woman glared at Ian, her eyes narrow and assessing. "If it makes you happy, I'm Trixie Bartlett," she said, "but that's all I'm saying. Everything else is none of your business."

Ian shook his head with frustration. "Well then, Ms. Bartlett," he said, "I want to know what you're going to do to discipline this boy, Thomas. You can't let him go around doing what he did today."

"How many times do I have to tell you? He said he wasn't involved." She threw back her mane of blonde hair, and gave him that same penetrating stare. "Look, I've got much better things to do than stand around arguing the toss with you. If you want to discipline anyone, start in your own back yard. If you let a boy that young wander around unsupervised you've got no one to blame but yourselves. Now I'd like you to get the heck off my property, and leave us the hell alone."

And with that she slammed the door in Ian's face.

"You just wouldn't read about it," Ian said later to his wife.

Both were preparing for bed. A blissful quiet had descended on the house. Matthew and Rose were sound asleep, and for now Matthew seemed no worse off for his ordeal. In the course of giving him a bath Sandra had questioned him a little more closely about what had transpired. Physically he seemed unharmed.

They had decided against taking him down the road to the emergency clinic, feeling that it would only add to the drama of an already chaotic evening. For Ian's part, he still felt stunned by his encounter. He did not know such heartless people existed.

Sandra sat at the dressing table, brushing her hair with slow deliberate strokes in the same way she had every evening of their married life.

"The whole situation seems very strange," Sandra said. "You reckon there was no sign of either Thomas or a parent?"

Ian shook his head. "No, there was only this Trixie, and I tell you she looks like one tough cookie. Hard as nails."

"So if she isn't the boy's mother, who is? And where was the boy's mother? And what is the boy doing living in a house with someone who's not his mother?"

"I don't know," Ian said.

"And there was no man around the place?"

"None in evidence. Lisa and Joan never saw a man earlier either. They both saw the woman we think is the mother. She arrived with the boy. Then Karen saw this Trixie person arriving when she got home from work."

"Weird."

"Families do come in all shapes and sizes these days. It's getting to the stage where the good old nuclear family is no longer a given."

Sandra was wide-eyed. "Do you think they're lesbians?"

Ian shrugged. "Don't know. Don't care. I certainly wouldn't want to ask, that's for sure."

"And what about the boy? It seems incredible to think of someone so young doing something so sinister."

As Ian took off his shirt he said, "We don't know that though, do we?"

"That it was sinister? How else would you interpret such behavior?"

"As a prank, like the police said. He did make out to Matthew that the whole thing was a joke."

"But it hardly was that," Sandra said. "I can't see anything in the least bit funny about pushing a defenseless four-year old boy into a shed and locking him in. Why are you all of a sudden defending him?"

"I'm not. I'm just trying to get my head around it. If this Trixie is anything to go by he certainly doesn't have the world's greatest role models."

"Say that again. It's unbelievable how rude she was to you. No apology or anything."

"I know."

"It makes you wonder what the world is coming to. It's a sad day when you're not safe on your own doorstep. I'm not sure I want to live cheek-by-jowl with people so rude, obnoxious and downright dangerous."

Ian said, "You know we can't do anything about that yet. We've set our goals and in order to reach them we have to wait a couple of years. We need to pay a bit more off the mortgage before we can consider moving."

"And what are we supposed to do in the meantime? Live in the company of gangsters and thugs?"

"According to her they've done nothing wrong. According to her we've got no one but ourselves to blame."

Sandra's eyes met Ian's in the mirror. She stopped brushing her hair mid stroke.

"And is that what you think? That it's my fault?"

Ian shrugged, his eyes darting away from hers as he turned to check the alarm setting on the clock radio.

"Well, do you?" Sandra demanded, turning on her seat to confront him. "Do you think I'm to blame?"

"Well, you were in charge when he disappeared," Ian said, his tone expressionless.

"And you think I meant to fall asleep?" Sandra asked, her voice rising by degrees.

"Of course not. But the whole thing wouldn't have happened if you'd not fallen asleep."

Sandra slammed the hairbrush down on the table. "Great," she shrieked. "So the whole world blames me for what happened."

"Shh. You'll wake the children."

"Well, that'll be something else you can blame me for, won't it?" Sandra snapped, gleaming tears welling up.

Ian came and perched himself on the end of the bed opposite her. He reached out and took her hand in his.

"Look," he said, "I don't blame you, and what's more I can't see the point in going over it. There are just too many 'what ifs'. I think we should just be very grateful that it didn't turn out any worse and that we got our little boy back safe and sound."

Sandra's tears fell faster. "But it was my fault," she sobbed. "I was so tired. I couldn't keep my eyes open a moment longer."

"Don't be too hard on yourself. You have to admit that Rose is a bit of a nightmare."

"And you're never home," Sandra said between sobs. "I have to manage everything on my own. Even today, when I needed you the most, you weren't there for me."

Ian stiffened and removed his hand. "You know I can't help that. It's the job. If I want to get anywhere with my career I have to put in the hours."

"But work sees more of you than we do."

"Sandra," Ian said, "we've been over all of this before. If we want to have a comfortable lifestyle, if we want to do all the things we've talked about, send the children to the sort of schools we would like to have had the opportunity to go to ourselves, then we have to make sacrifices. Short term pain for long term gain, remember?"

Sandra was silent.

"We've been over this plenty of times before. You did agree with me."

"I suppose," she conceded.

Ian patted her hand. "Let's go to bed, eh? It's been an exhausting day. I don't think this is the right time to be talking about any of this stuff."

Sandra sighed. "All right."

"It's for the best," Ian said. "Onward and upward."

Sandra folded back the duvet, exhausted to her marrow. As she went to climb into bed a cry filled the air. Rose.

Roger found Lisa perched on the edge of the bed. He sat beside her.

"I thought you would've been asleep ages ago," he said. "At least you *should* have been asleep ages ago. It's been an exhausting day for you."

Lisa waved the antacid packet at him. "It's a bit hard to sleep when you've got heartburn so bad you feel as though you must have a baby dragon inside you, practicing fire breathing."

"It won't be long now. Think on it as your heroic deed for the day."

"Hardly. Meanwhile, I've swallowed so many of these antacids you could sell me off at the local high school as a substitute for litmus paper."

Roger laughed. "Someone once told me that if you broke the human body down into all its minerals you'd only be able to sell yourself off for about four dollars fifty. Maybe I might get a bit more for you as litmus."

"Great," Lisa said, rolling her eyes. "Now you're starting to sound like Karen."

Roger grimaced. "Feel free to shoot me whenever that happens."

"I'll tell her you said that."

Roger lay down on the bed and stared at the ceiling.

"It's been quite an evening."

"I'll say. There are no words to express how I felt when I saw Matthew being carried up the road by that policeman. Such relief."

"It was a great moment. It's the hours before that'll stay with me the most, though."

"All that worry?"

Roger said, "In a situation like that worry sounds such a trivial word. Sandra's face was the personification of agony. A real hell on earth."

"I know. She looked like she'd forgotten how to breathe."

"And what about Ian? Have you ever seen anyone as arrogant as he is so…deflated? It was like the proud balloon that usually keeps his chest stuck out had suddenly been popped."

Lisa leant over and patted him on the cheek. "I still think you should have been an English professor," she said. "What a way you have with words sometimes."

"Ah, but instead I get to work my administrative magic for Tempo."

"A chain of menswear stores can hardly be compared to Shakespeare, however good a job you do."

Roger rolled over and leant on one elbow. "It doesn't matter to me," he said. "You know I've got about as much ambition as a two-toed sloth. What matters to me are you and our lovely baby. The biggest lesson from tonight is that family is paramount. You, me and our baby."

Lisa smiled. "It hardly seems real. Imagine us being a family."

"It is a bit strange. We've been together so long, just the two of us, nice and comfortable. It makes you wonder how we'll ever adjust to being parents."

Lisa shivered. "Scary word that."

"What, parent?"

"Yes. It sounds like a badge of responsibility. An all consuming, weighty and unavoidable mantle of responsibility."

Roger said. "Still, look how many people have done it before us and come out the other side."

"Yes, but look how many haven't. The amount of people who seem to get divorced once their children leave home, the amount these days that don't even get that far."

Roger reached up with his free hand and stroked Lisa's soft blonde hair. "Don't worry," he said. "I'm sure some of those people were having trouble long before babies came along. Who knows? Some of them might have decided to have a baby in order to draw them closer together."

"So you think we'll be fine?"

"Of course we will," Roger said.

"I have to admit that the idea of looking after a baby is overwhelming. I've never done this before. I barely know one end of a baby from the other."

"Ah, well, you're in luck there. No diagrams required. One end makes a big horrible crying noise. The other end makes big, horrible smells and messes. You'll have no problem at all."

Lisa laughed. "If only everyone out there didn't make it sound so awful. People - well parents, to be more precise - are always telling me about the terrible times they've had with their children."

"Kill-joys."

"You should hear some of the horror stories I've heard about giving birth. It's enough to put you off for life."

Roger laughed and patted her tummy. "Bit late now," he said with a lopsided smile.

"That's what I'm afraid of."

"Well, I say 'pah' to the critics," Roger said. "It's our baby and we're damn well going to enjoy it. Besides," he added with a smile, "if the baby is too unmanageable, we could always send it next door to live with Auntie Karen for a while."

CHAPTER FOUR

The Advent Birth Centre sat in the heart of a complex housing a whole raft of health providers who clung together in a medical enclave. In the course of a visit to the centre a person could, among other things, have their eyes tested, have a sample of blood taken, see any one of six general practitioners, be treated for infertility, have a root canal, or in the case of Lisa McLean, visit a midwife.

Calm and professional, everything smacked of the very latest in technology and efficiency. Patients were made to feel safe just by looking at the decor. Even the neat, economical gardens outside each facility gave the sense of careful nurturing, exuding the sort of confidence patients like to see in the medical profession.

In the waiting room sat a bevy of women in varying degrees of pregnancy. Lisa took comfort from the fact that she was by no means the largest in the room, but then reminded herself she did still have six weeks to go. She sat flicking the pages of a magazine, looking with one envious eye at the stick thin models and film stars that graced their pages. Had there ever been a time when she had been like that? When all her clothes didn't have to have strange little gussets to accommodate her ever-expanding waistline? When she could still see her toes?

All the while she took in small glimpses of the other women. She wondered if they all felt as nervous as she did about impending events. Did they worry - but not voice - their concerns that there would be something wrong with the baby? Did they wonder whether they were cut out for motherhood?

Amid all these thoughts, her turn came. Her midwife, Leslie Chalmers, was a homely woman in her early forties with three children of her own and a wealth of experience to match. Lisa found her very sympathetic, very thorough, and above all, very caring.

"You're looking much better, I'd say," Leslie said, as she ushered Lisa into her room.

Lisa smiled. "I'd say I feel it. I'm so pleased I decided to give up work. I didn't realize what a strain it was until I stopped."

"Your body knew," Leslie said. "Blood pressure never lies." They sat down. "Speaking of which, let's start there."

By now Lisa knew the drill. Over the next few minutes they went through the process of checking Lisa's blood pressure and ruling out any signs of pre-eclampsia.

"That's great," Leslie said as she finished making notes in Lisa's file. "Much improved. Finishing work seems to have done the trick. Been keeping your fluid levels up?"

Lisa nodded. "It's not easy. I feel swollen enough without adding fuel to the fire."

"Do your best. It's important. Weight?"

Lisa obliged by standing on the scales, but averted her gaze. Some things in life she would rather not know about.

"I'll get you to hop up on the table and we'll have a listen to how things are going in there."

"I'm afraid hopping is out of the question these days," Lisa said, heaving herself up.

"This gel will be a bit cold," Leslie said. "Usual story." She smeared it over a section of Lisa's abdomen then used the little device to listen to the sounds inside. As much as the sound might be likened to a washing machine, Lisa took reassurance from hearing her baby's heartbeat.

"Sound okay?" she asked.

Leslie nodded as she stretched a tape measure vertically over Lisa's bump, a tape measure that seemed to get shorter and shorter as each week passed by. "You can get up now."

Lisa once again heaved herself, straightened her clothes and resumed her seat.

Leslie went back to making her notes, then looked up and smiled. "Right, that's it. Everything seems on track. I'll see you again next week unless there's anything you want to discuss?"

"Not unless you count my irrational fear of childbirth?"

Leslie laughed. "You're hardly alone there. I doubt there's a woman on the planet who approaches labor without some degree of trepidation. How have your antenatal classes gone?"

"One more to go later this week and then we're all finished."

"No one had their baby yet?"

"Not yet. We're all wondering who will be the first."

"Have you found the classes good?"

Lisa chewed her lip thoughtfully. "Not bad. It sounds quite straightforward on paper, in the sort of way which defies both imagination and the laws of science."

Leslie laughed again. "We'll do our best to see that you're fine. Have you ever talked with your own mother about her labors? It doesn't always have a bearing, but it might help. Not to mention the fact that I find it quite interesting myself."

"I'm afraid she won't be any help at all," Lisa said.

"Because she lives in Wellington?"

"No, because she's never given birth. I'm adopted."

"Are you? I never knew."

Lisa shrugged. "Why would you?"

Leslie regarded Lisa with interest. "How do you feel about that?"

Lisa sat up in the chair and rubbed her back. "It doesn't bother me unduly. We don't know anything about my birth parents. Neither of them have come looking for me and I've never had any real desire to go looking for them."

"You hear of people hankering to find out even the simplest things. You've never been curious?

"No. Well, maybe just a little. But my parents were so great. I never felt any sense of displacement."

"Will they come up when the baby is born?"

Lisa shook her head. "Dad is scheduled for hip replacement surgery in two weeks' time. Mum will have to look after him. They did consider asking for a postponement, but he's been on the waiting list such a long time and is so uncomfortable that he can't afford to forego the surgery. He really needs it done."

"That's a shame. Still, those first few weeks are pretty busy. Coping with a new baby will make the time fly. I'm assuming Roger will be having some time off?"

"Just try to stop him," Lisa said. "Sometimes I get the impression he'd have the baby himself if he could."

"I bet you wish that too," Leslie said with a gentle smile.

"You're not wrong there."

"We'll see you next week, then. Don't forget, plenty of fluid, plenty of rest, as much sleep as you can manage."

Lisa smiled. "Yes, boss," came the meek reply.

Lisa drove to a small strip of shops in the middle of a neighboring suburb. These contained a dairy, bakery, takeaway shop, movie rental store, pharmacy, trendy cafe and the hairdressing salon where Karen worked. Lisa found an angle park out in front of the bakery, and eased herself from behind the wheel.

Karen looked up as Lisa entered the salon and waved her hairbrush in the air as she continued blow-drying her client's hair. Lisa expected to have to wait at least some time so sat herself on the sofa in the reception area.

Karen's newest trainee came scuttling over, her expression like a nervous dog.

"Do you have an appointment?" the girl asked.

"Only in a manner of speaking," Lisa replied. "I've come to have coffee with Karen."

"Oh." The girl looked confused. "Should I make it for you?"

Lisa has to stop herself from laughing. "No. It's a nice offer but I think we'll probably go next door to the cafe."

"Right." More puzzled looks. "Are you a friend of Karen's, then?"

"That's right. You haven't been here very long, have you?"

The girl shook her head, her lanky locks swaying. "Two weeks."

"Enjoying it?"

"Oh yes. Karen and Glenda are both awesome to work for."

"Have you just left school?"

The girl nodded. She pouted, and said, "It was boring."

Lisa wondered how long the novelty of this new employment would last.

"Ready then?" Karen asked, appearing at Lisa's side.

Lisa nodded and once again heaved herself into a standing position.

Karen said, "Don't need to use the bathroom before we go?"

"Oh, ha ha. Mock the poor pregnant one."

Karen turned on her usual cheeky grin. "Just checking."

"Truth be told, I did go before leaving the Birth Centre."

Karen laughed. "That'll see you right for another twenty minutes then."

"If I'm lucky."

As Karen held the door open for Lisa, she said to the young girl, "I'll be back in about twenty, twenty-five minutes. Mrs. Jarvis isn't due for half an hour, but if she comes in early whiz down and let me know would you? She's a pain if you keep her waiting."

As they walked along the footpath, Lisa said, "Looks like you've got your work cut out for you there, if you'll pardon the pun."

"Who, Mirabelle?"

"Mirabelle? Wow. That's some name."

"She's sweet really, but I think you might be right. She's the kid sister of my brother's girlfriend. I sort of got blackmailed into taking her on."

"That sounds intriguing. How so?"

"It's Mum and Dad's fortieth wedding anniversary coming up in April. Both Simon and I feel we ought to do something to help them celebrate since neither of them are likely to organize anything themselves. But of course neither of us wants to volunteer and take on the responsibility. So I said to Simon that I'd give in to his pestering about Mirabelle and give her a job if he'd assume responsibility for the party."

"Sounds like you blackmailed yourself into it."

"I suppose I did," Karen admitted. "Although I sort of forgot to mention that we did need someone at work, and fast. It was a convenient solution to not one but two problems. Now I have some help in the salon and I don't have to organize the anniversary bash."

"If you can rely on Simon to do the job."

"There is that," Karen agreed as they entered the cafe. "Only time will tell whether my two solutions will end up being two problems again."

They went up to the counter, ordered food and coffee, and sat down at a table against the wall to wait.

"How did things go this morning?" Karen asked.

"Fine. Everything seems to be on track."

"You'll be relieved about that. Nothing like the threat of hospital to get a person all anxious."

"The idea of bed rest, and in hospital to boot, did make me feel quite concerned."

"Not long to go now."

"I wish people would stop saying that."

Karen laughed. "Someone once told me that by the end you get so big and uncomfortable that you stop worrying about the labor. You get to the stage where you'd do just about anything to get the baby out. The lady I spoke to said she would have been happy if they'd cut her head off provided she didn't have to stay pregnant one more day."

"Could you be any more encouraging?" Lisa asked.

Karen shrugged. "You know me. A veritable smorgasbord of encouraging comments up my sleeve. How's the name selection process going?"

Lisa rolled her eyes. "It's not. Roger seems to like every flowery name under the sun. Ugh. Right now we're at a stalemate."

"You could flip a coin," Karen suggested. "Or what about drawing a name out of a hat?"

"We wouldn't even be able to agree on which names to put into the hat in the first place."

"That doesn't sound like you two. Where has all the peace and harmony gone?"

"Who knows? No doubt we'll settle on something."

"What about 'Number One'? Or 'Child A'?"

"Very inventive. How about 'Oi, you!' or 'Hey, you there'?"

"Now you're talking."

Lisa raised her eyebrows. "Well, I can tell you something for nothing. It won't be Mirabelle."

"Thank God."

At that point the waitress arrived with their order, fussed about a bit, then departed.

"Now," Lisa said, sipping her weekly treat of a single cup of coffee "could we talk about something else please? I feel like I've had just about as much baby talk as I can stand today."

"Right you are," Karen agreed. "Let's talk about me."

Lisa laughed. "Great. What's new?"

"Nothing."

"That was a nice short conversation."

"What, not even a little bit of sympathy? My life is a wasteland of adventure, excitement and romance. Can't you even commiserate?"

Lisa suppressed a smile. "Poor you."

"Oh, say it once more with feeling."

"Things will change. Look on the bright side. You have a thriving business, a nice home, a good family, good friends, and a good pair of legs."

"It sounds as though you're wearing Roger's rose colored glasses. My business might be thriving, but I'm not the sole owner. I still have to split the profits with Glenda."

"At least there are profits."

Karen made a dismissive gesture. "My home is not my own as you well know. It's going to take me two lifetimes to pay my parents back"

"Well then you'll get it as part of your inheritance before it's paid off."

Karen glared. "We are talking about my family here," she said. "They'll be wanting to control my life until my dying day, regardless of whether they are still alive or not. I'll probably front up to the solicitor's office for the reading of the will to find it's got more conditions and codicils than the Magna Carta."

"You don't even know what the Magna Carta is."

"You're right. It sounded good, though."

Lisa smiled. "I'm sure you're over-dramatizing the situation. I've met your parents a few times, remember? They seemed perfectly reasonable people to me."

"It's all part of the act. You have to see what goes on behind closed doors to appreciate the finer points of their awfulness."

"Say what you like about your family. After all they are exactly that: your family. I defy you to be so critical about your friends."

Karen sighed. "You've got me there. You and Roger do keep me sane. I'm sure I'm not nearly as good a friend in return."

"Not that rubbish again. Besides, we aren't your only friends."

"I know. I don't want to put you down or anything, but somehow having friends just doesn't make amends for the lack of a significant other."

"I still say Mr. Right has to be out there somewhere."

"Right now, I'd settle for Mr. He'll Do."

"Don't you have any eligible clients?"

"Believe me, being up close and personal with men's scalps is very off-putting. One look at all the greasy build up, or the showers of dandruff, and that's it. Either that or they're happily married. The good ones always are."

"You'll have to start getting out more. Why don't you join one of those singles organizations? You know, the ones where they host elegant dinners for six or eight, so that it's not as intimidating or downright dangerous as a blind date."

"What, with all the other sad bunch of losers?"

"I get the impression from the ads I've seen that it's not like that at all."

"Thanks for the suggestion, but no thanks."

"What about a night club?"

"When did you last go to a night club?"

Lisa shrugged. "Not since I was twenty-two."

"Precisely. Nor has anyone else. Not unless they've got habits to satisfy."

"I'm sure you're exaggerating. What about a holiday? You might meet the tall, dark handsome stranger of your dreams."

"Who'll turn out to be the taxi driver, or live in Siberia, or have a wife tucked away somewhere, or have some icky disease."

Lisa threw her hands up in the air. "That's it," she said. "I give up."

Karen looked repentant. "I'm sorry. Maybe a holiday might be a good idea, even just to have a break. I might even be able to scrape enough money together to do it." She chewed her lip thoughtfully. "Then again, I wouldn't want to be away for your big event. And then there's Mum and Dad's shindig to look forward to."

"Maybe you'll meet someone there?"

"Now you really are clutching at straws. No, I just have to get used to being on the shelf. Sweet thirty-four and never been kissed."

"Now you really are exaggerating."

Karen laughed mischievously. "You've got me there, I'm afraid."

Lisa drained the last of her coffee. "Things seem to have settled down in Maybury Place, haven't they?"

"Yes, thank goodness. I never want to go through another evening like that one."

"Joan's still outraged about the new residents. Ian told her that he went to see them after the police left that evening. The blonde woman, who you saw, was just as rude to him as she had been to Joan earlier."

"So it wasn't just a case of Joan rubbing them up the wrong way?"

"Apparently not. I must admit the same thought did cross my mind."

"Still seems fishy, though, the boy locking poor little Matthew in the shed."

"I agree. But Matthew seems none the worse for his ordeal. I guess you have to be grateful for small mercies."

"Wonder what's wrong with the boy?"

"Thomas? Perhaps he was a bit unsettled with the move. I've still seen no sign of a male around the place. Maybe he's traumatized after a marriage break up or something."

"No excuse, though. Especially since he's old enough to know better."

Lisa shrugged. "Who knows? What I do know is that Joan seems to have developed an unprecedented interest in her garden. It gives her the perfect excuse to spend time out there to get a better look. And not at her garden, if you get my drift."

"Only too well."

The intrepid Mirabelle interrupted their conversation.

"Mrs. Jarvis has arrived," she said.

"Right," said Karen, standing up. "Back to the grindstone."

"My turn to pay," Lisa said. "You go, and I'll settle up."

"Tell them to put it on my account," Karen said.

"I will not."

"Suit yourself. I'll see you later." Karen turned to go, then looked back. "By the way," she said, cheeky grin fixed in place, "thanks for the comment about the legs. Good to see you at least got something right."

The problem with gardens, Joan thought, lay in the ongoing need to give them attention. In truth she had turned a blind eye to her own, ignoring its tangled awfulness. But now that the heat of summer had faded, and the mood had descended upon her, the pull to be out there proved irresistible.

In fact Joan had found herself of late overtaken by an urge to tidy up many of her affairs. She couldn't pinpoint the reason behind this new urgency, only that she looked these days with a new discontent at things that had sat around incomplete for a couple of years. There were things in the house that needed fixing. They were minor things that you could quite easily live with: loose door handles, squeaky floor boards and a set of sagging shelves, but now seemed the time to put these things in order.

Today she had chosen to work on the small border garden beside the dividing fence with Number One, pulling out weeds, aerating the soil, assessing the general condition of the plants. The cosmos, petunias, pink and white lavatera, larkspurs and delphiniums were past their best and needed removing. She would then need to make some decisions about what she might buy to fill the holes.

A voice over the fence broke her train of thought.

"Hi ho," Sandra said. "Thought you could do with a break."

Joan looked up to see Sandra brandishing a glass of water.

"Indeed I could," Joan said, accepting the glass "Thirsty work, gardening."

"You've made some headway in the last week. Not that it looked so bad before."

Joan surveyed the scene. "Purely a matter of opinion. There's a lot more I want to do yet."

"When it's done you can come and make a start on ours. Ian never gets a chance to do it justice."

"He does seem to work long hours."

Sandra shrugged and glanced away. "Can't be helped," she said.

Joan took another sip of water and pointed at Matthew as he rode around on the concrete forecourt outside the garage.

"He's all right, is he?"

Sandra nodded. "I think so. We've talked about what happened once or twice. In his mind he seems to have come to terms with it. At the very least he knows now not to go off without me. In fact the main repercussion is that he's a bit clingy." She turned to Matthew. "Come and say hello to Mrs. Davis, Matthew."

He cycled slowly over. "Hello Mrs. Davis," he said without looking at her.

"Hello there, dear," Joan said. "Being a good boy, I hope?"

Matthew made a small face, and then cycled quickly away.

"Boys," Sandra said, by way of explanation. "Not very chatty, are they?"

Joan kept her opinion to herself. "How is little Rose?"

Sandra rolled her eyes. "Asleep, thank goodness. She has the face of an angel when she's sleeping but is a bit of a devil when she's awake."

"Never mind dear," Joan said. "Time will sort her out. It's early days yet."

"You sound like a professional," Sandra said. She looked quizzically at Joan and said, "You and your husband never had children, did you?"

Joan stiffened. "No," she replied. "There are some things in life that simply aren't meant to be."

"I'm sorry," Sandra said. "I didn't mean..."

Joan made a dismissive gesture and handed back the empty glass. "No," she said again, "I'm sure you didn't."

"I wanted to thank you again for the other night," Sandra continued. "Ian and I so appreciated everyone's help, but especially yours since you were treated so rudely by the new people."

Since they had already had this conversation a few days prior, Joan said, "You don't need to keep thanking me, Sandra. I was pleased to help. I would do so again in a heartbeat. You only have to ask. As for the new residents, I think the less said about them the better, don't you?"

Sandra was prevented from answering by the arrival of Maureen.

"Hello, hello," Maureen said, her tone almost bright.

"Afternoon Maureen," Joan said.

"Doing the garden?" Maureen asked.

Joan said. "Thought I'd get stuck in before the weather turns cold and the rain sets in."

Maureen frowned. "Very admirable. It puts me to shame." She turned to Sandra. "Everything all right now?"

Sandra smiled. "Yes thanks, Maureen," she said. "Matthew's a bit reluctant to let me out of his sight. Other than that everything is back to normal."

"Shaun was like that," Maureen said. "Always into scrapes, then he'd come running home to Mummy, get over it, and go straight back out there again. In fact he's still like that."

"He's a jockey, isn't he?" Joan asked Maureen.

"Yes, down Cambridge way. He doesn't come home very often. When he does there's usually trouble not far behind."

"I'm sure he was never as bad as that young reprobate you're living beside now," Joan commented.

"Shaun would never hurt a fly. He might not have the best sense in the world, but when it comes to people - and horses - you'd never find a gentler person I'm sure."

"So, no fall-out from the other night from your new neighbors?" Joan asked.

"None. They've kept to themselves. One of the women drives the boy to school every morning, but she seems to come straight back. I've yet to see her without dark glasses on, even if it's cloudy."

"And the other woman?" Sandra asked. "The one that was so rude to Ian?"

"Haven't seen a lot of her either. She goes out a bit, but neither of them seem to have proper nine-to-five jobs."

"What does Brian make of it?"

Maureen fingered her crucifix. "He's not big on neighborhood news. He reckons that as long as they keep to themselves we should let them get on with it."

Joan snorted under her breath. "Didn't make a very good start at that, did they?"

As Maureen went to reply the peace and tranquility of Maybury Place shattered as two men on motorbikes tore up the road and drove straight into the driveway at Number Seven. The hulking great bikes had throaty engines that throbbed out a primeval roar.

The men on the back of the bikes wore leathers and helmets that did little to lessen their intimidating presence. They were unlike anyone the women had seen in the street before. They parked, eased off their bikes and went up to the front door. Trixie appeared and ushered them inside. She paused on the threshold long enough to give her neighborhood audience a disdainful stare.

"Bikers?" Joan croaked. "What on earth are bikers doing visiting?"

Maureen and Sandra exchanged glances.

"I hope they aren't going to be regular visitors," Sandra said, casting a worried glance at Matthew, who had ridden over to see the source of the noise.

Joan pursed her lips. "This doesn't bode well," she said. "I've got a feeling in my bones. Where those women are concerned, we haven't seen anything yet."

The following morning Lisa became overwhelmed with the urge to bake. She had little experience since while she and Roger were both working they had favored eating anything that required the minimum of preparation. But she figured it was about time she reformed her ways. She was overwhelmed with a sense of sweet domesticity. The idea of donning an apron and throwing some baking into the oven could be a surefire way of turning her into a domestic goddess.

Upon examination of the cupboards she discovered the tried and true Edmond's Cookbook. Someone had given it to her at her kitchen tea. It had been sadly neglected ever since. Her enthusiasm for cooking in her early-married days had not taken long to wane. Flicking through it Lisa found several things that sounded more than a little appealing. On reading the required ingredients she found she didn't have half the things it said you needed. Finally she found a recipe that seemed easy enough and for which she felt prepared.

She went to try on her apron and was momentarily thrown when she couldn't reach behind her to fasten the ties together. Then, having littered the bench with the ingredients, she started to read the directions.

"Cream the butter and sugar until light and fluffy," Lisa read. She took out her mixer, washed the dust out of the bowl and threw the butter and sugar in. She turned the machine on and stood watching as the beaters combined the ingredients and waited for it to look suitably light and fluffy.

It stayed looking unappealing and stodgy.

She waited some more, but still no improvement.

"Stupid thing," she said, turning off the machine.

She was wondering what she ought to do next, when she heard a knock at the front door.

Sandra stood on the doorstep.

"Hello," Lisa said, mustering up a smile in the nick of time.

"Hi. I hope I haven't caught you at a bad time."

"No, no," Lisa said. "Come on in. In fact you might be able to help me."

"That sounds interesting."

Lisa made a face. "I'm afraid it isn't. Come along to the kitchen and you can tell me what I'm doing wrong."

They entered the kitchen and Sandra's brows rose at the sight of everything everywhere.

"Looks like you're having fun."

"Hmm. Ever had times when you thought you had a really good idea, only to discover how wrong you were?"

"Practically every day."

Lisa smiled. "I'm having one of those."

"What's gone wrong?"

"It says to cream the butter and the sugar until it's light and fluffy, but you could use mine as a temporary boat anchor I think."

"Let's see? Yes, not great."

"What have I done wrong?" Lisa asked.

"Did you use softened butter, or use it straight out of the fridge?"

"Out of the fridge. Why? Wasn't I supposed to?"

"It works better softened. And you need to have your machine on a higher speed too. It fluffs it up more."

"And how am I supposed to know that?"

Sandra shrugged. "Cookbooks always assume you've got some knowledge, or else they have a page of tips buried somewhere that you've never read. After all, nobody reads a cookbook like an ordinary book, do they?"

"So do I need to start again?"

"No. Just throw the eggs in, beef up the speed, and it'll probably come right."

"Thanks."

Sandra looked at her sharply. "Not nesting are you?"

"What?"

"Strange desires to do domestic chores. It's a sign of nesting. It could mean the baby is on its way."

"It better not be. I've still got six weeks to go."

"It could be early. If the baby comes two weeks early, then you've only got four weeks to go."

"And if it's two weeks late, I could have another eight."

Sandra sent her a wry look. "Not very predictable, though, babies. Either before they're born, or after. Have you bought all the furniture you need?"

"Mostly. We're talking about getting the room ready this weekend, or maybe the next."

"Leaving it quite late, aren't you? What about prams and car seats and the like?"

"We've settled on what we're going to buy. There's a lot to choose from, isn't there?"

"There is. If you want any tips, just say. We experienced mothers can always tell you what works and what doesn't."

Lisa managed a weak smile. "Thanks."

"Speaking of thanks, that's why I've come. To say a belated thank you to you and Roger for all your help last week. I've been meaning to come every day, but what with one thing and another, I haven't had the chance."

"We were just pleased it all worked out in the end. Joan said Matthew's doing really well."

Sandra smiled. "He's a resilient boy."

"What about you? Have you recovered?"

Sandra made a quick gesture with her hands. "Every time I think about it I get chills up and down my spine. But as Ian says, you can't live your life thinking about the 'what ifs'."

"Easier said than done."

Sandra nodded. "Men don't seem to dwell on things like women do. For them, if it doesn't work, just forget it; if it hurts too much, shrug it off."

"Very true. Where's Rose, by the way?"

Sandra laughed shortly. "What, worried I might have lost the other one? No, Mum's at home looking after her for me."

"You're lucky to have her so close."

Sandra looked at Lisa thoughtfully. "Your mother's in Wellington, isn't she?"

Lisa nodded. "At the moment I feel as though Mum and Dad may as well be on the other side of the planet. While it was my decision to move here, away from my family, at times I wonder what on earth I could have been thinking."

"You'd never have met Roger then, would you?"

"Too true. I guess you can't have everything."

Sandra agreed. "Some things are more important than others. Your priorities change. Right now, for instance, good old basic safety is pretty high on my priority list. Two weeks ago, the high things on my list were money, and trying to get a bit of time to myself."

"Oh?"

"Well, look at last week. Admittedly, if Matthew hadn't gone out to look at the truck nothing might have happened, but you'd think that in a suburb like ours a kid would be safe to go out on the street for five minutes."

"They say nowhere is safe these days," Lisa said.

"Nevertheless. There's something distinctly odd about those people."

"Joan said they gave Ian short shrift."

"That's putting it mildly. Not even a whiff of an apology. We wonder whether it's just the tip of the iceberg. Yesterday I was out in the street, talking to Joan and Maureen, when a couple of bikers came roaring down the road and into there." Sandra rolled her eyes. "I'm telling you, they looked like gang members to me. Big and mean and a bit unwashed looking."

"Maybe they were there to do some sort of job?" Lisa suggested.

"They had a distinct lack of tools and equipment with them, if that was the case. Then, to cap it off the police were there again last night."

"Really? When?"

"Ian went out to put Matthew's trike away about nine o'clock, wandered down to the letter box to see if there was any junk mail, and saw a police patrol car sitting in Number Seven's driveway. They were there some time because when I looked out half an hour later, the car was still there."

"Perhaps they were following up about last week."

Sandra rolled her eyes again, reminding Lisa of a character from a melodrama. "I doubt that very much. We got the distinct impression they'd done all that they were prepared to do on the matter. Case closed. So you've got to wonder what on earth is going on there, don't you? Joan said to us she had a bad feeling about them and do you know, for once, I think I agree with her."

Roger came home later than usual on a Friday night, bound as he was by an obligation to spend at least an hour at the ritual drinks session held at Head Office. It was a chance for wider management, of which Roger was a part, to congregate and make boastful claims about their achievements for the week, and even more boastful claims about which activities they would be engaged in over the weekend.

Roger would never be called unsociable but he often found himself irritated during these sessions. He enjoyed his job, in a mundane sort of way. There was nothing else he would rather be doing for a career since he had a natural flair for organization and methods. But as for standing around bragging about it, well, he simply couldn't be bothered. The opportunity for people to blow their own trumpets, long and loud at times, constituted the type of spectacle Roger would do anything to avoid.

As for all the hype about weekend activities, there again Roger had little to contribute. He wasn't a great outdoors man, although he enjoyed getting out and about as much as the next person. He didn't sail, hunt, shoot, fish, play rugby, abseil, hang-glide, or white water raft. In fact he liked nothing more than to have the weekends at home pottering around and spending time with Lisa. Nothing wrong with that, one might think, except that it made him sound unsubstantial and unmanly and unmotivated.

So, with a sense of relief he left for home on a Friday night, a relief that turned to happiness the moment he turned the car into the peaceful refuge of Maybury Place. He let himself in through the back door, slipped off his shoes, and listened for signs of life. The kitchen bore traces of Lisa's handiwork. The benches were littered with baking ingredients and equipment, with mess everywhere, just as there had been for the previous three nights.

Roger found Lisa curled up as best she could on the couch, a box of tissues balancing on her stomach, watching the end of a soppy DVD she'd hired, and sobbing her eyes out. Her intense focus on the action meant she hadn't even heard Roger come home. He could do little more than to shake his head in disbelief at the sight of his blubbering wife. She who had never cried at anything much before had been reduced to an emotional wreck by the sheer fact of being pregnant.

"Roger!" she said, her face lighting up as she caught sight of him. "I'm so pleased you're home."

"Me too," he said, coming over to embrace her. He bent down awkwardly to do so, then perched himself on the coffee table in front of her. "Movie nearly over?"

"Oh, it's all right," she said, leaning over to the remote control to switch it off. "I've already watched it twice today."

Roger raised his eyebrows. "Twice? I thought you were going to make a start on sorting out the baby's room."

Lisa looked guilty. "Hmm," she said, "but I thought I'd have one more crack at baking."

"So I saw. Didn't you think that three days in a row was enough? We'll have food coming out our ears."

"If only we did," Lisa said. "Nothing I've made has been a success."

Her face was a picture of sadness. She reminded Roger of a small child trying to come to terms with a large disappointment.

He patted her hand. "Then why bother? Don't do it if it makes you unhappy."

"I was determined not to let it beat me. If Sandra can do it, I can do it."

"Forget Sandra. Why is it so important?"

Lisa sighed. "She knows everything about everything, especially parenting. Even when it came to baking she knew what to do. She makes me feel so inadequate."

"She wasn't so adequate last week when I was sitting in her living room while her son was missing," Roger said. "And as much as we agreed that you can't be judgmental about what happened, you have to also question her parenting skills too. She's far from perfect, Lisa."

"I know. But she seems to wear this secret look that tells me that she knows everything and I know nothing, especially when it comes to talking about babies. And right now, I know it's true. I do know nothing about babies."

"Lisa, we've been over this before. Don't worry about it. You'll make a great mother."

"But how will I know what to do?"

"You'll learn. We'll figure it out together."

She attempted a small smile. "Always the optimist."

"I don't think I am being optimistic about this. We're both intelligent adults, we've done the classes, it's one baby. I'm sure we'll be fine." He patted her hand again. "Meanwhile, you've got nothing to prove to Sandra, about baking, or anything else for that matter."

"Really?"

"Really."

"And you don't care that I can't bake for peanuts?"

"Not a bit. Not for peanuts, or even with peanuts. After all, you don't want me getting paunchy or anything. Better if I steer clear of too much baking."

"Implying that one fatty in the family is enough?"

"Implying nothing of the sort," Roger said firmly. "You're very quick to twist things around these days, my darling, and it's time you stopped. I love you, you're not fat, and you've never looked more beautiful. How many times do I have to tell you?"

Lisa looked repentant. "Okay, okay." Then a mischievous expression flitted across her face. "Do you love me enough to help me clean up the mess in the kitchen?"

Roger looked resigned to his fate. "Go on, then."

"And help me cook the dinner?"

He rolled his eyes. "Maybe. If you're good. Come on, I'll help you up."

He had just pulled Lisa to her feet when the doorbell rang.

"Who could that be?" he asked. "It seems to get more and more like Grand Central Station here every day."

"Only one way to find out," Lisa said, "but whoever it is, don't take them into the kitchen under any circumstances."

Roger laughed, and went to open the door. It was Maureen Haskell, looking thinner than ever in a wispy dress that was clearly doing nothing to stave off the cool evening air.

"Maureen," he said. "How are you?"

"Hello, Roger," she said her voice as thin as a reed. "Not too bad, considering."

"Come in."

"Thanks. I won't keep you long, but I wondered if Lisa was home."

"Sure. We're in the lounge."

Maureen crept up the hall behind Roger.

"Hello, Lisa."

"Hi Maureen. How are things?"

"So so. You all right?"

"Fine. Has something happened?"

Maureen, Roger noticed, looked unsteady on her feet.

"What is it, Maureen? he asked. "Look, have a seat, and tell us what's wrong. Do you want a drink? I'm sure there's some brandy around if it would help?"

Maureen nodded. She subsided into a chair and Roger pressed the drink into her hand. She took a minute sip, holding the glass in her hand as though the mere pressure of her fingers might be enough to crack the tumbler.

"Better?"

She nodded again.

"Think you can tell us what's happened?"

Maureen swallowed another small sip. "We've been robbed," she said, her voice tremulous.

"Robbed?" Roger and Lisa chorused in surprise.

Maureen nodded yet again, the power of speech having deserted her.

"When?" Lisa asked.

"This afternoon, I think. I didn't go out until late morning. When I came back, at about four-thirty, I found the place in a huge mess."

"And was there much taken?" Roger asked.

"Not that we can tell. We haven't got anything of much value in the house. Even the television and DVD are quite old now. Older than must be desirable, because they're still there."

"Really?" Roger said. "But they made a mess? As though they were look-ing for something?"

"Yes."

"And does Brian know?"

Maureen played with her necklace nervously. "I called him straight away and he came right home. He's hopping mad. Keeps asking me if I locked the door. Which I did."

"You don't have an alarm system?"

Maureen let out a staccato burst of laughter. "You'd think we would have, Brian being an electrician and all that, but like I said, we don't have anything valuable. He said it was a waste of time. And money."

"And have the police been?"

"We've called them. They say they'll be around, but burglaries are a dime a dozen. It doesn't sound as though it's a high priority." She looked bashful. Emboldened by the warmth of the alcohol she took another larger swig of drink. "I don't think Brian shouting at them over the telephone helped."

"Never mind," Lisa said. "They'll come."

"I know," she said. Her tone was resigned. "In the meantime I thought I'd do something useful, like ask if anyone saw anything. You were home this afternoon, weren't you, Lisa?"

"I was," she said, "but I'm sorry to say that I saw nothing." A flash of guilt crossed her face. "I spent most of the afternoon lying down, quite in another world, I'm afraid."

"You weren't to know."

"Perhaps some of the other neighbors might have seen something? What about Joan?"

Maureen shook her head. "She was out too."

"Geoff?"

"He doesn't appear to be home at the moment. His jeep is missing from the driveway and there aren't any lights on."

"And Karen won't be of any help," Lisa added. "She'll still be at work. They were going to stay back and have a few drinks with a couple of their regular clients."

Maureen looked downcast.

"What about the new neighbors?" Roger suggested.

Maureen's face mirrored her doubt. "To be honest, I'd rather not ask them. I don't mean to cast aspersions but in the space of the last two weeks we've had an abduction, seen gang members in the street, the police calling, and now a robbery."

Roger frowned. "You think they might have had something to do with it?"

Maureen shrugged. "Not them, perhaps. Maybe one of their callers. They do seem to have a lot of people coming and going. This week alone I've seen four different men come and go in cars, and that doesn't include the bikers that Joan and Sandra and I saw."

"All men?" Lisa asked.

Maureen nodded. "That I've seen. It makes me wonder if that policeman didn't have a point when he talked about Neighborhood Watch last week. Perhaps it's time we had something like that."

Roger and Lisa were silent for a moment before Lisa said, "I'm sorry we can't be more helpful."

Maureen put her empty glass down on the coffee table. "Not to worry," she said again. "It was just a thought. I'd better get going."

She stood. Her dress was a cascade of wrinkles that she smoothed down with a nervous hand. "Hopefully the police will arrive soon. In the meantime there's always the dinner to cook, isn't there?"

CHAPTER FIVE

Before he knew it Roger found himself going about his Monday morning routine, more like a condemned man than a willing employee. The weekend had flown by in a whirl of preparations as he and Lisa had worked toward trying to get baby's room ready for its upcoming arrival.

"What do you think you might do today?" Roger asked, as he carried his drained coffee cup into the kitchen to put it in the sink.

"Not baking that's for sure," Lisa said with a smile. "The way I see it, if what everybody says is true, I'm not going to have any time for such things when the baby comes. In which case why change the habits of a lifetime?"

"That's more like it," Roger said, returning her smile. "So what will you do instead?"

Lisa shrugged. "I've got an appointment with Leslie this afternoon. It's Karen's usual every second Monday off so I might see her a bit later. There are still one or two things that need finishing in the baby's room that we didn't get done over the weekend."

"Not that much. We worked pretty hard yesterday to get it finished."

"According to Sandra we should have everything organized by now. We had better not dare disobey."

Roger frowned. "I thought we'd sorted out all that rubbish about Sandra Fleming."

Lisa's face broke into a mischievous grin. "Had you going for a minute there, didn't I?"

Roger rolled his eyes. "You could pop over to see Maureen if you get the chance," he said. "She did seem quite shaken up on Friday."

"She always seems a bit shaken up to me," Lisa said. "In some ways, she didn't seem too much more upset than usual."

"Still, it's not a nice thing to happen to anyone. And, loathe as I am to 'cast aspersions', as Maureen put it, you have to admit that things seem to be spiraling a little out of control since Trixie and her cohorts moved in."

"And I can't say I was too impressed with the noise they made on Saturday night. What with being responsible for the disappearance of a four year old boy and having music blaring until two o'clock in the morning, they're not making an effort to endear themselves to the rest of the neighbors are they?"

"I quite agree. For people who seem to have an unusually high desire for privacy, they weren't too reticent on Saturday night, were they?"

"Yes, but in a furtive kind of way," Lisa said. "When I saw Joan yesterday she said she'd watched as people arrived. She reckoned they still only opened the front door for the smallest amount of time."

"There's definitely something funny about those people. Which reminds me, I've been thinking about something that Maureen said on Friday night, about Neighborhood Watch. I wonder if there may be something in that idea."

"You mean for us to set one up in the street?"

Roger nodded. "I haven't got the foggiest idea what's involved, but maybe it's time we banded together a bit more, looked after one another a bit better. It's not as though we don't know everyone in the street."

"And you don't think that's enough?"

"I don't know. If you got a chance you could raise the idea with Joan. See what she thinks. Maybe even ask a couple of the other neighbors and try to gauge support."

"You want me to talk to Joan?"

"I'm not asking you to run naked through the street."

"We definitely wouldn't want Neighborhood Watch in that case, would we?"

"Ha ha. Don't forget you're the one who's always sticking up for Joan and saying she's just a lonely old woman. Time to put your money where your mouth is kiddo. Get her involved in something. Besides," he added with a grin, "anything's got to be better than baking."

By mid morning Lisa had tidied up all the odds and ends left over in the baby's room, and could now officially say that it was ready. She suppressed a desire to run straight over to Sandra Fleming's and tell her in person, even though she had been quite serious when she'd told Roger she was over her feelings of inadequacy.

She did, however, have a desire to talk to someone. She dialed Karen's number but there was no reply. Whatever Karen's plans were for her day off, they clearly didn't include staying home this morning. Lisa sank down on the sofa, tempted to have a rest, but it occurred to her that maybe the rot was setting in. She then considered going to see Maureen, but things looked closed up next door.

She felt so restless, so filled with the need to do something that she decided that she would go to see Joan after all, raise the suggestion of Neighborhood Watch, and see where that took her. She looked out into the street. Joan's windows were open and the net curtains wafted gently in the breeze. Lisa slipped on some shoes and headed across the road.

She knocked on the door and waited barely ten seconds before Joan appeared.

"Lisa, my dear," she beamed. "How lovely to see you! Do come in."

"Thanks."

Lisa followed Joan into her lounge. It was stuffed full of rigid, proper looking furniture, and a swathe of fragile looking ornaments depicting scenes from a bygone age. Joan, it seemed, displayed a propensity toward all things pink, the color of which was incorporated into the heavy drapes, the floral carpet and even the lounge suite itself.

"Sit down, sit down," Joan said, her enthusiasm for Lisa's visit apparent. "A lady in your condition doesn't need to spend any extra time on her feet."

Lisa gave a small smile as she complied. "I'm beginning to think that if I sit much longer I might just take root."

Joan's carefully sculpted eyebrows shot up. "Nonsense, dear. Enjoy the peace and quiet while you can."

"I am. I just never bargained on having so much time off before the baby's birth."

"What is it now? Are you down to a month to go?"

"Five weeks."

"So are you missing work?"

Lisa inclined her head. "In some ways. I don't miss having to get out of bed in the mornings, and I feel bad when Roger still does." She gave a small smile. "Mind you, now I have to get up for other reasons instead, so I don't get off entirely scot-free."

"Indeed," Joan said. "But what about work? Are they missing you?"

Lisa laughed. "My old boss phoned last week, begging me to come back because my replacement is driving him up the wall. Being an optometrist's receptionist isn't complex, but so far my successor has managed to break a whole case full of expensive sample glasses, lose the orders of several customers, crash the computer system half a dozen times and double-book several appointments."

"Heavens."

"I feel a bit sorry for the girl," Lisa confessed. "She was thrown in the deep end and probably has had little training."

"I hope this old boss of yours wasn't serious about you going back."

"Oh no. He was very worried when I was feeling so unwell and was adamant I do nothing to jeopardize either my health, or the baby's. He was just feeling sorry for himself."

"I'm glad to hear it. Mind you, you'd be lucky to be getting much rest with all the shenanigans going on in this street. I know we talked about it yesterday, but I still can't quite get over those...those...people...making such a racket until such a late hour on Saturday night."

"Or Sunday morning, as the case may be."

"Precisely," Joan said. "And then there's poor Maureen. I saw her first thing as she headed out. She still seemed very cut up about the robbery. It's really rocked her."

"The idea of someone in your house, rifling through your things. It's creepy." Lisa paused then said, "Actually, that's part of the reason I've come over today."

"How so?"

"When Maureen came over to see Roger and me on Friday night, you know, to see if we'd noticed anything suspicious, she said the incident had made her think about what the police officer had said when we were at the Flemings."

"About what?"

"Neighborhood Watch. She said she wondered if it hadn't got to the stage where it might be a good idea."

Joan straightened at this. "You mean us establish one here? In Maybury Place?"

Lisa nodded.

"I must say," Joan said, "that it sounds a very tempting proposition. If ever vigilance is required, I'd say it would be now."

Lisa nodded again. "Roger asked me to see if you were interested. He suggested that if you thought it a good idea, we might look into organizing it."

"Between the two of us? Oh, my dear I would be delighted."

"The thing is," Lisa said, looking down at her stomach, "I couldn't exactly say how much use I would be to you, but even if I help get it off the ground?"

"Of course. I understand perfectly."

Lisa could see that Joan's brain was already into overdrive. She wondered if she could get up and walk out now.

"Where do we start?" Joan asked.

Lisa shrugged. "Perhaps we could get in touch with the police officers who came to the Flemings."

"Oh no, dear," Joan said. "I can't say I was particularly impressed with either of those two, especially the woman. What an attitude she had! I was tempted to go down to the local station and complain."

Lisa raised her brows. "Maybe that's just what we should do. Go down to the local police station and make enquiries."

"Or we could call. Why go when you can phone?"

Lisa smiled. "Why indeed?"

"Although perhaps getting in touch with the police might be a bit pre-mature at this stage," Joan suggested. "We would naturally have to canvass for support."

"Do you think we'd get much interest?"

"Of course. You're in, as am I. I would imagine both the Flemings and the Haskells would also be very interested in light of their recent difficulties."

"Even Brian?"

"Well, perhaps we are being a bit presumptive, but Maureen would sure-ly be a starter. What about your friend Karen?"

Lisa could easily picture Karen's face upon being told, but lied and said, "Oh, I'm sure she'd be keen."

"So that's five out of the eight."

"What about Geoff?"

Joan looked thoughtful. "I wouldn't like to make any assumptions where he's concerned either, but his general reserve doesn't mean a lack of caring. He seemed genuinely worried when Matthew disappeared. He even came by the following morning to check whether Matthew had been found."

"And so you'd ask him?"

"No problem."

"And then there's Gordon Price."

Joan sniffed with disdain. "Well, I wouldn't count on him. The only person that old buzzard cares about is himself."

"But we can't not ask him," Lisa said, well aware that neither Gordon nor Joan could stand the sight of one another.

"Can't we?" Joan asked. Seeing the look on Lisa's face she said, "All right, if we must, but I'm afraid you'll have to ask him, as well as Karen."

"Sure. We aren't thinking about asking the new residents, are we?"

"Saints alive, I should think not. If it wasn't for them I doubt that we'd be going to such lengths."

"Just checking," Lisa said in a very small voice.

"Anyway, that covers everyone. So, if you ask Karen and Mr. Price, I'll ask the Flemings, and Geoff Milne."

"What about Maureen? Do you want me to ask her as well?"

"No, no. I'm bound to see her again today. Besides, we don't want you doing too much, do we?"

Lisa shook her head.

"Of course we would have to have somewhere to hold the meetings," Joan said, her mind now going off in another tangent.

"I was thinking that, for a start at least, one of us could host the meetings," Lisa said. "It might help to generate enthusiasm if people feel they don't have to do anything."

Joan held her mouth in a straight line. "Yes, well, there are certain people who seem to live their whole lives hoping they won't actually have to do anything. I'm not sure such an attitude is altogether healthy. But, by the same token, you're probably right."

"So which of us should do the honors?"

"Well, my dear, I hope you don't think me inhospitable, but I'm afraid the idea of having that old fool from Number Two under my roof just sticks in my craw. It will be bad enough having to invite him in the first place."

"I thought you said you didn't think he'd come."

"He'll probably come just to spite me."

"In that case, we'll do it," Lisa said. She looked at her stomach again. "If we start as early as next week, there shouldn't be a conflict of interest."

"And I can always bring the supper so you don't have to go to any trouble."

"That would be great," Lisa said, thinking of her bungled baking attempts.

Joan stood up. "Speaking of which, why don't I make us a nice cup of tea to drink while we continue going over details?"

"Lovely."

"Tea?"

"Yes, just milk. No sugar."

"Right, well, just relax. I'll be back in a moment," Joan said. She gave what could only be described as a small bow and took herself off to the kitchen.

Silence engulfed the room, save the ticking of a carriage clock on the mantelpiece, and the distant sounds of cups and saucers being rattled in the kitchen.

Lisa looked around her with interest. To her, Joan was something of an enigma. For someone who seemed intelligent and articulate, and genuinely caring - albeit in a nosey kind of way - she had little or no friends that Lisa knew of, and few interests outside of the home. This seemed a contradiction. Lisa wondered what drove a woman like this to lead such a limited lifestyle.

The room, crammed as it was with ornamentation, betrayed little of her life. Thinking of their own living room, Lisa could picture at least a dozen objects that carried sentimental value for Roger and her and also in their own way told a tale about their lives. There were one or two quality souvenirs from trips they'd had overseas, several prints on the wall of Bay of Islands scenes, where they'd spent their honeymoon. A group of photo frames bore shots of family and friends at various occasions, including Roger and Lisa's own wedding.

Joan's living room had none of this.

That was until Lisa noticed one photograph, in a sturdy silver frame, perched on a shelf amongst a group of ornaments. Lisa stood up and went over to it in order to get a better look.

It was an old, war-era studio photo, of a man in uniform, a young man, perhaps in his mid twenties. He looked peaceful, almost serene, something that seemed in sharp contrast to the fact that he was kitted out in military garb and was perhaps preparing to be shipped overseas. One last portrait before embarkation maybe?

Joan came bustling in with the tea tray and set it down on the coffee table.

"I've got us some chocolate biscuits," Joan said as she straightened the tray. "I've always been partial to chocolate."

Lisa looked around, photograph still in hand. Joan looked up. The expression on her face left Lisa feeling as though she had somehow intruded into Joan's privacy.

"He's a good looking young man," Lisa said lamely.

"Yes, he was that."

"Was this taken in the Second World War?"

"Of course," Joan said. "Just how old do you think I am?"

Lisa hesitated, but curiosity got the better of her. "Is it your husband?"

Joan nodded.

"How long has he been gone?"

"A while. Long enough for me to feel like I'm living a different life."

"What was his name?"

"Frederick."

"Were you married then? When the photo was taken, I mean," Lisa said, as she put the photo frame back into position. She gave Frederick one last look. She noticed there wasn't a speck of dust on anything.

Joan shook her head. "Not until quite a while afterward. He was a bit older than me, you see."

"Have you no other photos of him?"

"There was a fire," she said, her voice choked with emotion. "In our old house. That was the only one saved because it wasn't with the others."

"Oh, Joan. What a shame."

Joan seemed to remember herself, and straightened. "It can't be helped. In life, one thing is certain. You can't go back. No sense in reliving the past. Now, here's your tea, dear. Shall we get on?"

"It seemed so sad, just that lone photograph of him," Lisa related to Karen later. "And I felt so awful for making her remember."

"You weren't to know."

Lisa shrugged. "Maybe. But I should have known better than to stick my nose in where it wasn't wanted."

"That's never stopped Joan. Why should it bother you?"

"Now you're being uncharitable," Lisa chided.

Karen gave her a steely look. "Great. Now she's got you feeling sorry for her."

"Well, I do. She seems so lonely. Looking around her living room gave me the impression she'd never even had a life."

"She must have," Karen said. "After all she was married to good old Frederick for however umpteen years. That must count for something."

"Yes, but there was no trace of him. It must have all been destroyed in the fire. I can't help but wonder what happened."

"Maybe he started it. Years and years of badgering and nagging, and he thought he'd turn her into a bonfire."

"Karen!"

"Just joking."

Lisa sent her a disapproving stare. "For all we know they were devoted to one another." She paused, then said, "He was a good looking young man you know, although funnily enough, there was something familiar about him."

Karen made a dismissive gesture. "Why did you go over there in the first place? Surely you weren't that desperate for company?"

"It was Roger's idea, or Maureen's idea, or the policeman's idea. However you want to look at it, it wasn't my idea."

"Eh?"

"Neighborhood Watch. The policeman asked us if we were in it, that night at the Flemings. Then Maureen said she wondered if we ought not consider it in light of their burglary and the increasing number of strangers in the street. Then Roger said he thought the idea had merit, and that Joan and I should organize it."

"Good old Roger. He wasn't drunk at the time, was he?"

"You mean at breakfast this morning? No, stone cold sober. Anyway you know Roger. He's not a hard drinking man."

"He's obviously not a hard thinking man either, otherwise he would never have suggested such a ludicrous idea."

"Why is it so ludicrous? You have to admit that things don't seem as safe as they once did around here."

"I will admit that ever since the new people moved in things have been strange, but Neighborhood Watch? Don't you think we all see enough of each other as it is?"

"You get police advice," Lisa told her in a winning tone. "About what to do and what not to do to make your place safer."

"Great."

"It just gives things a bit more structure."

"Structure. How appealing."

"Could you be any more enthusiastic?"

"No, I could not."

"So you won't come, then?"

Karen sighed. "I didn't say that."

Lisa's expression brightened. "So you will come?"

"I didn't say that, either."

"Wonderful," Lisa said. "Just let me know when you make up your mind."

Karen laughed. "All right, all right. Count me in. But really I should be focusing on other things. After all, attending a Neighborhood Watch meeting is no way to meet a man now, is it?"

Just over a week later the inaugural Maybury Place Neighborhood Watch meeting took place. It had taken a bit of to-ing and fro-ing to establish a date, time and place that suited everyone, but they'd finally all agreed on Wednesday night.

Lisa was a little perturbed when the heavens opened at about half past five in the afternoon, heavy rain cascading down in an impenetrable sheet. She began to fear that nobody would turn up. It wouldn't have worried her except for the fact that the local community constable and a representative of the Neighborhood Watch organization were due to be there.

She pictured herself, Roger and Joan sitting there like idiots, stammering apologies because nobody else had bothered to turn up. It was not a pretty sight.

In the end her fears were unfounded.

Joan came bustling over at seven o'clock. She quickly established herself in the lounge, plumping pillows and straightening magazines, while Lisa and Roger sat by and watched her. Her movements were brusque, and she talked at much the same pace, oblivious to the fact that her actions might somehow offend the hosts.

"I spoke to Sandra this afternoon," Joan said. "She said one or other of them would be here. It depends on when Ian gets home from work." She glanced at Roger over her shoulder. "He seems to work a lot longer hours than you do."

Roger could think of nothing to say to this. Besides, Joan seemed indifferent to a reply and carried on talking.

"Maureen will also be here, but not Brian. He has to see a man about a dog, or some such. No surprise there. Not a man for community spirit, Brian Haskell."

"What about Geoff?"

Joan had finished tidying and made herself at home.

"Oh, he had a meeting with clients at six, but if it all goes well, he'll come." She looked pointedly at Roger. "Another one who seems to work every hour God sends."

"Karen will be here," Lisa said, thinking to herself that if Karen didn't show up she'd go around and drag her there, kicking and screaming if necessary.

Nobody mentioned Gordon Price. Lisa had asked him along but he'd been evasive. Lisa had made sure he clearly understood the details but did not press for a commitment. Gordon did only what Gordon wanted. No amount of pleading would change his mind.

The constable and the Neighborhood Watch representative arrived at seven fifteen, as arranged.

There was a bit of a bustle in the doorway, with Joan vying with Roger for space in the cramped hallway. Lisa watched from the safety of the lounge doorway.

"Come in, come in," Roger said.

"I'm Joan Davis," Joan said, quickly stepping around him, and proffering her hand.

"Jessica Higgins," the policewoman said. She was blonde, attractive, with an open face and her hair scraped severely back. She was in her early thirties at most. She wore her police uniform. She carried her hat in one hand, and a briefcase in the other, but stowed her hat under her arm leaving her free hand to pump Joan's with vigor. "And this is Joe Riley, representative from the Neighborhood Watch organization."

"Pleased to meet you," Joan said. "Should we call you Constable Higgins?"

The policewoman laughed. "Just Jessica. No one is in trouble here."

"I'm Roger," he interjected.

He shook hands with both Jessica and Joe. Joe, in contrast to his companion, was neither young nor attractive. He had a grizzled face and was on the wrong side of sixty. He had a sharp look that implied he missed little. In consequence he seemed an ideal member for such an organization as Neighborhood Watch.

"Come through and meet my wife," Roger said, herding the little gathering into the lounge.

Introductions were made, seats were found, and Jessica gave a brief run-down on the agenda for the evening. They then chatted until the first guest arrived.

When the knock at the door came, Lisa volunteered to answer it.

She found Maureen on the threshold, looking suitably careworn, although she had made an effort to tidy up her auburn locks into some semblance of order.

"How are you?" Lisa asked.

"Fine," Maureen said.

As she stepped out of the darkness Lisa noticed two things: first it had finally stopped raining, which went a long way to bolstering Lisa's confidence about the evening; and second a noticeable bruise flourished at the side of Maureen's left eye.

Maureen's laugh was brittle. "I walked into a cupboard door," she said. "You wouldn't believe a grown woman could be so stupid, would you?"

"It must have hurt."

"At the time, yes, but it's amazing what time and a bit of arnica cream can do to soothe the pain."

"Come along in."

Lisa was about to shut the door when Karen appeared on the doorstep, followed in quick succession by Geoff Milne.

"Fancy meeting like this," Karen said to him.

He gave her a tolerant smile, but looked away.

"Evening Lisa."

"Thanks for coming, Geoff."

"Anything to keep the peace, both literally and figuratively."

"I hope it won't be too excruciating," Lisa said.

She was yet again about to shut the door when she noticed Gordon marching with purpose up the front path. She turned to Karen, and said, "Show Geoff through, won't you?"

"Yes ma'am," Karen said, for once the picture of obedience.

Lisa turned to greet Gordon.

"I'm pleased you could make it," Lisa said by way of welcome.

Gordon snorted. "Someone has to come along and make sure that busybody from across the street doesn't take over the whole meeting."

Lisa gave him a wry smile. "I suppose we all have our different callings in life," she said.

He grinned at her. "Damn right."

Since she could see no sign of either of the Flemings Lisa closed the door and said, "Come through, Gordon. Everyone's in the lounge."

As they entered the room, Lisa heard Gordon mutter to himself. "God, there she is, presiding like the bloody Queen of Sheba."

Joan looked up as though she had heard. She sent Gordon a quelling stare. Not to be outdone, Gordon stared back. Lisa stepped in and found

Gordon a seat.

"Are we all here, then?" Jessica asked.

"We're waiting on one more," Joan replied.

"Perhaps we could make a start anyway?" Jessica suggested. "Unfortunately both Joe and I have to be away by eight-thirty, and there's quite a bit to cover."

Joan was in the middle of saying, "Of course," when there was yet another knock at the door.

It turned out to be both Ian and Sandra.

Joan beamed at them as Lisa showed them into the lounge. "Fancy you both being able to make it," she said.

Sandra smiled. "I arranged for my mother to come and look after the children so that at least I could come, since Ian was tied up in a meeting."

"But the meeting finished early," Ian explained. "Since Diane was already there, we thought we'd take advantage of the fact to come along and hear what it's all about."

"You're just in time," Jessica said to them with a warm smile. "We were about to get started."

By eight-forty both Jessica and Joe had departed, and the rest of the residents were invited to stay for coffee. To Lisa's surprise all agreed.

"Well, that wasn't quite what I expected," Ian said, when everyone gathered back around to talk.

"Yes, but you have to admit that there were some very interesting ideas on improving home security," Joan said, her tone defensive.

Maureen said, "I know that I'll be talking about some of the measures to Brian when he gets home. As we've recently discovered, you just can't be too careful."

"Do the police have any idea who the perpetrators were?" Geoff asked.

Joan snorted. "We've got a fair idea, haven't we?"

Blushing, Maureen said, "Actually, the police believe the robbery might have been motivated by a particular reason. Friday, which was the day of the break in, is the day when Brian pays most of his staff. They think it was most probably the wages they were after."

"Which explains why nothing was really taken," said Roger.

Maureen nodded. "The thing is, though, Brian never brings the money home. He usually goes to the bank mid morning and hands over the wage packets at lunch time."

"Do people really still get paid in cash?" Ian asked in disbelief.

"Oh, yes," Maureen said hurriedly. "It...er...means less bother and book keeping."

Collective eyebrows were raised.

"So you feel pretty confident that the break-in couldn't have anything to do with the residents from Number Seven?" Roger asked.

Maureen looked sheepish. "I don't really think so, no."

"Well, that doesn't excuse the other behavior we've seen from those people," Joan said. "And how do you know? They might have found out about the wages."

"Oh, come on, Joan," Roger said. "That does seem a bit far fetched."

Joan sniffed. "Maybe. There's still the matter of Matthew's disappearance, followed by the endless stream of characters that come and go from the house."

"Not to mention the party," Lisa said.

"And the boy skateboarding up and down the road at all hours," Joan added.

"Skateboarding?" said Geoff. "That's hardly a crime now."

"It is if you ask me. It makes a huge racket, the thump, thump of the wheels along the footpath. They've banned it from the local shopping centre, but that doesn't seem to be taking things quite far enough."

"So you think we should be putting up a 'No Skateboarding' sign at the entrance to the street, right below the one they've given us to put up saying we're a Neighborhood Watch zone?"

"Good idea," Joan said.

Geoff shook his head in disbelief. "Now that really is going too far," he said. "The boy has to have some recreation. Surely it's better than sitting for hours in front of a TV or video games."

"Or kidnapping defenseless pre-schoolers," Sandra added.

"What he needs is a good dose of military school," Gordon said. "That'd soon sort him out."

Joan looked as though she sorely wanted to agree with him, but because the comment came from Gordon she ignored it altogether and said, "No one can deny that they're a disruptive influence in the street."

"No," said Ian. "But what can be done? Matthew was abducted, and the boy didn't get so much as a rap over the knuckles with a wet bus ticket. If the police can't do anything, how can we?"

Roger said, "And I have to say that you can hardly take them to task for having too many visitors. However undesirable they might look."

"Yes, but bikers," said Joan. "Once you start seeing that sort of element in the street, it's just the thin edge of the wedge."

"They're not all bikers, though, are they?" Lisa said. "In fairness you have only seen them the once."

"But what about all the other callers?" Joan asked. "All men, I hasten to add."

"You've got to ask yourself what they're coming for," Karen said, her expression wry.

"What? You think they're coming for something underhand?" Sandra asked.

"Or under sheet," Karen giggled.

Joan's face was incredulous. "You're not trying to suggest that they're... that they're..."

"Prostitutes?" Karen finished. "Why not? I was reading an article in a magazine at the salon the other day that said that a lot of sex workers are moving to the suburbs these days. It's safer, they reckon."

"Safer for whom?" Ian asked, clearly shocked at the idea of a brothel being set up in the quiet sanctuary of Maybury Place.

"Of course, it might not be that," Karen said. "It could always be drugs."

"They all stay too long for that," Gordon said.

Everyone looked at him in surprise.

"How do you know that, Gordon?" Roger asked, suppressing a smirk.

"Got a friend, see. From the RSA. Blow me down if he didn't end up with a drug house right across the road from where he lived. I saw it myself when I visited. All these young punks pulling up in their flash cars, with that foul noise they call music blaring. They'd stop, get out of the car, go inside, and within a minute or two they were back out, into their car, and gone."

"Where was this?" Lisa asked.

"Hatton Road. You know, on the other side of the shops."

"Wow," said Sandra. "I never pictured things like that going on around here."

"It's no good, I tell you," Gordon said. "Fair put the willies up my pal, and like me, he's seen some things that'd make your hair curl. Mind you, it took him a little while to put two and two together. Nobody ever actually pulled up in front of the house, you see, so as not to let on. They'd always park a little bit down the road, or outside my mate's house. In the end that's what tipped him off."

"And what happened?" Roger asked.

"These drug pushers didn't own the house, of course. That sort never do. The police always catch up with them eventually, at which point they simply move on to greener pastures."

"So the police evicted them?"

Gordon shook his head. "Nah. It's like the young feller was saying about the wet bus ticket. Plenty of raids, maybe even an arrest or two, but at the end of the day it's up to the landlord to evict them. It was him that had to be appealed to for help."

"Yes, well, we've obviously established it's not a drug house," Joan said, sick of Gordon monopolizing the conversation. "That situation's nothing to do with what's going on here."

"Hold on a minute, though, Joan," Ian said. "Gordon might just have something."

Joan pursed her lips. "I can't imagine what."

Gordon looked outraged, but was prevented from retorting by Ian continuing his train of thought.

"Think about it for a minute. Gordon said that the type of people who live in a drug house don't ever own the houses they live in. Doesn't it stand to reason that prostitutes wouldn't either?"

"Sex workers," Karen said. "The p.c term is sex worker."

Ian rolled his eyes. "Whatever."

"You're suggesting that maybe Trixie and friend are renting?" Joan asked.

"You have to admit that there isn't an air of permanence about them."

Joan considered this. At length she said, "That might make sense. After all there was some considerable time between the Marshalls moving out and those…women…moving in. Perhaps the reason for the delay is because they're tenants, and that the real owner only just got around to letting the place."

"There's no way of knowing, though, is there?" Geoff asked.

"Well, I don't know about that," Gordon said. "My mate Spike must've found out who the landlord was. Either that, or the police did, because they did go, those drug dealers. Eventually."

"So how do you find out who owns a place?" Sandra asked.

No one knew.

"I could ask Spike," Gordon said. "See what he can remember."

Joan muttered something under her breath that cast doubts on the veracity of any information obtained from a friend of Gordon's, especially one with the dubious name of Spike.

"Good idea," Roger said to him. "It seems like the only way we'll ever know whether they're the actual owners or not is to find out."

"And then what?" Geoff asked.

"Let's find out first," Roger said, "and then decide. After all, if Trixie really does own the place there isn't much that can be done. Not by us, anyway."

"What about a petition?" Joan asked.

"And say what?" Gordon countered. "Stop annoying us, or else? Signed by all nine of us? What d'you think that'll do?"

Joan raised her chin. "Does anyone else have anything positive to say?"

All were silent.

"Right, well, I think it's time we adjourned this meeting. Why don't we all have a think about what can be done, and work on trying to find out whether the place is rented or not, and we'll meet again in two weeks' time? Wednesday again, at seven-thirty, here at the McLean's, if that's all right with them?"

Roger nodded. "Can't see why not."

"Everybody?"

Most people nodded in agreement and with that the meeting adjourned.

"Good grief!" Karen exclaimed, when Lisa eventually answered her knock at the door. "What happened to you?"

Lisa looked puzzled. "What? What are you talking about? Nothing's happened to me."

"That," Karen said, pointing to her stomach. "Didn't I only see you yesterday?"

"You know you did. What are you on about?"

"You're enormous. Tell me when you're due again?"

"Just under two weeks, as well you know." Lisa's shoulders drooped. "I had hoped I was imagining things. I woke up this morning, got out of bed and felt as though I'd put on about ten stone."

"It looks like it."

"Thanks."

"No problem. Any chance you're going to invite me in, or shall we conduct this conversation entirely on the doorstep?"

Lisa shook her head, as if to clear her thoughts. "Sorry," she said. "Come on in. I don't know where my brain is today."

"Maybe it fell out of your head and into your stomach," Karen suggested, as she followed Lisa into the living room.

"Maybe."

They both sat down. Karen gave Lisa a penetrating look. "Are you feeling all right? You don't look that well."

"I'm not. All of a sudden I feel tired and anxious and heavy, and ever so slightly sick."

"Maybe we overdid it yesterday with all that shopping," Karen said.

"It had to be done, though, didn't it? A one-day-only sale on all the things that we had yet to buy for the baby. It was too good an opportunity to pass up."

"And was Roger pleased with all our purchases? The pram, the highchair, and the car seat?"

"Very. If anything, I think he felt a bit peeved that he couldn't be there himself. But it was Monday, and there were a couple of very important meetings he couldn't get out of."

"That doesn't sound like Roger."

"No, it doesn't, does it? The thing is, he's gearing up now to have time off when the baby comes. There's heaps to do if he's to walk away and leave everything in order for the guy who's filling in. It's just been the end of the financial year, so he has to make all kinds of reports and whatnot."

"Tell me about it. Glenda and I have got to start cooking our books for the accountant. Why the tax man has to be so damned fussy I don't know."

Lisa managed a small smile. "What's a couple of grand here and there, between friends, you mean?"

Karen smirked. "Something like that."

"Perhaps you need to take a leaf out of Brian Haskell's book, or in his case just don't bother with the books at all."

"I know," Karen said. "Could you believe that, when Maureen said about the way he pays wages? Nobody knew what to say!"

"I wouldn't be surprised if that guy had more fiddles than a country and western band. You wonder how poor Maureen puts up with him."

"Maybe she likes being a doormat."

"Nobody likes being a doormat," Lisa said. "You can see that just by looking at Maureen's face."

"Well, look at the alternative. Single lonely spinsterhood, like me."

"Still no prospects on the horizon?"

Karen looked coy. "Actually, now that you come to mention it..."

Lisa sat as bolt upright as she could manage. "Don't tell me you've met someone? How could you not tell me? All that time we spent together yesterday and not a word."

"Well, to be honest, there isn't really anything to tell," Karen admitted. "It's more of a prospect on the horizon, as you put it, than anyone definite."

"Like a mirage?"

"No, not like a mirage. A real, bona fide, single guy."

"Tell me more. Name, age, occupation, where you met him."

"If I tell you, you're never going to believe it."

"Why not? Just out with it, will you? The suspense is killing me."

"Well," Karen said, "I met him right under your very nose."

"What! You mean yesterday? You're right, I find that very hard to believe, especially with you going around pretending there was something wrong with you."

Karen threw back her head and laughed. "Oh, the look on your face," she said. "It was priceless."

"I could tell the sales assistant didn't know what to make of you. She kept sending you nervous little glances and it was practically impossible to have a serious conversation with her with you pulling faces in the background."

Karen pulled just such a face as a reminder.

Lisa buried her head in her hands. "You're impossible. I can't remember when I was more embarrassed."

"I can."

"Yes, and all because you were there at the time, creating the embarrassment. Why I stay friends with you I just don't know."

"Because you love me," Karen said, a mushy look on her face.

"Maybe," Lisa said grudgingly. "However, at the moment I'm not so interested in who I love, but in whom you love. Now out with it."

Karen smiled a secret smile. "Well, love is much too strong a word at this stage. In fact, up until two weeks ago I barely even gave the guy a thought."

Lisa screamed with impatience.

"All right, all right," Karen said, holding up her hands. "It's Geoff."

"Geoff?" Lisa echoed, her face a picture of confusion. Then clarity struck her. "What? Geoff Milne, from across the road?"

Karen nodded.

"But...but..."

"But what?"

"He's so...so..."

This time it was Karen's turn to scream. "So what?"

"So quiet, I suppose. So reserved. So very unlike yourself."

Karen shrugged. "They say opposites attract, don't they?"

"Do they? Is that really true? Or do those people end up like two magnets, repelling each other?"

Karen looked crestfallen. "So you think I'm an idiot?"

"An idiot? No, not an idiot. But, Karen, he doesn't seem like your type."

Karen shook her head. "Yes, well, my type, as you put it, don't ever seem to pan out, do they? They're all fun loving, love 'em and leave 'em guys, who aren't interested in scary concepts like commitment."

"And you think Geoff is? He seems to have managed to get to this age without being snagged. What would he be? Thirty-six or seven? Maybe even thirty-eight? A man doesn't get to that age and still be a bachelor for nothing."

"Maybe he's shy."

"Maybe he's gay?"

Karen shook her head. "No. I've got a sense about these things. He's not playing for the other team."

Lisa sighed. "What makes you think he might be interested in you?"

"Well," Karen said with care, "we hit it off at the Neighborhood Watch meeting."

"Did you? I can't say that I noticed."

"We talked a bit while you and Roger and Joan were organizing coffee."

"Wow. Love at a Neighborhood Watch Meeting. That's got to be a first."

Karen gave a wry smile. "And there was I joking that it was no way to meet men."

Lisa laughed. "So, I'm assuming I'm not going to have to twist your arm to come to the meeting tomorrow night, then, am I?"

"Oh no," she said. "In fact, I'm quite looking forward to it."

Lisa wondered briefly, at around seven o'clock the following evening, whether people's zeal for another Neighborhood Watch meeting would still be intact. Granted, it was not raining this evening, which meant one less deterrent. And the meeting was bound to be shorter, for no other reason than there was nobody there to give them a formal talk about the merits of home security, and of keeping an eye on one another's properties.

A punctual Joan arrived at seven fifteen. Roger and Lisa sat back in their lounge and waited for the pillow fluffing and magazine straightening to start, but it became apparent that the same amount of care need not be taken when one only expected the locals.

Karen arrived next, looking cheeky and expectant. It was clear to Lisa that she had taken some time over her appearance. Lisa thought she did not seem as relaxed as usual, and that there was an air of bravado about her quick one-liners.

Maureen followed. She seemed to have developed the unhappy knack of injuring herself again. She brushed aside all comments of concern, took a seat in the corner, hunched herself into her voluminous cardigan and engaged Roger in conversation.

The fourth knock at the door was Geoff and Gordon, deep in conversation about the merits of pre-war architecture. Geoff had his hands buried in the pockets of his jeans. He watched Gordon with some interest and with more patience than Lisa knew she had at the moment. Gordon, intent on what he was saying, waxed lyrical about the way things were in the old days.

"Evening," they both said to Lisa as she let them in, and were scarcely over the threshold before they were back to the topic.

Lisa followed them down the hall into the lounge. The two men exchanged brief pleasantries with the group, but took seats together on the couch, and quickly resumed where they had left off.

Lisa noticed that as soon as Geoff entered the room, Karen's eyes went straight to his, and there they had stayed. It was clear she had hoped to catch his attention, probably had her prettiest smile at the ready, but he did not glance her way. Lisa's heart ached for her friend. She couldn't help feeling that Karen had got it bad.

Lisa went to sit down, when the last knock came at the door. She looked in Roger's direction hoping to see him making for the door. All the to-ing and fro-ing had started to make her feel a bit unusual. Roger, however, remained deep in conversation with Maureen, his head angled toward her to catch what she was saying.

Lisa found Sandra waiting.

"Hello," she said. "I hope I'm not too late."

"Not late," Lisa reassured her, "although you are the lucky last." She looked past Sandra into the inky night. "No Ian tonight?"

Sandra shook her head. "He had hoped to be here. In fact, Mum's come to baby-sit, ostensibly so we could come together, but he got tied up at the last minute. Some big crisis or another with one of his major clients. If they don't get the computers fixed by morning, the whole business will turn to custard. I'm not expecting to see him this side of midnight."

"Goodness. I hope he's well paid."

"Never well enough, believe me. So, how are things in the McLean household? I must say you're looking a bit peaky."

Lisa stifled a sigh. "I'm often a bit tired in the evenings."

Sandra rolled her eyes. "Me too," she said. "And in the mornings, and in the afternoons, and, well, pretty much all the time. You think you're tired now. Just wait until the baby comes. You won't know what's hit you."

"Come on in, won't you?" Lisa said, resisting the urge to pick up an umbrella off the hat stand and ram it down hard over Sandra's head. She wouldn't know what had hit her either.

Once they entered the room, Joan started coughing with such flair she could have had a career on the stage.

"Attention, everybody, attention," she said regally. "I must say, it's wonderful to see such an excellent turnout this evening. I'd like to, on behalf of Lisa and Roger, welcome you here tonight, and to the second inaugural Maybury Place Neighborhood Watch Meeting."

"Get on with it," Gordon muttered under his breath.

Karen giggled. Joan sent him a withering look, the sort that could strip wallpaper, but Gordon looked triumphant nonetheless.

Roger whispered to Lisa, "How can something be both second and inaugural?"

Joan, not catching what he said, looked his way as though she expected much better from him. Roger had the good grace to start looking attentive, if not wholly repentant.

"So, I guess the best place to start would be to review procedures from the last meeting," Joan said.

Lisa coughed.

Roger took the hint and said, "Maybe all the things that Jessica said are still fresh in most people's minds, Joan."

Everyone nodded in agreement.

"Well...but...shouldn't we... Very well, then, although at some stage I think it would be helpful to go over things again."

"Good idea," Roger said. "However, I think most of us are only thinking about the one issue at this stage, aren't we?"

More nods.

"Quite right, I suppose," Joan said but it seemed clear from her expression that the meeting had taken a turn she had not prepared for. "So, then, after first meeting two weeks ago, what have we all found out?"

Silence ensued.

"What? Has nobody anything to report?"

"We are talking, of course, about trying to establish whether or not Ms. Bartlett and her unknown friend are indeed the owners of Number Seven, or merely tenants," Roger added helpfully.

"I'd bet my bottom dollar they're tenants," Gordon said.

"Yes, but it's proof we require, not wild assumption," Joan said, her tone at its most patronizing.

Maureen fidgeted as usual with her crucifix and said nervously, "I'm afraid I couldn't think of anything."

Sandra said, "I wondered about the Electoral Roll, but of course all that shows is where a person lives, not whether or not they actually own the house where they live."

"Not to mention the fact that the Roll is only printed once in a blue moon. Even if they're on it, it would show an old address, not a new one," Roger said.

"It was a good thought, though," Joan said. "What about the rest of you?"

Lisa grimaced. "I'm afraid I've had other things on my mind," she confessed.

Joan looked at her with maternal affection. "Not to worry. Plenty of other folk to get stuck in and help."

"I've been a bit busy with work, Joan," Karen said. "End of the financial year is a nightmare for we self employed folk."

"I suppose that applies equally for you too then, Geoff?" Joan questioned.

He shrugged. "A bit, I suppose. I must confess I can't really see the point of all this. Things have settled down over the last two weeks, haven't they? Surely it's all a storm in a teacup."

Joan looked outraged. "I can't say that abductions, wild parties, bikers, and men in and out of there like...like...I don't know what, can be dismissed as easily as saying it's a storm in a teacup, Geoff."

"People are entitled to have guests, though, Joan. You can't persecute people for having friends over."

"But are they? I thought we had decided last meeting there was every likelihood that all manner of despicable things going on there."

"Weren't you just banging on about wild assumptions?" Gordon interjected. "We don't know that's what they're up to, however suspicious it looks."

Joan ignored him and reached down for her handbag. She opened it, fished around inside, and brought out several sheets of paper, all covered in her neat, efficient handwriting.

"Let's see, then," she said. "Thursday, twenty ninth of March, normal school routine with woman out in her sports car with the boy, and home by nine fifteen. First visitor, a male, nine forty five. He leaves ten twenty five. Next arrival, another male, at eleven ten. Third visitor, another male, comes at one twenty, out at one fifty. At this point there seemed to be a break in proceedings until four fifteen when guest number four arrives, stays about half an hour, then leaves." Joan looked up. "Shall I go on? Shall I read you the entire file, all fourteen days worth, all forty four men that have come and gone over that time, including the bikers, who came back together and stayed an hour?"

Everyone was stunned, although whether it was more because of what Joan had revealed, or more because of the fact that Joan had catalogued it all like some amateur detective from a B Grade movie, Lisa didn't know. Lisa experienced a giant twinge.

"You've documented it all?" Roger asked, finding his voice at last. "All fourteen days?"

Joan nodded.

"And in that time there were forty four men in and out of that house?" Sandra asked, her voice as stunned as Roger's.

"That I saw."

"Blimey," Karen said. She looked at Geoff. "Even you'd have to admit that's an awful lot of visitors."

"I can't believe you did that, Joan," Geoff said.

She sniffed.

"What will be next? Standing outside on the footpath and asking these men for their particulars?"

"If that's what it takes. I believe we need to be vigilant."

Geoff let out a short laugh, although there was no amusement on his face. "Vigilance I can cope with. Vigilante-ism is something else again."

Joan spluttered and Roger quickly intervened by saying, "Well, it's clear we need to rethink things. Meanwhile, we never heard if Gordon found anything out from his friend, er, Spike, wasn't it?"

Gordon nodded. "Wasn't asked, was I?" he said, looking with loathing at Joan.

"So was Spike of any help?"

"Nah," Gordon admitted. "He said it was the cops that had them moved on in the end. They found out who the landlord was and the landlord had them evicted."

"So is that our only option of redress?" Maureen asked. "We just complain to the police?"

"And say what?" Geoff asked. "Having visitors, even a lot of visitors, having a house warming party and knowing bikers does not in itself constitute a criminal offence. I think the only thing the police would do is have a good laugh."

"Geoff has a point," said Roger. "Besides, the police are clearly regular visitors to the house already. They are probably far more aware of what's going on than we are."

"So we're back to square one," Joan said her voice as flat as her expression.

"Apparently so," Roger said.

Lisa, who had been feeling progressively stranger and more uncomfortable as the evening went on, said, "I hate to break up the party, but I'm afraid I'm going to have to."

All eyes were on her with interest.

"You see," she said, cringing. "I'm pretty sure I've gone into labor."

CHAPTER SIX

Joan looked at her sandwich in disgust. It sprawled on her plate, dry and lifeless. She couldn't think what on earth had possessed her to make it in the first place. But since the clock told her lunchtime had arrived - thus indicating the designated time to eat - she had gone through the motions. She had spread a thin layer of margarine on a slice of kibbled loaf with usual precision, and added to this a couple of meager slices of her favorite cheese.

So it sat there, like a reproach, waiting for consumption. Joan just couldn't bring herself to go through the process of chewing and swallowing. Not when she had so much else on her mind. Not when matters of life and death were hanging in the balance.

She glanced at her kitchen clock. Twenty past twelve. How could it be twenty past twelve and there yet be no word? What could be taking so long? Surely, if things had happened, then someone would have let her know. After all, she couldn't help feeling as though she had a right to know.

She drummed her fingers with unconscious impatience on the kitchen table. They danced up and down as if by their own volition. It was something that she had done since very young. It was funny that all through the intervening years, she could still hear the authoritarian voice of her mother commanding her to cease and desist such unladylike behavior forthwith. As though her mother, to this day, sat perched on her shoulder with a plethora of useless saying and admonitions.

She had not thought about her own mother for quite some time. Perhaps it had something to do with the circle of life, the need to look backward as well as forward. She thought now of the one who had given her life, but very little besides. Nothing of any worth.

Like love.

Or affection.

Or approval.

Still, she told herself, she was free of all that now - the hurt, the recriminations. Things were different in those days. Her mother had been dead and buried the best part of thirty years, her father, twenty-five. There was no one left to pass judgment on her, to continue to throw her life's mistakes back in her face, to call her ungrateful and undeserving.

Joan glanced at her sandwich again then back to the clock. Twelve forty-five now, and still no word. Perhaps no one was going to tell her after all. Perhaps some conspiracy had been formulated to keep her out of the loop. She made an impatient sound and could stand it no longer.

She went into the hall and looked at the telephone, willing it to ring. It did not. It sat there in its neat efficient little way, on its freshly dusted hall table, the doily straight, note pad at the ready with the pen laid at a pleasing angle, there for use if need be.

The question she faced: whom should she call?

Should it be Roger? No, not a good idea.

Would Sandra know?

Surely no one would have informed Maureen before her?

What about Karen?

Karen wasn't Joan's favorite person, in spite of the fact that Lisa and Karen were such good friends. There was something about the girl that Joan found a little hard to take. Too glib? Too fresh? Too cheeky? Maybe even all three. Moreover, Karen lacked a sense of decorum that seemed to come to Lisa as easily as breathing. However, under the circumstances, Joan figured she might just be her best bet.

She had to look Karen's number up in the telephone book, and couldn't for the life of her think of the girl's last name until finally it came to her. Livingstone. She was sure it was Livingstone. Sure enough, there it was Livingstone, K. 4 Maybury Place.

Joan dialed the number. No reply. Then she remembered Karen would be at work, at that hairdressers she part-owned over on Edmonton Avenue. Cutting Edge, or some such silly name. All hairdressers seemed to have a propensity toward naming their salons supposedly clever names.

She found the number, dialed, and waited for an answer.

"Cutting Edge," said the nasal voice. "Mirabelle speaking."

"I want to speak with Karen Livingstone," Joan said.

"Did you want to make an appointment?" the girl asked in her whiny voice.

"No," Joan said firmly. "I just want to talk to Karen Livingstone."

"Are you a friend?"

Joan considered this for a moment or two. "No," she said.

"Could I take a message?"

"No. I want to talk to Karen, if I could, please."

"She has a client with her."

"Well, would you mind interrupting her because I would like to speak with her?"

"It might be better if I got her to give you a call."

Joan felt her stress levels rising. "It is most imperative that I speak with her."

A moment of silence followed. Joan pictured the cogs of this girl's brain turning like rusted wheels.

Joan said, "Perhaps if you could tell her that Joan Davis is on the line?"

Joan could hear a shuffling from the other end of the phone. "All right," the girl said, her tone so reluctant as to be bordering on insolence.

A clunk rattled down the line as the girl lay the telephone heavily down on the desk, followed by a long delay during which Joan leaned against the wall in the hall and looked at her front door. She could see that, up in one corner above it, some spider had made itself a web, quite without her approval. She would soon teach it the error of its ways.

Through the telephone the sounds of the salon drifted down the wire. The noise of a blow drier being used, the distant chatter and sounds of laughter, and beyond that, a staccato beat issuing from the hi-fi system.

At length and with much scraping of the receiver, Karen came on the line.

"Joan," she said. "What can I do for you?"

"Have you heard?" Joan asked, all patience lost. "Is there any news?"

"Of Lisa?"

Joan resisted the urge to shout, "Of course, you imbecile. Why else would I be calling?" Instead she mustered up every ounce of civility she could find and she said, "Yes, dear."

"Not yet, I'm afraid."

"Goodness. Surely the baby must have come along by now."

"Well, Joan, you and I probably know about as much as each other about this business, but I've heard a few horror stories in my time about the length of time babies take to be born. Thirty hours, forty hours, sometimes more."

Joan did a rough calculation in her head. They were up to about seventeen hours already. Not long in the scheme of things, but long enough. Her heart ached for Lisa. She just couldn't help it.

"Roger hasn't called at all? Not even to check in with you?"

"No. Not a word. I wouldn't imagine him wanting to leave Lisa, even for a second, and he doesn't have a cell phone. You know Roger. The less modern contraptions the better."

"Did he tell you that he'd call you, from the hospital, once there was news?"

"Oh yes," came back the lofty reply. "They went on one of those tours of the delivery suite. There's a little room where you can go and call, to tell everyone the good news. He was so organized he went off with one of those plastic coin bags banks use, full of twenty cent pieces."

Joan had been excluded from hearing and seeing all these arrangements last night, as upon Lisa announcing that the baby was on its way, most people had made prompt exits. Gordon had fled the scene as though his backside was on fire; Maureen had sidled out with the promise of prayers. Sandra had given all the advice she could think of before going back to the bosom of her own family.

Joan had hovered, offering to clean up, lock up, whatever was required, only to find that all of these things had been entrusted to Karen. Not only that, she had a helper, a somewhat surprising helper in the form of Geoff Milne. Geoff who, after being - it must be said - rather confrontational during the meeting, managed to outstare Joan in such an unassuming manner that she had no option other than to leave them both to it. Joan had no idea of a friendship existing between him and either the McLeans or with Karen, but since activities in the street seemed to be getting stranger by the day, she'd shrugged it off, had given her good wishes, and departed.

"And he'll call you there, at the salon? He won't wait until you're back home?"

"He'd better not," said Karen, her voice full of the promise of malice. "Look, Joan, I'd better go. I've got Mrs. Robbins with her hair full of perming rods, and the timer's beeping."

"Of course, dear. You will let me know, won't you?"

"Naturally. You'll be the first to know. Well, after me, that is."

Joan rang off and sighed. It was the story of her life.

Lisa lay on her side on the hospital bed, her back to the window. Her face rested on the pillow, angled so that she could see her baby, swaddled into near invisibility, sleeping peacefully in the little perspex crib by her bed.

Outside, the sun streamed down, sending its warm rays of welcome to the sleeping infant. From the ninth floor maternity ward, a brilliant view spread out over the city and out over the water. The thick glass windows muffled any trace of sound from the world beyond. When you looked out, from a position of lying down, you could only see the blue sky, and a trace of white, puffy clouds being blown along by the breeze. It felt like being suspended in the sky.

These were details that had absolutely no interest for Lisa. She had her gaze fixed on her baby. In the ward room where Lisa had been brought, two other mothers fussed with their infants. Both had been there for a couple of days, during which time they seemed to know everything about one another, and be so at ease with their babies as to make Lisa feel lost and inadequate. But at the moment it was visiting time, and both women were ensconced behind their curtains, talking rapidly to the people who had come bearing gifts to see them.

The curtain around Lisa's bit of rationed space was open. She longed to pull it around and shield the two of them from the world, but she was tired to the point of exhaustion. She could not muster up enough energy to make the effort.

She willed herself to stay awake, not wanting to miss a second of the first day of this new life but in spite of the noise, and her own resolve, she could feel her eyes drooping.

Suddenly she was aware of a presence, and opened her eyes.

A nurse stood at the side of her bed reading her chart. Lisa thought she looked about the same age as herself. She had russet brown hair that was pinned up at the sides, and a kind, open face covered in a smattering of very obvious freckles. When she realized Lisa watched her, she smiled and said, "Sorry, didn't mean to wake you."

Lisa generated enough energy to reply, and said, "I was just resting my eyes."

The nurse grinned. "Sure you were." She put the chart back into its place and said, "I'm Delwyn. I'll be looking after you now." She looked at her watch, pinned to her uniform. "Well, until eleven tonight, that is."

"What happened to the other nurse? I can't remember her name."

"Mary. She's gone off duty but she'll be back in the morning."

"What time is it?"

Delwyn looked at her watch as though she hadn't just looked at it moments before. "Half past three."

"Really? I seem to have lost all sense of time."

The smile came back. "I wouldn't expect that feeling to go away any time soon, especially if your baby decides night is day and day is night."

"Do they do that?"

"Some do. They sleep all day, and are up all night."

Lisa looked over at the slumbering bundle. She'd only seen the baby's eyes for a couple of minutes. Since the birth there'd been nothing but sleep, sleep, sleep.

"So you've had a little girl, then," Delwyn said. She lent over and gently lifted the wrap away from the baby's check so that she could get a better look. "She's quite a respectable weight for being a little early. Have you come up with a name yet?"

Lisa nodded. "We're going to call her Grace. Grace Elizabeth."

"She's beautiful."

Lisa concurred. Grace had the face of a miniature angel, with soft, smooth skin and delicate features.

"Roger said he thought she'd come out looking like a prune, but she's not like that at all."

"Roger? He's your husband?"

Lisa nodded again. "He's gone home to change and to bring a few things in for me. I thought I was organized but I don't seem to have brought in half the things that I really need."

Delwyn smiled. "Do you think you'll stay in for a few days?"

"Oh, yes," Lisa replied, wanting to laugh out loud at this. The way she was feeling, they'd still be here in a couple of months. She'd barely even held Grace, felt frightened by the idea of picking her up, to the point where she felt as though she needed permission to do so. On top of this came feeding, changing, bathing. The idea of going home with no supportive instruction at hand seemed inconceivable.

"You'll be in over Easter," Delwyn said.

"The idea of Easter doesn't seem real."

"No, I can imagine it wouldn't."

Lisa looked back at Grace. "I haven't fed her properly yet. My midwife tried to help me feed her about half an hour after Grace was born, but she wasn't really interested. She's been asleep since."

Delwyn picked up Lisa's chart again. "Babies tend to sleep a lot during the first twenty four hours. People often think they've got these perfect little angels, but in most cases that doesn't last. There's growing to be done, and tummies to be filled. It's inevitable that they'll let you know all about it."

"So, should I just wait until she wakes up then?"

Another glance at her watch and the chart, and Delwyn said, "No. I think we'll wake her up soon. Maybe after four o'clock, when visiting is over."

"Should I do that myself?" Lisa asked, panic rising within her. "Will you help me?"

Delwyn smiled with practiced patience. "Of course, if you need me to. Just ring the bell if you want to get going. Otherwise I'll be back to see you when I get myself sorted out." She looked at the chart yet again. "Now, what about you? Need any pain relief?"

Considering the fact that Lisa's body felt as though it had been run over by a tractor, the answer should have been an unequivocal and resounding yes. Yet the pain relief she'd had during labor had made her feel groggy and a bit unwell. She felt as though she would be in need of all her faculties when the time came for feeding.

"No," she said.

"I'll let you get back to resting. Don't forget, ring if you want anything."

With that she departed. Lisa nestled her head into the pillow again, feeling a little constricted and uncomfortable on the single hospital bed, which creaked ominously if she moved too much.

She lay there looking at Grace, who had not so much as batted an eyelid, and marveled that her body had produced such a wondrous thing. It had to be the most surreal experience of her life. To think that in the course of a few hours she had gone from being an ordinary adult to being mother. To now be responsible for such a beautiful helpless being simply could not be.

Her heart overflowed with both love and fear. She could not fathom how she would ever be worthy of undertaking the mission of parenthood. Yet love and an attachment that had started way before she had ever set eyes on Grace somehow made everything right. As much as she worried about her own capabilities, she knew that she would never and could never abdicate her parental responsibility of her own free will. As little as she knew, she would find a way. She would learn everything she could, be the best mother she could.

Perhaps it wasn't so strange that at such a moment as this she should think of her own beginning. One day, long ago, she too had lain in some hospital crib, but the eyes that had looked on her had not been the ones she had grown up to know. She knew nothing about the circumstances of the woman who had given her life, but it seemed unimaginable that anyone could turn their back on their own flesh and blood and simply walk away. Lisa knew she could never do it. She even found it difficult to comprehend.

She let her mind drift, and her eyes droop, and she ought to have dropped right off. After all she had not slept in close to thirty-two hours. Yet sleep remained elusive, something that had less to do with the noise of the other mothers and more to do with the way she felt inside. The whirl of emotion, the upheaval of her body, and an edgy feeling she had not experienced before made her feel as though someone had given her a shot of adrenaline.

So she resolved just to rest. Delwyn would be back soon to help wake up Grace. And then a whole new chapter of her life would begin.

"Gordon Bennett," said Karen, putting down a bunch of flowers so that she could strip off her coat and jumper, "it's like a furnace in here."

Lisa screwed up her mouth in mock sympathy. "I know. I think that they try to keep things womb-like for all the newborns, no matter how uncomfortable it makes anyone else feel."

"Glad to know where I rank in the scheme of things, then," Karen said with a grin. "Now, speaking of newborns, where is my little cherub?"

"Sleeping," Lisa said. "And so she ought to be after keeping me up half the night."

Karen peered into the crib. "Oh, very nice," she said. "Look at those long eyelashes!"

"I know. Amazing, aren't they?"

"I suppose Roger's been out and bought the shotgun already? He'll be needing it if she stays that beautiful."

Lisa smiled with pride.

"What color are her eyes?"

"Blue, silly. All newborn babies have blue eyes."

"Do they? I thought that was just an old wives' tale."

"They're a really interesting blue. Not the sort of blue you ever see on a grown up, so I'm guessing they'll turn brown like Roger's."

"What, no baby blues like her mother? Don't tell me she'll be dark haired like him as well?"

"I don't know. At the moment she's got no hair to speak of so only time will tell. Maybe one blonde in the family is enough."

Karen settled herself on the designated visitors' chair and gave Lisa one of her penetrating looks.

At length she said, "Well, you don't really look any different now you're a mother."

Lisa laughed. "What did you expect? That I would suddenly start to look matronly?"

Karen shrugged. "I don't know. I must say that you do look tired, though."

"Gee, thanks. I knew I could count on you for the usual boost to morale."

"And, as usual, no problem."

"I defy anyone to look energetic after having only had three hours sleep in the last two and a half days."

"Is that all? Sod that for a game of cards."

Lisa flicked at a piece of fluff on her dressing gown. "The ironic thing is that I should be absolute knackered, exhausted to the point of collapse, but somehow I seem to be surviving."

"If that's all the sleep you've had, I'd say you were damned near perky."

"I think perky might be overstating it a little. Actually, it seems unfair that my body has just been through the most traumatic event of its life and you aren't even allowed to rest afterward."

Karen gave her another searching stare. "How was it, then?"

"What, labor?"

Karen nodded.

"I'm not sure you really want to know," Lisa replied. "I wouldn't want to put you off for life."

"Oh, so you'll be joining the usual group of mothers with their horror story births?"

"I wouldn't say that. My midwife said that for a first delivery, it all went remarkably well. Not as quick as some, not as long as others. Roger and I both thought it went better than we had expected."

"A big concession on Roger's part I'm sure. You'll sign up to have a few more, then?"

"Steady on. The way my body feels at the moment, I may well never recover from this ordeal."

Karen screwed her face up in disgust. "Don't tell me any more."

There was a small silence as Karen looked around the ward, at the equipment on the wall behind Lisa's bed, there for some unknown emergency procedure; at the little locker beside the bed with a water jug on top and the toilet bag half poking out of the drawer; at the bunches of flowers that were beginning to gather on the windowsill; and over her shoulder at Lisa's other inmates.

"Very cozy," she said.

Lisa sighed. "I can't wait to go home."

"How long are you going to stay in?"

"If it wasn't for the fact that I was proving to be such an incompetent, I'd be home in a flash. This breast-feeding business is a nightmare."

Karen grimaced. "I don't think you'd better tell me anything about that, either." She straightened, and said, "In fact, for a neat change of subject, how about we get on with present time?"

"Oo, goody."

"There are flowers, of course," Karen said, indicating the bunch she had deposited earlier, "and then in my bag, I have the rest of the surprises." She fished around. "Now, let me see…here's one for the new bubs."

Lisa took the square package, wrapped in sweet pink paper covered in baby motifs, and began to open it.

"Oh, get on with it will you," Karen ordered. "None of this undoing the sellotape bit by bit. The suspense is killing me."

Lisa laughed. "How could that be? You bought and wrapped it. Oh, a Buzzy Bee."

"All self respecting Kiwi children should have one, or so at least the lady in the shop assured me."

"Not the same shop where they think you're a lunatic?"

It was Karen's turn to laugh. "No, no. I think, upon reflection, that it will be quite some time before I show my face in there again. Not that I should imagine I'll have the need."

"It's lovely. Thank you. Thanks, too, for the flowers."

"Hardly original," Karen said, eyeing the other bunches on the window-sill.

"That doesn't make them any less special. Anyway, just think how they'll brighten the house when we get home."

"You'll spend the next three weeks clearing up pollen and petals."

Lisa made a face. "You're always a ray of sunshine, but I thank you anyway."

"But wait, there's more."

"Not a set of steak knives?"

Karen delved into her bag again, and pulled out another parcel, wrapped in the same baby paper. Lisa obliged by unwrapping it at top speed, and found inside a gorgeous little pink dress.

"Oh, Karen," Lisa breathed. "It's beautiful. Thank you so much."

"But wait, there's even more," Karen said again. At the very bottom of her bag her hand found what it was looking for. "Easter eggs. For you and Roger. I couldn't think of a single thing to get him and I thought you might miss out otherwise. It's a kind of 'killing two birds with one stone' present."

Lisa laughed. "I'm overwhelmed. Surely there mustn't be any more room in that bag of yours."

"There isn't. You aren't going to tell me you're not supposed to give eggs until Sunday, are you?"

"No. To tell you the truth it will be nice to have something sweet to munch on if Grace has me up half the night again tonight."

Karen put her bag down and sat back. "The neighbors send their love."

"What, all of them?"

"Well, mostly just Sandra and Joan. I haven't seen anyone else."

"They aren't thinking of sending themselves, are they? As well as their love, I mean."

"Not Sandra. Too busy. As for Joan, I can't vouch for her. She was so anxious to know what was happening she even called me at the salon for news. It seemed like taking the need for gossip a bit far, if you ask me. Even for Joan."

Lisa frowned. "You weren't rude to her, I hope."

Karen laughed. "I was the model of politeness, I promise. Scout's honor."

"Except you never were a scout, were you?"

"I'm sure that's quite beside the point. Actually, there was one other person who sends his best wishes."

"Oh?"

"Yes, Geoff."

"Oh, ho, ho. Seen him, have you? Is there something you should be telling me?"

"Well," Karen began, "it probably didn't register with you when you were busy going in to labor, but when you and Roger left for the hospital, Geoff and I stayed behind to tidy up."

"That couldn't have taken long. We hadn't even got around to making anyone a coffee."

"I made Geoff one," Karen said, her expression arch.

"Do tell."

"Actually, there's not much to tell really. Simply that I offered him a coffee, he accepted, and we chatted for a while."

"Is that all?"

"Yep. Except to say that it was a really good conversation and he seemed as interested in me as I am in him."

Lisa eyebrows drew in, her expression skeptical. "Are you?" she asked. "Are you really?"

Karen nodded. "He isn't anything like what I thought. Sure he's not the noisiest guy in town, but he can hold down a conversation - and is interesting - and even you would have to admit that he's not so terribly unattractive."

Lisa shrugged. "Handsome in a mousey kind of way, is how I would put it."

"Mousey? Ugh! What an insult."

"All right, perhaps mousey is a bit undignified." She looked at Karen. "So, the big question is, has he asked you out yet?"

Karen chewed her lip. "Not yet," she said, "but let's just say I have high hopes."

Gordon could not believe how much junk mail he had in his mailbox. Pamphlets from grocery stores, from department stores, from electrical goods shops, from the local bakery advertising a special on hot cross buns, together with two from different specialty gardening firms that would come and fleece you in the name of cutting your grass for you.

Then there was the big DIY centre that had opened up a couple of miles away, promptly putting out of business the place where Gordon had gone for the last twenty five years, as if they expected him to darken their doorstep. There was one from the local optometrists, that place where young Lisa had worked, and one from the garden centre which had sprung up beside the new DIY palace, announcing they would be open practically every second of Easter weekend if he should have the slightest inkling of a need to go there.

"Don't they realize it's supposed to be a holiday, for Christ's sake," Gordon muttered to himself. It irked him as much for the poor pamphlet deliverers as for all the people these shops employed. It was better in the old days, when people still knew how to stop.

Gordon went to turn on his heel and take all the offensive literature, and shove it, unread, into the recycling bin, when he caught sight of Roger McLean walking down the road. He decided to wait and give his congratulations. He leaned on the fence in anticipation of Roger's arrival.

"Hello there, Gordon," Roger said, his grin broad.

Gordon had never met a man who smiled as often and as readily as Roger McLean. At first he had distrusted this, but he'd come to see in Roger a young man for whom openness and contentment came by nature, and this in turn reflected on his face.

"The young lass across the road informs me that congratulations are in order," he said.

"Who, Sandra? It was good of her to let you know. I meant to let you know myself only I've been spending practically every second at the hospital. With the baby being early I've also had to work a couple of days to get organized so that I can be on holiday for when the girls come home."

"I s'pose that'll be in five minutes. No staying in for a two weeks like it was in the past."

"Well, not exactly five minutes, but we're hopeful Lisa will be home by the end of Easter."

"Can't recall what Sandra said she was called, your new little one."

"Grace. We've called her Grace."

Gordon nodded. "Nice," was all he could manage. "Where are you off to?"

Roger smiled. "I'm sneaking out for a bit of exercise. What with spending time cooped up in the hot hospital, then coming home and eating quick snack-type foods, I'm beginning to feel a bit sluggish. I've run out of milk, so I thought I'd combine getting some with having a bit of a constitutional."

"S'pose I ought not hold you up," Gordon said.

"Not to worry," Roger replied. "Plenty of time."

"Did want to ask you about these meetings. Now that your young missus has had your baby, will they keep on going?"

Roger considered this. "Yes, I should think so, although perhaps not at our house any more. I guess we'll have to see how things go. Why? Were you hoping they wouldn't?"

Gordon cracked a smile at this. "Well, I've got to say they've been a bit more interesting than I first thought. 'Specially when a certain someone gets taken down a peg or two. That architect fellow goes up in my books practically every time I see him. He's not afraid of putting Joan in her place."

Roger couldn't seem to help smiling in return. "Still," he said, "the point of the meetings is to make Maybury Place a safer place to live."

"There is that, to be sure," Gordon conceded. "Those folk at Number Seven are nothing but a liability to the street. Had the cops there last night, again. Lord knows why, although we've got a fair idea, haven't we? And that young punk stuffed a whole lot of dog droppings into my mailbox. Not that you'd be able to tell the difference between that and the rest of the crap that gets put in there," he said, waving the wad of pamphlets under Roger's nose.

"Really?" Roger asked, with raised brows. "Did you see him do it?"

"Nah, but I know it was him, all right. Told him off, I did, for throwing litter down as he walked home from wherever he'd been. That gave him a reason, see. Little bugger should be shipped off for National Service."

"I don't think they do that any more, Gordon."

"Course they don't," Gordon snapped. "But the way the country has gone to the dogs, they should bloody well reintroduce it. And with the way those two floozies at the end of the street are carrying on, I'm not sure they shouldn't have it for the likes of them an' all. Not in favor of women on the battlefield, you understand. They're too emotional for war. But a bit of hard training certainly might toughen them up a bit. Might make them think twice about their ways, too."

Gordon looked at Roger, daring him to disagree, but when there was no response he said, "Right then, better let you get on with it. Send my regards to your young wife."

On the return journey Roger took his time. Not because he did not relish the thought of going back to the hospital, although of course he would be pleased when he no longer had to; nor because he was reluctant to face the mess he'd ended up making at home from whizzing in and out at breakneck speed - not pausing long enough to wash a dish or sweep a floor - but because it was blissful to be alone, even for a moment, without the pressure of having to be something else for someone else.

Evening began to fall, and although the temperatures were still unseasonably warm, the air held just enough chill to make it invigorating. Only the barest few leaves on the deciduous trees had begun to turn, making it difficult to believe it could be fall.

Walking along the road past numerous houses with the traffic humming by, Roger let his mind wander. It had certainly been a busy couple of days. So busy, in fact, he'd hardly had a chance to enjoy, let alone experience, fatherhood.

He knew that he was unlikely to ever forget the moment his child came into the world - the relief, the cessation of pain for Lisa, the attentive and watchful eye of the midwife, the scarcely disguised clinical atmosphere of the hospital, the sounds that emanated from other rooms within the delivery suite. All of these things had disappeared when he had first seen that little face, the small, perfectly formed body, those tiny limbs, the sheer helplessness of the newborn babe.

His Grace.

His child.

It was incredible.

Since that moment he had taken every available opportunity to hold her in his arms, although the chances were proving to be quite few and far between. His visits often coincided with either sleeping or feeding times, or he would turn up to find other visitors there to claim the right. His family, in particular, had been most taken by the newest member of the McLean family, were relishing the joy of the first grandchild.

Roger felt a bit sorry in that respect because Lisa's parents were unable to make the journey north. With Charles recovering from hip replacement surgery it would be impossible for either he or Victoria to visit for some time. Roger knew that Lisa felt the keen loss of their presence.

At the moment, though, all of Lisa's time and energy focused on learning the skills of motherhood. It seemed ironic that much of what parents had said to them about what they were in for had thus far proven to be true. Roger wondered which other preconceived ideas they held about parenthood would be challenged.

He and Lisa had spoken at length about the sort of family life they wanted to have, not full of rules, but of course with certain standards. They had talked about what they would and would not do, what they had seen others do that seemed right or wrong, but now that the baby had arrived perhaps their ideas and judgments might not end up being so sound.

As Roger turned the corner into Maybury Place a sleek black car drove out of the driveway from Number Seven, past Roger. The driver was a well-to-do looking businessman who glanced at Roger as he waited to pull out into the main road then glanced quickly away, as though not wanting to be recognized. Business, it seemed, still kept going, even on Easter Saturday.

Gordon had disappeared back indoors but just the thought of him made

Roger smile. He snapped and snarled like a little bulldog, and the idea of him finding dog turd in his mailbox was unbelievable. It was shameful that younger people could have so little respect for someone who, in his time, had put his life on the line for King and Country.

Roger passed Karen's house, although she was not yet home after visiting Lisa at the hospital. Visiting hours finished at four o'clock so she had presumably gone to the store on her way home.

As he neared his front door Roger heard a familiar voice.

"Yoo hoo! Roger!" called Joan.

Roger stopped fiddling with his keys, paused, fixed a smile on his face, and turned around.

"Joan, hello," he greeted, as she trotted up the path, wearing, Roger noticed, a fluffy pair of pink slippers on her feet. He realized she'd been watching out for him.

"Oh," she breathed, "I'm so pleased to catch you. I've called a few times, but of course you've scarcely been home since little Grace was born, have you?"

"No," he said. "My feet have barely touched the ground."

"It's all so exciting. Tell me, how is Lisa?"

Roger gave a small smile. "She's pretty well, Joan, but very tired. Grace hasn't quite got the hang of the fact that you're supposed to do most of your feeding during the day, and sleep at night. She's got it totally the other way around."

"And of course hospitals are murder to try to sleep in, aren't they?" Joan said. "I know that when I was unfortunate to be in one, oh, quite some time ago now, I could scarcely sleep a wink."

"Yes, you're right. Lisa says the very same thing. I'm sure things will improve once she comes home."

"Which will be?"

Roger shrugged. "Tomorrow? Monday? One or the other. I think it depends what Lisa's midwife says and how things go overnight tonight."

"And the baby? Little Grace? Is she well?"

"Quite well, thanks. Apart from this sleeping thing she seems to have taken to being out in the big wide world like a fish to water."

"Oh, good, good. And you, my dear? Not getting too exhausted with all the to-ing and fro-ing?"

"It's not too bad. In fact, I probably should be getting a move on if I'm to get back there in reasonable time."

"Of course, of course. I just wanted to convey my congratulations. Naturally I've bought a little present, but would love to give it in person. I wonder, would I be allowed to visit? At the hospital?"

Roger could just imagine the look on Lisa's face if he told her he'd given permission for Joan to visit. He looked thoughtful as he said, "I'm not sure. She isn't having visitors if she can avoid it. It's this tiredness thing. Then of course sometimes it isn't a good time because she's still coming to grips with feeding, and all that kind of thing. Perhaps, since she'll be home any day, it might be better to wait?"

Joan's face fell for a fraction of a second before she remembered herself. "Of course," she said. "I quite understand."

"I'll definitely pass on your best wishes," Roger said.

"I hope you will. Well, I suppose I had better let you get on your way. Just say the word if I can be of any help."

"Thanks. Oh there is something. I saw Gordon earlier. He asked me about what is to become of these meetings. I told him I wasn't sure, but I think we can all agree on the necessity of them keeping going for now. At least until we decide what to do about certain elements in the street. However, to be honest, I think that neither Lisa or I will really be in the position to sort it out, so I'm afraid we'll have to ask you to shoulder the load on your own for a while, sorry."

"Oh. Oh, yes I see. Well, I suppose needs must when the devil drives. Not," she said quickly, "that I'm implying your little Grace is a devil, or anything like that."

Roger grinned. "I'm quite sure she'll have her moments. Meanwhile, if it's all right with you, I'll leave everything in your capable hands?"

Joan nodded vigorously. "Don't worry," she said. "Just leave it all to me."

By the following evening Joan regretted she had ever uttered those words. What had seemed like a good idea at the time had proved to be a bit of a burden.

"You know, Jess," Joan said to her ever faithful feline companion, "you have to wonder about people's idea of civic duty these days. I'm beginning to think that it is no wonder that the world's in such a state when your own neighbors won't even come to the party and help you out."

Her problems began when she had returned to her house after telling

Roger not to worry. While he went off carefree, her worries increased a good deal. If Roger and Lisa were not prepared to have the meetings at their house any longer, then an alternative venue would have to be found. As she had said to Lisa when they had undertaken the whole Neighborhood Watch venture, she could not tolerate the idea of having to invite that man under her roof. Gordon Price was a coarse, belligerent old fool. She failed to see why she should extend hospitality to someone she could not abide. If she had it her way, they'd be trying to run him out of the street as well.

So Joan had set about finding an alternative venue.

The first person she had asked the following day was Sandra. Joan could see her outside, pulling out some weeds by the mailbox, and it was just too good an opportunity to miss.

To Joan, she seemed quite a logical choice. There would be no need for Sandra to ask her mother to come and baby-sit, and if Ian happened to be late home from work he could quite conveniently join in when he arrived. She would be there for the children, should they need her, and Joan was more than prepared to make a light supper if Sandra was not willing to oblige.

In fact, she found Sandra not willing to oblige at all.

"Oh, Joan," she said. "I just don't think it's a good idea. Having people in the house is bound to be more disruptive than having Mum around to baby-sit."

"I shouldn't imagine we would make that much noise," Joan had countered.

Sandra pursed her lips. "Maybe. Maybe not. But if Matthew gets wind that there's people in the house, there'll be no persuading him to go to bed."

Joan longed to say, "Surely you just make him go to bed," but something told Joan that such a suggestion wouldn't go down too well.

"Ever since the, er, incident, Matthew gets easily upset. He gets affected by all sorts of things that never used to bother him at all," Sandra continued. "He's only a couple of weeks away from going to school. My first priority has to be to ensure things are as settled and stable as possible."

"But you are still keen to attend the meetings?"

"Oh, yes. We both are if we can. Just not at our house. Besides, Mum loves coming to look after the children, even if they are asleep."

Joan then upset the apple cart by wondering out loud whether Matthew would end up at the same school as Thomas, a thought that had not previously occurred to Sandra. She became very agitated, and had taken herself inside to talk to Ian about such a horrifying possibility.

Next on her list of preference came Maureen, whom she spied coming home after attending Mass.

Maureen had frowned, her fingers going straight to her necklace. "I don't know, Joan."

"It would be no trouble. I'd bring supper, make coffee, run the meeting as usual."

"It's not that.

"You really wouldn't have to do a thing or provide a thing, except, of course, somewhere for people to sit."

"It's not that either."

At that point Joan had become a little exasperated. "Well, what is it, then?"

Maureen left off playing with her necklace and began to fold the little leaflet she had brought home from church, giving all the parish notices, her fingers moving as though she gripped her rosary.

"It's Brian," she admitted at length. "I'm afraid he would not be pleased if he learnt I'd invited all the neighbors over."

"But surely it's your house as well? And for such a worthy enterprise?"

"I'm afraid Brian would not see it that way."

Joan noticed that Maureen's voice had become very faint by this stage. It seemed to Joan that Brian Haskell was nothing more than a bully, and she longed to tell Maureen just to stand up to him. Once again she sensed her advice would fall on deaf ears.

Instead she tried again. "But he's under no obligation to come to the meetings himself. Besides, I thought you said he goes out on a Wednesday night."

"He does. I'm afraid it's the principle of the thing that Brian would object to. As I've told you before, he thinks we should mind our own business."

So Joan had left Maureen to finish her trip home, and had taken herself back inside.

Strike two.

That left only Geoff or Karen, since her desire to not have Gordon Price under her roof was matched only by an equally strong desire to not set foot under his either.

She contemplated her choice. Both Geoff and Karen were single, and therefore could have no objection on the grounds of family, be it spouses or offspring. Both had comfortable homes, and could not surely be squeamish about the prospect of having to make coffee for guests, nor have the neighbors over to their house.

Of course, Geoff had shown an alarming attitude toward the rest of the group's desire to be rid of Trixie and company, but this outlook had not deterred him from attending the meetings. His willingness to play their advocate had unnerved and annoyed Joan but that did not preclude asking him to host the meetings. Failing that, she would have to ask Karen, although it did not sit particularly easily with Joan either.

In the end both let her down, each citing work as an excuse.

"The thing is, Joan," Geoff said, his gaze direct and unchallengeable, "I have to make work my priority over everything else. If a client wishes to have a meeting on a night when we have scheduled Neighborhood Watch, I'm afraid Neighborhood Watch would have to take a back seat."

"It wouldn't be a problem to organize an alternative venue at short notice, I'm sure," Joan said.

Geoff looked doubtful. "At times there might be very little notice at all, an hour or two at most. Frankly, I don't think it would be worth putting everyone out for such a possibility. It's better that you find another venue."

Karen said, "To be honest Joan, I'm not the greatest housekeeper when I'm working. I like to get up at the last possible second, leave everything lying around, and deal with it later. Much later. The idea of having to come home after a day of standing on my feet for eight hours or more, and then run around like a maniac trying to make the house presentable is positively frightening. Give me Chinese water torture any day."

Joan had tried to object, to offer a counter argument, but one look at Karen's face told her the folly of persistence. At the very least it confirmed what she had always suspected about Karen Livingstone. The girl was bone-idle.

"Why don't you have it at your house?" Karen had said as a parting shot.

Now, sitting in the lounge at home and looking at Jess, Joan could not help but despair at the inevitable. For in truth her desire to see the back of the residents of Number Seven had grown to such an extent that she would have to make the ultimate sacrifice and host the meetings after all.

She just wished the whole idea didn't give her such a dreadful feeling.

CHAPTER SEVEN

Easter Monday dawned fine and clear, but within a couple of hours the weather changed. Florid clouds appeared at intermittent intervals and showered down heavy torrents of rain before departing as fast as they had come. These clouds swept up from a southerly direction bringing with them an altogether cooler air stream than had been felt of late. Inside the hospital the temperature sat at about twenty-five degrees, reminding Lisa of a summer day.

Roger had not long arrived, bearing with him the little capsule car seat into which Grace would soon be stowed, ready for her first trip into the outside world, and home. Presently she slept a blissful sleep in the only home she had ever known, unaware that all of their lives were about to be turned upside down.

"I can't believe how much stuff I seem to have accumulated," Lisa said, shoving things into her bag. "Surely you didn't bring in that much extra."

Roger's eyebrows shot up. "I'm pretty sure I brought something extra in with me every time I came," he said.

"And what are we going to do with all these flowers? I mean, they're lovely, but how on earth are we going to get them all home? And when we do, where are we going to put them all? The place will look like a funeral parlor."

"Don't be silly. I'll make a few trips to the car with all this stuff and then you and Grace will be the last leave. That way you can potter around getting ready, and we won't end up carrying everything at once. You just need to take it slow and not get wound up."

Lisa sat down on the edge of the bed and sighed.

"I don't know why I feel the way I do. A big part of me is longing to get out of this place. I've had all I can take of sleeping on this squeaky bed, of being woken up by other people's babies. And don't get me started about the food. But at the same time the thought of leaving terrifies me. At least in here if I'm not managing I can ring the bell, and someone will eventually come and give me a hand. There's no such luxury at home."

"I'll be there to help for the first couple of weeks," Roger said. "And don't forget that Leslie will be coming to do home visits, as well as being available on the phone."

"It's hardly the same."

"What about Sandra? She's a mine of information. I'm sure she'd be more than willing to pop over if you were having trouble."

Lisa made a face. "Gee, thanks."

"Well. I'm just saying there is help available if you need it. You won't be coping on your own. Now, why don't you start getting a bit more organized and I'll start taking some of this lot out to the car?"

After several trips Roger had everything stowed in the car and Lisa's discharge papers were signed. They were about to attempt popping Grace into the car seat, when Delwyn came by.

"You're off?" she asked, her smile warm.

Lisa nodded. "We're trying to work out the intricacies of the car seat. We put Grace in but she just seemed so small. Her head keeps flopping everywhere, and the straps are too loose. Roger is trying to tighten them."

"Have you got any cloth diapers?"

Lisa nodded again.

"You might like to try rolling one up like a long sausage and putting it around her head. It'll stop her flopping about so much. Needless to say, she won't need that safety measure for long. Before you know it, she'll be out of the capsule altogether."

"I can't imagine that."

"I bet you couldn't imagine leaving hospital with your new baby either, could you?"

"No, you're right about that. Getting ready to take Grace home is pretty unreal."

In fact, when she had imagined bringing her baby home, she had pictured herself taking the baby on a tour of the house, showing it every nook and cranny, explaining things as she went. Back in the real world, Grace could only see a very short distance and would probably be asleep when they got back anyway. The baby she had been picturing in her mind was in reality more like six months old.

"You'll be fine," Delwyn said. "You've been doing really well these last two days. I think you'll be pleasantly surprised at how much easier it is to cope when you're home in your own environment. Besides, you can't stay here forever."

"Can't I?" Lisa asked, with a small grin.

"Of course you can't. Nor would you want to. I'm only in here for eight hours at a time, at which point I'm dying to get home."

"Ah, yes, but without the newborn baby in tow."

Delwyn laughed. "There is that. Well, I'd better get on. Just thought I'd look in and say goodbye."

"Thanks."

"Hope everything goes well. You too, Roger."

He turned, face flustered with mental exertion. "Thanks, Delwyn. Thanks for all your help."

Once Delwyn had left, Roger and Lisa placed the still sleeping Grace in the car seat capsule. She stirred, opened her eyes and frowned at them, resenting the intrusion into her slumber. In the end they managed to get her comfortably and correctly stowed and were ready to leave.

This, then, was the first day of the rest of their lives.

They had only been home four short hours when there was a knock at the door. Joan stood on the threshold, laden with gifts and bursting with enthusiasm. Roger simply did not have the heart to send her packing.

"I saw you come home," she beamed. "I hope I'm not too early coming over, but I simply could not wait a moment longer. It isn't a bad time, is it?"

Roger stifled a sigh.

"No, Joan, come on in. Grace is settled in her bassinet and Lisa and I are just finishing a bit of late lunch in the lounge. Come on through."

"Oh wonderful," Joan said as she followed Roger down the hall. "It must be so nice having both of them home."

"Indeed it is. I'm not going to miss visiting the hospital."

"Oh, Lisa," Joan cried when she saw her. "How well you look." She placed all her bits and pieces down and went to bestow a kiss on Lisa's cheek. "Congratulations. A little girl. Well done. You must be so proud."

Lisa bore the kiss with stoicism. "Thank you, Joan. How are you?"

"Most well. All the more so for seeing you. And of course I do hope I will be permitted a small peek at the baby before I go."

Lisa gave a weak smile but said nothing.

"Well, then," Joan said, settling herself in the chair by which she had put her gifts, "let me see." She gathered up her things and with theatrical flair said, "Presents."

"That's very nice of you, Joan," Roger said. "Would you like a cup of tea while Lisa looks at them?"

"Not if it's any trouble."

"Not at all."

"In that case, tea would be lovely."

"I'll leave you to it," Roger said, pretending not to see Lisa glaring at him for making such an easy escape.

"Now, first things first. A gift for the baby. Nothing as grand as gold, frankincense and myrrh, although I do like to think of myself as just a little bit wise."

Lisa smiled with every ounce of politeness she could muster. She took the neat package out of Joan's hands noting the precision with which it had been wrapped. She unwrapped it with corresponding care as Joan watched her every move.

"Oh a soft toy," Lisa said, thinking of the growing pile they already had. "It's lovely. I'm sure Grace will love it."

"I bought her something else, too," Joan said, handing over another package, which looked like - and indeed was - a couple of books, with old-fashioned illustrations.

"I know they won't be much use to you for a while, but before long Grace will be ready to start learning her numbers and alphabet."

"Thank you, Joan. The illustrations are lovely."

Joan withdrew a plastic bag full of muffins. "And I made you these. I thought you might be able to make use of them what with having visitors to call. They'll freeze too, if you think you might not use them straight away."

"You shouldn't have."

"Nonsense. A new resident is an exciting event in the street. Or at least it should be, shouldn't it?"

Roger came in with Joan's tea and said, "Here you are, Joan. I hope it's not too strong."

"As it comes is fine."

"Speaking of neighbors, did you hear what happened to Gordon?" Roger asked.

Joan bristled. "No."

"He reckons that the young boy from Number Seven, Thomas, put dog poop in his mailbox after Gordon told him off for littering."

Joan reddened, perhaps from the mention of excrement, and floundered for words. It was clear she did not know whether to cheer and applaud an act that should not be sanctioned, or feel sorry for Gordon and outrage toward the perpetrator. She contemplated it while she sipped her tea, and in the end the latter won out.

"But that's disgusting, not to mention scandalous and downright disrespectful. What has he done about it?"

"Nothing. What can he do? He didn't see Thomas do it."

"But still, an act like that should not go unpunished. He should go and knock on their door and complain."

"Do you really think that would do any good? Look what happened when Ian tried to talk to them after Matthew disappeared. He got the door slammed in his face."

"Nevertheless, they can't be allowed to get away with it."

"I don't think you'll have any luck persuading Gordon to go calling," Lisa said, knowing full well that Joan would do anything rather than have a direct conversation with Gordon.

"He's probably worried about being taken for a potential client," Roger said. "I'm sure they're always on the lookout for new business. I know I'd think twice before knocking on their door."

Joan drained the last of her tea. She looked distinctly uncomfortable. "Yes, well, I probably shouldn't keep you much longer. I've intruded long enough. You'll have unpacking, and probably lots of sorting out to do for the baby."

Lisa said, "I'll probably just go to bed. I didn't sleep very well in the hospital. I have to rest when Grace does otherwise I miss out."

Joan stood and looked expectant so that Lisa had little choice but to say to her, "Come and have a look at her, then."

She led the way to Grace's bedroom, and carefully opened the door. There she lay, swathed in blankets, in her lace-covered bassinet.

"Oh, beautiful," Joan mouthed, tears coming to her eyes. "She's perfect," she whispered.

Lisa smiled and nodded in agreement.

After they said their farewells, Roger and Lisa watched Joan bustle back across the road.

"You know," Roger said, "I sometimes get the impression that Joan thinks she's part of our family. She'd probably move in if she could."

"Saints preserve us," was all Lisa could say.

"And so, did you have to have an epidural then?"

Lisa looked at Sandra with a bland expression, wondering how many more of these intense and personal questions she was going to have to endure before it was safe to tell the woman to mind her own business.

Sandra wasn't actually paying any attention to Lisa. She had Grace in her arms and was busy cooing at her, and probably, Lisa presumed, frightening the life out of the poor wee thing. Lisa had to swallow the desire to poke her tongue out at Sandra while she wasn't looking. She then wondered to herself which one in the family could be called the bigger baby.

Meanwhile Rose had managed to wiggle her way over to Lisa and Roger's stack of CDs and was busy laboriously pulling them out one by one and throwing them onto the floor. To this Sandra was quite oblivious.

"No," Lisa finally replied.

"What? No pain relief at all?"

Lisa sighed. "Yes, gas, and a bit of pethidine."

"Wretched stuff. It made me very unwell when I had Matthew." She laughed. "It's funny how much you remember, and how much you forget. Here we are, now only seven weeks out from Matthew starting school."

"Will he be going to the local primary school?" Lisa asked, grasping on to the topic like a lifeline. Anything to avoid reliving the birth in technicolor for the sake of Sandra's curiosity.

"Yes. It's a good school with good education reports, and even the very latest in computers and that sort of thing. You can't start learning new technology too early, you know."

"Will there be other children Matthew knows going there too?"

"Most will go on there from kindy, including the two little boys he plays with every day." She looked up at Lisa. "And I did have one chilling moment when I thought there might be someone else going as well."

"Oh?"

"That boy, Thomas, from Number Seven. I must confess that it hadn't even crossed my mind as to where the boy goes to school, except perhaps for picturing somewhere that looked like Borstal. You know, all bars on the windows and cold draughty rooms with wooden, splintered seats; the archetypal East German woman wrestler for a teacher, complete with military style uniform, hair pulled back into a bun, and hairs growing out of her chin."

Lisa grimaced. "And is he?"

"Huh?" Sandra said in mid coo. Lisa couldn't help feeling as though she'd had quite enough of Sandra tormenting her baby.

"Is Thomas going there, or not?"

"Not. At least not at the moment. Who's to say that pair of sluts won't take him out of where he is now."

"And presumably you know where that is?"

"Oh yes. When Joan first asked me if Matthew would end up being at the same school as Thomas I went cold all over. I thought about it all weekend, and just couldn't rest. And of course it's been the school holidays, so I couldn't even call the school to ask them."

"They wouldn't tell you, would they?"

"Probably not. All that privacy nonsense they trot out these days. It's designed to give power to the few and leave the rest of us in the dark. Besides, when I thought about it, I wasn't even sure of the boy's last name. We know Trixie is Bartlett but we're pretty sure the boy belongs to the other woman. We don't know her name at all."

"But you were able to find out?"

"Oh yes. Not her name, of course, but the school where he goes. There's no way I'd let that rest. So with the new school term having commenced there seemed only one way to find out for certain."

"Which was?"

Sandra looked over at Lisa again, with a smug look on her face. "I followed them. Both Joan and Maureen said that the boy and the woman leave at the same time every day. So I got organized, packed the children in the car, and waited until they drove away."

Grace started to cry. Lisa sprang to her feet as though her seat had started to combust and went over to remove Grace from Sandra's arms. She nestled her daughter against her shoulder and Grace soon settled.

"And where does he go?"

"Miles away. You know that posh school on Pineridge Road? There. It must cost a fortune to send the boy there. I know damn sure they mustn't be getting their monies worth, the way he carries on. My question is: how can they afford it? And why there?"

Lisa shrugged. "Perhaps business is booming?"

"You can say that again. The way those two plough through the clients, it won't be long before the council will have to come and reseal the road."

"Maybe they used to live in that area before they moved."

"It's pretty affluent. I can't imagine people in that area tolerating their shenanigans any better than we have," Sandra said, finally going over to rescue the CDs from Rose.

"Are you thinking of moving? Lisa asked, the fingers of her free hand crossed behind her back as she continued to walk Grace around, gently rocking her up and down.

"No. Not now," Sandra said with a sigh. "Chance would be a fine thing to be able to move up a step or two, maybe to a house with a couple of extra bedrooms and a family room. A pool would be great. I can't say I'd mind being able to send Matthew to a school like the one where Thomas goes either. You should have seen Ian's face when I told him." She brushed the hair back off her face as she settled Rose on her knee to play with her house keys. "What about you and Roger?"

"Oh, no. We like it here, even though we aren't very impressed with the new neighbors. We wonder whether they'll stay long. They don't seem particularly settled, and we haven't exactly embraced them with open arms."

"I'd say they get enough of that on a professional basis, don't you?"

Lisa made a face. "Don't," she said. "I don't even want to think about it."

"And is Roger enjoying being back at work?"

"Like a hole in the head. He reckons nobody lifted a finger while he was away, so he's busy making order out of chaos."

Sandra grinned. "He's happy as a sand boy, then?"

Lisa returned her smile. "Actually I think he is. As much as he'd quite happily stay home and play with Grace all day, he enjoys his job more than he makes out."

"Typical man. Just look at Ian. You'd think he'd taken a vow of faithfulness to his company, and not to me, for all the look-in I get. By the way," Sandra said, "Grace has gone to sleep on your shoulder. You'd better watch that. It's a bad habit to get into. Before you know it, she won't go to sleep anywhere else."

"I'd better put her to bed, then," Lisa said with as much patience as she could muster.

Still, she should be grateful in one way. At the very least it presented Lisa with a valuable opportunity to get Sandra out of the door.

"Hellooo," Karen called from the back door. "Is it safe to come in?"

Karen had taken to letting herself in the back door since Grace had come home. Taken too, to refusing to come into the house if there was the smallest possibility she might be called upon to change a dirty diaper, or help wind Grace, or any one of a number of baby related chores.

"Come in you coward," Lisa said, appearing in the kitchen. "It's quite safe."

"Great," Karen said, nipping inside. "Hope you don't mind a visit."

"Not if there's the slightest chance you might be prevailed upon to help me cook the dinner."

"No chance," Karen grinned. "It's me you're talking to, remember?"

Lisa went over to look in the fridge. "Not that there's much in the way of dinner," she said, pulling out a sad bag of limp mushrooms, a wedge of cheese, and a withering capsicum.

"Oo, omelet," Karen said. "Great. I love omelet."

Lisa looked back into the fridge. "Good idea. By some small miracle there are even some eggs and milk here. Tell you what, you can stay, provided you help cook."

"What? Are you starting now? Where's Roger?"

"Some emergency meeting. There's an Australian firm sniffing around, looking at the idea of a takeover. The very idea's got the wind up everybody, and so there's an emergency strategy meeting for senior staff, to try to put together some sort of action plan. Attack, Roger said, is the best form of defense."

Karen made a face. "That sounds awful. Give me Mrs. Jarvis any day. How's Grace?"

"Tiring. Asleep, thankfully. She seems to have decided that she's hungry every two hours, and wails the place down until satisfied."

Karen's look of mock horror outdid her last. "That sounds awful, too. Give me Mrs. Jarvis followed by the depressing Mrs. Dexter, over and above the joys of breast-feeding a baby."

"I'm getting used to it. Anyway, you haven't heard the worst yet."

"Oh?"

"I had saintly Sandra Fleming over today. She gave me a lecture on the benefits of breast-feeding, before conducting the Spanish Inquisition about the birth, then rounded it off by chastising me for letting Grace fall asleep on my shoulder."

"Well, that seems like a capital offence. That woman can be a right cow.

Where does she get off?"

Lisa made a self-deprecating gesture. "She does mean well. I know I shouldn't be so catty about her. The truth of the matter is that I should be grateful for all the advice I get. Don't forget she's been through this twice herself, so does know a thing or two about babies."

"Sod that. She also knows a thing or two about letting her four year old wander unsupervised about the countryside, unless you've forgotten. Sanctimonious prig."

"Of course I haven't, and I get the impression she'll never forget that either," Lisa said, and went on to tell Karen the story of her following Thomas and his mother half way across town.

"Blimey," Karen said. "That seems a bit desperate, doesn't it?"

Lisa shrugged. "Anyway, Sandra was only the tip of the iceberg in terms of visitors. Joan came again on Monday, popping in with yet more baking."

"Muffins, again?"

Lisa nodded. "Luckily Grace was very testy at the time and I could pretty much dispense with the formalities and get rid of her straight away."

"Three cheers for Grace."

Lisa smiled. "Well, they do say that every cloud has a silver lining, don't they?"

Karen laughed. "I think you've been living with Roger just a little bit too long. So, who else came?"

"Maureen. She brought some little booties that she had knitted herself that for some reason won't stay on Grace's feet, and some Catholic tracts about babies with pictures of mournful angels on them. In fact I think the angels are supposed to look holy, but I'm sorry to say in reality they just look a little bit depressed."

"A bit like Maureen herself, then. A fitting gift, if you don't mind me saying so."

"Poor Maureen. You try living with the likes of Brian Haskell."

Karen raised her eyebrows. "He seems like the perfect husband to me. He's practically never there."

"Yes, well, she was very sweet, and nostalgic for her own babies."

"What, the ones that never darken her doorstep from one year's end to the next?"

"I think the daughter lives in Australia. She could hardly pop in, could she?"

"And what about the son?"

"He's into horse racing."

"Like his dad, then."

"No. On the back of one, silly. He's a jockey, remember? Maureen said he's had a few wins lately."

"Bully for him. He still doesn't visit his mother, though, does he?"

"You're a fine one to talk. Look how hard you avoid going to visit your parents."

Karen put her chin up defensively. "That's only because they're control freaks. Maureen's such a doormat, neither of her children could ever accuse her of that."

"All I'm saying is that you never know what goes on behind closed doors. Now, here make yourself useful and cut up these mushrooms."

Later, when the simple meal was prepared, Lisa and Karen sat down in the dining room to eat.

"I can't stay too long," said Karen. "Neighborhood Watch meeting tonight."

"Is it? Of course. I'd forgotten all about it."

"I take it neither of the McLean's will be in attendance."

Lisa laughed. "You're on fire tonight, Einstein. In precisely twenty minutes I'm expecting that small daughter of mine to wake up and want feeding again, after which I am going to bed. No, don't make a face. I don't care if it'll only be eight-thirty by then."

This time Karen laughed. "I'm assuming Roger isn't going to make it back either?"

"Not from the way he was talking. They were ordering a meal in, so I very much doubt it."

"I hope he's getting something more exciting than omelet," Karen said, pushing the fluffy yellow egg around her plate.

"Stop moaning. You're lucky I let you stay at all."

"I wonder who will be there tonight?"

"Like Geoff, you mean? Still no word from him?"

Karen shook her head and sighed. "I was so sure I'd read the signals right. I thought it was only a matter of time before he asked me out, or at least came over to my house on some small pretence so that I could ask him in for coffee."

"Maybe it still is only a matter of time, only you haven't allowed enough."

"How long does it take to ask a girl out?"

"Come on, Karen. He's hardly the chattiest of men, now, is he? Perhaps he's shy and is still working up the courage to ask you."

"But is he? Is he really shy? You don't see him having any trouble standing up to Joan, now, do you? Nothing shy about him at those Neighborhood Watch meetings, is there?"

"I suppose not. And he was very pleasant when he popped over to say congratulations about Grace."

"You mean he came here? To your house? And you never mentioned it?"

Lisa looked blank. "I didn't think to. Just the same as I didn't think to mention that Gordon had been to see us as well. He was very funny. He'd put on a tie and everything, and came with a bunch of pink camellias he'd picked from that big bush by the side of his house."

"Who, Geoff?"

"No, you fool, concentrate. I meant Gordon. There were ants in the camellias and they ran out of the flowers, across the kitchen bench where I'd put them, and ate the remnants of one of the lots of muffins Joan had baked."

Karen smirked. "Perhaps he'd trained them. You know, seek and destroy ants trained to annihilate anything Joan-related."

Lisa laughed. "You think perhaps they're the advanced party, and it won't be long before he sends a whole platoon of the things across the road to wreak havoc in Joan's pantry?"

"Wouldn't put it past him. They can't stand the sight of each other."

"It's worth going to the meetings to watch the fireworks between those two alone," Lisa said.

"You have to wonder what they've got against each other, don't you?"

"Search me. All I know is, there certainly won't ever be a love match between those two."

There was a small silence.

"And what about Geoff and me?" Karen asked.

Lisa held her hands up in an expansive gesture. "There are some things in this world where only time will tell."

Maureen arrived at the meeting first. Joan ushered her down the hallway with an anxious expression. The air was redolent with the smell of baking and of furniture polish, and that strange smell the vacuum gives off when you run it for too long.

Everything, it seemed, had been cleaned to within an inch of its life. Maureen wondered where she should put herself for fear of ruining the perfection Joan had created.

Karen came next, bearing the news that neither Roger nor Lisa could make it.

"I don't suppose we could expect them with the baby being so new," Joan said. "I had wondered whether Roger would be able to come on his own. He seemed to indicate to me that he might."

"Oh," Karen said airily, "it's not the baby. He's tied up at work. They've got some catastrophe in the making, and had to stay at a meeting."

Joan couldn't for the life of her imagine what sort of catastrophe a chain of menswear shops could have. Especially not with the sort of prices they charged.

Geoff let himself out of his house and breathed in the cool evening air. It made him want to go and take a walk. He was so busy right now that he really did not have time to waste by going to yet another one of these meetings, where the only real thing to be exchanged was a lot of hot air. At least a walk would be productive if for nothing other than giving him a chance to clear his head. Give him a fresh perspective. Maybe even some inspiration.

When he got to the path leading up to Joan's front door, he wavered ever so slightly, the temptation to just keep walking very strong. But then, out of the shadows stepped Gordon Price, giving Geoff the distinct impression that he had been lurking there for some time, just waiting for him to arrive.

"Safety in numbers," Gordon said with a rare grin.

Joan's sense of relief at being able to usher the two men into her house without having to acknowledge the presence of Gordon was palpable. She directed them into the lounge then excused herself with a story about having to check on something in the kitchen. The less time she had to spend with him the better.

Maureen looked out through Joan's net curtains, into the street when Gordon joined her. He appeared ill at ease. Maureen suspected she could smell a whiff of alcohol on his breath. She supposed he had needed a bit of Dutch courage.

"I can't help wonder why," she said, "they'd give such a grand name to such a small street. Don't you think there's something interesting about the name Maybury?"

"Search me," Gordon said, eyeing her up with suspicion. It crossed his mind that he might not have been the only one to have had a tipple before coming tonight.

"I've often thought it should have been called something else, something little, like Short Street, and not Maybury Place," she said.

Was she a crackpot? Gordon wondered. Who would ever think such a thing?

Instead he said, "It's named after a former mayor, Franklin Maybury. There's a Franklin Street on the other side of the shops, too."

"Really? Well, of course I know where Franklin Street is, but I never knew about the mayor."

"Before your time," Gordon said.

Gordon remembered him well. He'd been a bit of a crackpot, too.

Geoff sat himself down on the couch beside Karen.

"Hello."

"Hello yourself. How are you?"

"Pretty good," he said. "Actually, too damned busy, if the truth be told."

"All rosy in the world of architecture, then?"

"Something like that. I've never had so much work."

"It's a wonder you could get away," Karen said her tone as bland as her expression.

Geoff raised his eyebrows. "I've been meaning to call you."

"Oh? Whatever for?"

He coughed. "I suppose I thought you might like to go out one evening."

"Did you? What, with everyone else?"

"No. Just the two of us."

Karen fingered her sleeve. "Right then," she said, not looking up. "I suppose you should call me when you're free."

"I will. I'm not sure when, but I will."

"Oh, Sandra and Ian," Joan said when she answered the door. "What a treat for us to have you both here. Neither of the McLeans could make it."

"I'm not sure I can stay," Ian said, waving his mobile under Joan's nose. "I'm on call, you see, but I'll stay as long as I can."

"Good, good. Come on through. Everyone else is here."

"Well, then, down to business," Joan said as they all found seats.

Joan thought they seemed a much smaller gathering than when Lisa and Roger were in attendance. But then, of course, her lounge was bigger than theirs. And less cluttered.

"Firstly, thank you all for coming," Joan said. She drew the line at actually welcoming them, just in case Gordon Price should get the wrong impression.

"Now," she said, picking up the file she had organized earlier, "we've had a letter from the Police."

She looked up at everyone to gauge whether she had gained their interest. She had. "It was from that nice community constable who came to our first meeting, Jessica Higgins. She's sent some information on protecting ourselves at night. Probably more appropriate for you young ones gadding about after dark than for some of us here, but important nonetheless. Perhaps, take one, and pass them on?" She handed the leaflets over to Maureen on her left.

"She also apologizes for the fact that they've been unable to let us have that etcher she told us about. You know, the one you use to etch your name or whatever into the back of your television and DVD player, and that sort of thing. To make it easier for your goods to be identified, to stop thieves selling them and to make it easier for the police to return them to you, should you be unfortunate enough to be robbed."

"Which, of course, isn't supposed to happen if we're all doing our jobs right," Ian said with a good deal of levity.

"So, when will this etcher thingy be coming?" Maureen asked, the thought of her own break-in still fresh in her mind.

Joan color rose, embarrassed on behalf of the police. "Well, now," she began, "they really can't say."

"Why?" Geoff asked. "What's the problem?"

"It appears the thing has been stolen."

"What?" Karen said with a laugh. "Stolen from the police? Surely not a very good advertisement for their skills, is it?"

"Perhaps someone should have etched the etcher," Ian said with a grin.

Karen laughed again. "Well, you know what they say. If you've got an etch, scratch it."

Everyone laughed, except Joan. She was stony-faced, and said, "I fail to see the humor in this. Crime is rampant. We all have to do our part to stem the tide. Including supporting the police in their endeavors."

"That's why we're all here, isn't it? Sandra said quickly. "To do our bit?"

"Is it?" Gordon asked. "I was under the impression we were here to get those couple of tarts from the end of the street run out of town."

"Or at least out of our street," Karen added. "Let's face it. That is the main reason for us being here, isn't it?"

Joan bristled. "There was Maureen's robbery as well. And the fact that we've joined up with Neighborhood Watch means we have the opportunity to improve our personal security in all sorts of different ways. We would be fools not to take notice of all the information they have given us."

"So we won't be talking about the tenants from Number Seven, then?" Geoff asked.

"Who said they were tenants?" Ian asked. "I thought we were yet to determine that."

"As a matter of fact, I have a feeling Geoff might well be right," Joan said.

"Have you found something out then?" Maureen asked.

"I have. I got to thinking that there must be some way to find out who owns a particular property. With or without asking the police."

"They'd never tell you," Ian mumbled.

Joan glared at him for interrupting her. "As I was saying," she said heavily, "I got to thinking about how to find out, when I remembered about when I sold my last house. Before I moved here, I mean."

"A sorry day for us all," Gordon said under his breath.

Joan ignored him. "You see, when the house sold, I had a couple of letters from moving firms, addressed to me personally."

"And?" Geoff said.

"Well, don't you see? It would be easy enough for them to find out who is moving, or thinking of moving. You only have to look in the paper, or one of those property rags they're always shoving through our letter boxes."

"Better that than what Gordon had shoved through his," Karen interjected with a grin.

"All the addresses of houses up for sale, particularly those having an open home, are printed there for anyone to see," Joan continued, deciding to ignore Karen as well. "But how would they know who lived there individually, to be able to personalize the letter?"

"How indeed," Ian said.

"So I called them up and asked them."

"And?" Geoff said again, irritated by the fact that Joan was making the whole thing into something resembling a five-act play, pausing for effect after every sentence she uttered.

"The information comes from the council. Off the rates notices. You simply call the council, quote the address, and Bob's your uncle, they give you the ratepayer's name."

"Which is?" Sandra asked.

"In this case, a bit of a mystery. I got told the house is owned by a trust. It's known as GEM Trust."

"GEM Trust?" Ian echoed. "Nothing very telling about that name, is there?"

"Except that the owners sound rich," Karen said.

"You'd have to be to own a rental property," Ian replied.

"How do we know that the trustees aren't Trixie and her offsider?" Sandra asked.

"We don't," Joan said.

"You'd have to find out the name of the trustees then?" Maureen asked uncertainly. "In order to know who owned the house?"

Joan nodded.

"Seems to me like we're no further ahead," Gordon said. "Another waste of time."

"I don't suppose anyone knows how to find out about the names of a trust's trustees?" Joan asked hopefully.

Everyone shook their heads.

"Right," she said. "Back to the drawing board, if you'll excuse the expression, Geoff. Next plan - find out how to find out and we might be one step ahead about deciding what to do once we do find out. If you follow my drift. Cup of tea, anyone?"

"She doesn't half rabbit on," Gordon said to Karen while Joan and Maureen went to make the tea.

Karen rolled her eyes, but said nothing. She was keeping an eye on Geoff, who had been buttonholed by Ian. They were talking computers. Specifically programs for architects.

Nothing she could contribute to.

Not that she had any right, yet, to go over and include herself in their conversation.

For the first time in her life Karen was determined to play it cool, even though a major part of her wanted to run across the road to Lisa's house, shrieking, "He asked me! He asked me! He asked me!" at the top of her lungs.

"Cor," Gordon said. "What do you make of this place?" He indicated Joan's baby pink lounge with an expression as though he had just discovered another surprise package in his mailbox.

"Bit much," Karen said. "Makes me feel a bit claustrophobic."

"Makes me sick to my stomach."

Karen wanted to suggest that any nausea Gordon felt might just as well be attributed to whatever alcohol he'd imbibed before he came over this evening, but her heart wasn't in it to make fun of the poor old codger. She wondered for a moment if she was in danger of becoming as softhearted as Lisa.

Next thing, she could be out buying baby clothes.

"She hasn't got much in the way of family stuff," Gordon said, thinking of his own place and the banks of yellowing family photos his wife had put all over the house. Photos he'd never had the heart to put away, even though dusting them was a bloody nightmare each month.

"Lisa told me that a lot of Joan's stuff was burnt in a fire. A lifetime of memories with her husband, all up in smoke. Lisa said Joan told her that the fire destroyed their wedding photos, all the photos of their holidays, and their houses, all the important occasions in their lives."

"Probably did it himself. Wanted to torch the memories."

Karen remembered that she had said much the same thing herself, but didn't let on to Gordon.

"Lisa said that in the end there was only one photo of Joan's husband left. Must be that one over there, on those shelves."

They wandered over to take a better look, to gaze upon the face of the man who had been unfortunate enough to suffer a lifetime of love from the unlovable Joan Davis.

Karen lifted the frame down. He looked an honorable fellow too, staring back at her in his military uniform, full of youthful enthusiasm.

"Poor bugger," she said.

"Say that again. Give us a look."

Karen passed the frame over to Gordon, who peered myopically at it.

"Eh?" he said, peering closer.

Karen thought he looked like he'd seen a ghost.

"What is it Gordon?"

"Well, I'll be buggered," he said. "Haven't seen that face in over fifty years."

He looked at Karen. "There must be some sort of mistake," he said, "'cos this isn't Joan's husband."

"It is, I tell you," Karen insisted. "Lisa told me the story herself, not two months ago. Straight from the horse's mouth."

"Nup," Gordon said. "This here's Frederick Davis, and he died in the Second World War. At El Alamein, right alongside hundreds of other New Zealand soldiers. I know, because I was there. I saw the body myself. This poor blighter never spent a lifetime with anyone, let alone an old battle-axe like Joan Davis."

Karen's mouth drooped in surprise. "But they have the same surname, don't they? Couldn't you have made a mistake?"

"No way. Happen he might have been her brother, but he was never her husband."

Karen looked from the photograph to Gordon, then back to the photograph.

"I don't believe it," she said.

"Only one way to find out," Gordon said, a wicked twinkle in his eye. "Let's ask the grieving widow herself."

As if on cue, the lounge door swung open, and Joan strode in carrying a tray laden with cups and saucers.

"Maureen's just coming with the tea and coffee," she said. "Help yourself."

Her eyes scanned the room, looking for the best spot to deposit her tray, when her gaze fixed upon Karen and Gordon.

"Just looking at the snap of your poor husband," Gordon said, his chin up, his expression defiant.

A look of sheer horror crossed Joan's face and Karen could see that the game was up. The tea tray slipped out of Joan's fingers and went crashing to the floor, but Joan was oblivious to it. Her eyes were fixed on Gordon's, like a possum transfixed by the oncoming headlights of a fast approaching car.

CHAPTER EIGHT

Outside in the darkness, the streetlight in front of Joan's house cast a strange aura on the ground. The crisp clean air bore a distinct hint of winter. An eerie silence weaved its way about, punctuated only by the footfalls of the neighbors as they made their way back to their homes. Everyone had emerged too stunned to speak.

Diane Wilson, surprised to find her daughter and son-in-law back from the meeting, looked up from her novel with a look of expectation on her face.

"Over already? Run out of things to talk about?"

Both Ian and Sandra flopped down on the couch in unison, Ian expelling the air from his lungs in a great long sigh.

"After tonight, I'm not sure the neighbors will ever run out of things to talk about," he said.

Diane's eyebrows shot up. "Oh?"

Sandra shook her head in disbelief. "It all seems so odd," she said. "Weird, even."

"What? What's odd? Will one of you please stop talking in riddles and tell me what on earth is going on."

Ian shrugged. "We scarcely know ourselves. One minute we were all sitting around chatting while Joan was making the tea. Next minute Gordon's waving a photo around under Joan's nose, she drops the entire tea tray, and then starts screaming like a banshee for us to all get out of her house."

"What? I never heard a thing."

"Well, it's a wonder you didn't, Mum. I don't think I've ever seen anyone that hysterical in my entire life. Including me. And I know I was definitely on the verge of it that night Matthew disappeared."

"What on earth was it all about?"

"If only we knew. Ian had been talking to Geoff about computers. We'd just moved on to talk about what Geoff thought of the property market at the moment, and where people seemed to be investing their money. Maureen was out in the kitchen with Joan, and Karen was talking to Gordon Price like they were old friends. What about, I don't know."

"Well, it stands to reason it must have been about the photograph. The one of Joan's husband," Ian added. "Gordon said as much before Joan dropped the tray."

"And then he said to Joan she was nothing more than a liar, pretending to be married, when all along it was a sham. Gordon said he knew that for sure because he'd been there the day the man in the photo was killed, back at El Alamein."

Diane looked confused. "So what was he saying? That Joan, the eyes and ears of Maybury Place, has been pretending all this time to have been married to a man nobody around here has ever seen or heard of, and that it just so happens someone else in the street turns out to know exactly who he is?"

"Something like that," Ian said.

"That's quite some coincidence. But why would Joan do such a thing? It's not as though it's a cardinal sin to have never been married, is it?"

Sandra shrugged. "That's what I've been wondering. Why would Joan do such a thing? Who cares if she was ever married or not?"

Ian made an expansive gesture. "Maybe it mattered to Joan. Extra respectability and all that stuff."

"Could be," Sandra said. "Perhaps people make assumptions about older unmarried ladies that Joan just didn't want."

"Like they're dried up old prunes, you mean?" Ian asked with a smirk.

Sandra suppressed a smile. "Actually, I was thinking along the lines of being an acid tongued old spinster, left on the shelf. Someone that nobody else ever wanted."

"It doesn't sound so that attractive put like that," Diane said. "However, spinsterhood was a lot more common in those days than in my generation. There were just so many young men killed in the war, and many more wounded and traumatized. I suppose pickings were pretty slim."

"Even here in New Zealand?" Sandra asked.

Diane tilted her head. "Perhaps not as much as in Britain, but enough for the impact to be felt, even here."

"But to go to the lengths of pretending to be married? It seems a bit of an over reaction," said Ian.

"She even has a whole cover story," Sandra added. "I've talked to Joan about him several times over the years, and she'd tell me all sorts of little things about him. Likes, dislikes, places they'd visited together. Even the fact that they had never had any children of their own."

"No wonder. That certainly would have been the ultimate immaculate conception of the twentieth century."

"There is one thing I would like to know though," Sandra said. "Just who was it, the man in the photo?"

"Search me," said Ian. "Although with the look of absolute triumph on Gordon's face, you can bet your bottom dollar we'll all know in the fullness of time."

Sandra mulled this over. "Kids okay, Mum?"

Diane avoided her eye. "Oh, yes."

"Don't tell me Matthew woke up."

Diane brushed an imagined piece of fluff off her sleeve. "It was nothing. Just a bit of a bad dream. A quick cuddle and he settled right back down."

"It's getting to be a real habit," Ian said, his face hardening.

"He's still getting over all the upset with that boy," Sandra replied. "I'm sure he'll come right in time."

Ian snorted. "So you keep saying. It seems to me as though he's had time enough. He'll never grow up to be a man if you keep treating the boy like a sissy. Enough is enough."

Geoff hated supermarket shopping. It was tedious and uninteresting, a necessary evil. Of course he knew that these days even buying the groceries could be done through the wonders of the internet. All you had to do was log in, order up big, and sit back waiting for some spotty teenager to drive everything much too quickly down the road from the supermarket to your front door. For a price.

It wasn't so much the premium payable that dissuaded him from using such state of the art facilities. It was more a need to get out of the house for reasons other than business, to walk down the aisles and have the tactile experience of picking things off the shelves, weighing up the pros and cons, and then exercising his power of choice. To stop and take a look at the outside world, even admire one or two of the ladies pushing trolleys up and down the aisles, and to shake his head with a whisker of regret over his own solitary existence.

Only a whisker, mind you.

Life had been so hectic of late that he hadn't even had the chance to catch up with his one or two good friends. If it wasn't for endless client meetings, and interminable Neighborhood Watch meetings, he knew he could quite easily become a hermit.

His thoughts turned, as they often did lately, to Karen. He could not pinpoint the attraction besides the proverbial moth-to-flame scenario. Of course she was pretty, and her skin looked so smooth that a part of him longed to reach out and touch it, but in all other respects she was the antithesis of him. He was reserved, she gregarious. He could not shake off his seriousness; she could seldom be serious at all. Where he liked peace and tranquility, she seemed to thrive on chaos and disorder.

They were like chalk and cheese.

However, while she should have been like fingernails down the blackboard, he found himself amused by her dry wit, intrigued by the things she said, finding himself wanting to know more about what made her tick.

Geoff rounded the aisle and was about to start contemplating the relative merits of toilet cleaners when he caught sight of Gordon Price heading toward him at full speed. There seemed no way to pretend he hadn't seen him so Geoff prepared himself for the onslaught.

Gordon was dressed in his usual civvy uniform, checked flannel shirt rolled to the elbows, baggy trousers which hung on his frame - which had probably been a perfect fit when he'd purchased them in the late seventies - sturdy boots encased in a thin film of grime. Not to mention matching dirt under his fingernails. He carried one of the supermarket's own plastic shopping baskets, in which he had yet to place anything.

"Spot of luck seeing you here like this," Gordon said as he approached.

He almost danced up and down with glee as he spoke, reminding Geoff of a marionette with someone unseen pulling his strings. An elderly Thunderbird, perhaps.

"Hello, Gordon. You're well?"

"Couldn't be better if I tried," he crowed. "I've had the best couple of days in decades. Oh, just the thought of that stuck up old biddy's face! Every time I think about it, I pretty near laugh my socks off."

Indeed Geoff thought he'd never seen as big a smile stretched across the old man's face. The usual dower expression had vanished, ushering in a new, more comical looking Gordon.

"Wasn't it great?" Gordon added, when Geoff was not forthcoming with his own opinion.

Geoff managed a lopsided smile. "I'm not so sure about great," he said. "In fact, to be honest I'm not even sure I understand what all the fuss is about."

Gordon was aghast. "Not understand? How could you not understand?"

"Well..."

"Don't you see? It's completely unbelievable. There she is parading around as though she owns the entire street, looking down her nose at the rest of us. Pretending to be mourning the loss of her poor dead husband." Gordon's voice rose as the excitement got the better of him. "And there's me thinking, lucky bugger, even if he'd ended up somewhere much worse than this world, he'd still be better off, when all along she was never married in the first place."

"But are you sure, Gordon? You couldn't have been mistaken?"

"What do you think I am? Soft in the head or something? When you've seen the sort of things I've seen in my lifetime, things that would make your hair curl, things get etched on your brain. People, names, places, death. Things no one can forget in a hurry."

"And you served with Joan's husband? In the war?"

"Not her husband, her brother. Frederick Davis. Bloody shame, poor bastard, died like so many others on foreign soil with the sand off the desert trying to cover him up before he even hit the ground. Criminal it was."

"Yes, not exactly history's finest hour."

"It was when we won, though, wasn't it? Just as well we did," Gordon said, pointing a bony finger at Geoff, "or you, sonny Jim, might very well be speaking German or Japanese now, instead of the Queen's English."

"Indeed."

"Can't say I've felt this triumphant since we won the war. If only someone had had one of those new fangled video recorders. The look on her face when she realized the game was up is something I know I could watch again and again."

"She was pretty devastated, though, Gordon."

Gordon raised his chin in defiance. "Serves her bloody well right for pretending to be something she isn't. Parading around like Lady Muck in the duck yard. It was time someone took her down a peg or two."

"I still don't see what business it is of ours what Joan does or doesn't do."

"None of our business? Maybe not, but it's not very honest, though, is it? Why, even those tarts living next to you are more honest than Mrs. Davis. They don't pretend to be anything other than what they are."

"The truth is though, Gordon, we don't really know what they are do we? It's all supposition and conjecture," Geoff said as evenly as he could manage. "If you ask me all this Neighborhood Watch thing is starting to get a little bit out of hand. People do have a right to privacy, Joan included. It's all very well to be neighborly, but when you start invading people's privacy it's another story." He gave Gordon a direct look then added, "And that's something in which I will not be involved."

Maureen flicked through the pages of a weekly magazine she'd been given by the surly girl Karen employed to sweep up hair and answer the phone and who had just washed Maureen's hair with such vicious vigor that her scalp still smarted.

Before her she saw glamorous movie stars and stick thin models, local celebrities with stiff, forced smiles. She scanned implausible stories both fact based and fictional. She read the outlandish recipes that nobody would ever make in a million years and averted her eyes from the horoscopes of which she did not approve.

Losing interest, she wedged the magazine in between the amalgamation of hairbrushes, combs, scissors and hair spray scattered on the little table in front of her. She sighed. If such publications were the plumb line of how a person should be living her life, then Maureen surmised that her life probably resembled the leaning tower of Pisa by comparison.

She avoided looking at herself in the mirror that hung on the wall above the table. She had no wish to see her hair hanging in limp rat's tails around her face - a face ravaged by time and gravity so that looking at it felt more like looking into the eyes of a stranger. She couldn't help wishing Karen would hurry up.

She examined her fingernails in quiet contemplation, the words of the rosary not far from her mind, when she realized Karen was bidding her previous client adieu and heading Maureen's way.

"Now then, Maureen," Karen greeted. "How are you?"

"Not too bad, all things considered. Yourself?"

Karen pulled over a small stool and sat herself down. "All the better for taking the weight of my feet. It's been one of those days today. Not so much as a chance to dash to the toilet."

"Well, if you need to go..."

Karen laughed and began playing with the wet tendrils of Maureen's hair, shaping it this way and that, as though she dreamed of cutting it into some ridiculous style like one of those poor people who volunteer to be transformed for a hairdressing competition.

"Ah, perhaps I exaggerate just a little," she said. "So, what can we do for you today? It's not often we see you in here, so I'm guessing it must be a special occasion?"

Maureen managed a bashful smile. "To be perfectly honest it's my birthday. I just fancied a bit of a spruce up."

"Really? Many happy returns. What a pity we don't have any champagne floating about. We haven't even got so much as a glass of wine in the fridge."

Maureen glanced away. "It doesn't matter."

"What about a cup of tea? Or even go the whole hog and have coffee? Please tell me Mirabelle at least offered you one or the other?"

Maureen felt herself reddening. "Not exactly."

Karen frowned. "No, well, it's hard to get good help these days. I don't suppose you've ever thought of getting a job, have you? Don't fancy doing a few hours here?"

"What, me? I don't think so. I'd probably be useless."

"Oh, I think you might be underestimating yourself there, Maureen. In comparison to Mirabelle you'd most likely earn yourself 'Employee of the Year' in no time."

Mirabelle drifted past, and Karen said sharply, "Cup of tea for Mrs. Haskell, Mirabelle. At a guess, I'd say white, no sugar."

Maureen nodded. She didn't really want a cup of tea but felt it would be churlish to refuse.

"Now, back to this hair of yours. What did you have in mind?"

"Just a bit of a trim really. Nothing too fancy."

"No highlights? No yearning for a new style?"

Maureen shook her head. "I think I'm a bit past new styles."

"Fair enough." Karen grasped a pile of Maureen's lank locks and attached them to the top of her head with an enormous clip, then reached for her scissors and started snipping. "So, tell me, what are you planning to do to celebrate?"

"I'm not sure really. Shaun said he would try to make it up tonight. The racing schedule is pretty busy so he finds it hard to get away, but apparently there's something wrong with his horse. There's a chance he won't be racing at all for a couple of weeks."

"He doesn't get home much, I take it?"

"He hasn't been home in nearly a year. Not since just after my last birthday."

"What? Not even for Christmas?"

"No. There are big races on Boxing Day and over New Year, so it's difficult for him to excuse himself. Especially when it's only to have Christmas dinner with his dad and me."

Down came the clump of hair before Karen deftly twisted it into another place. Mirabelle arrived with the tea and placed it down with such force that some of its contents spilt onto the magazine. Karen sent her a withering look but the girl seemed oblivious to the reprimand.

"I hope he does make it home then," Karen said. "It will be nice for you to see him again."

Maureen managed a smile. She fervently hoped it would be nice. Last year, when Shaun had come, he and his father had had cross words over the drying remnants of Shepherd's Pie and Shaun had stormed out in disgust. Now he only rang when he knew his father would not be at home. It was funny, but she couldn't for the life of her remember what the argument had even been about.

"Now," Karen said. "Do tell what you make of developments in the street."

With a sigh, Maureen said, "I don't know what to make of them. It all seems so strange. One minute I was out in the kitchen talking to Joan about the relative merits of different chocolate biscuits, and the next thing I knew we were being tossed into the street."

"Yeah, she really did her bun, didn't she? It was like something out of a soap opera."

"Well, you can hardly blame her. I mean to say, it must have been very embarrassing to be found out like that, and to have it revealed by Gordon Price to boot. She's always had very little time for him."

"So you feel sorry for her?"

"Of course. I mean I know she deceived us all, but to be so humiliatingly exposed like that. It was a bit too cruel, I think."

"You don't feel she brought it on herself?"

"Maybe a little. If only we knew why she did it. There seems so little to be gained by making up a story like that."

"Gordon thinks it's because she likes to be superior to everyone, and that there's no way she could do that if people thought she'd never been good enough for anyone to marry."

Maureen shook her head at this. "But that doesn't sound like the Joan I know. The Joan I know is quite deliberate about everything. She would never do anything arbitrary because she wanted rise in others' estimations. Especially if a chance existed that she might be found out."

"You haven't seen her?"

"No. To be honest, I'm starting to get a bit worried about her. I've tried phoning, tried going round and knocking on the door, but she doesn't answer. As far as I'm aware she hasn't left the house in over a week."

"What? Not at all? Not to peg out her washing or go shopping or find out the latest gossip?"

"Not for anything, as far as I can work out."

"Do you think she's actually there then? I mean if the place is all shut up and there's no answer, who's to say she didn't just up and leave. It would be an easy business to pack a case, phone a taxi and simply take off."

"Maybe. Except for one thing."

"Oh?"

"Her cat. She loves that cat. It's all the family she's got. I know she would never have left it to its own devices. Not without arranging for someone to take care of it."

"She could have taken the cat too. Put it into some cattery somewhere."

"I saw it this morning," Maureen said. "It meowed as I knocked on Joan's door again."

Karen looked thoughtful. "And it didn't seem desperately hungry?"

"No more than any other cat. Just a bit lonely."

"She couldn't have asked Sandra to feed it?"

"I saw Sandra two days ago and she said she hadn't seen Joan since the night of the meeting. I'm sure she would have said if Joan had asked her to feed the cat. Oh, and she did say she'd seen a light on in the lounge two nights ago, but other than that, nothing."

"So she's definitely there."

Maureen nodded.

"How long do you think she'll keep that up for? I mean to say, she can't hide forever. She's going to have to come out sooner or later."

Maureen shrugged. "I just hope she's okay, that's all."

He stood amongst the bushes, lurking in the darkness, craving its cloak of invisibility. He hunched himself into his jacket to ward off the cold, shoving his hands into his pockets for warmth. He longed for a cigarette but wanted to show nothing of himself lest he be seen.

His eyes had adjusted to the dark now, and although objects were still gloomy shapes he could work out what they were more or less.

From his vantage point he could see clearly the house at Number Seven, had watched a statuesque blonde woman draw the curtains in the front room a few minutes earlier.

She had paused for a moment and looked out into the street, almost as though expecting someone overdue. For a split second her eyes had traveled in his direction. He wondered if she would see him, but she did not. He had heard rumors that she was a good time girl, and wondered briefly about the going rate but he wasn't really interested. Not while there were other fish to fry.

He leaned against the fence, could almost feel the hard, splintered wood pressing through the thickness of his jacket. His breathing had become slow and regular, and he could feel the steady beat of his heart. He knew that he must be patient.

Time passed. How long, he wasn't sure. He dared not give himself away by looking at his watch. Any movement might be enough to attract unwanted interest. It was long enough though, for him to have begun to feel his toes, although whether it was because of having stood for some time, or because of the cold, he could not determine.

A car turned into the street, two beams of light sweeping up the road straight at him. He held his breath, tried to make himself look thinner. His heart rate increased. He could feel the adrenaline pumping. The desire to run for all he was worth built by the second and threatened to reach a crescendo when the car pulled up just a few feet from where he stood.

Not just any car.

A police car.

He stifled a cry. His mind raced. Perhaps the blonde woman had seen him after all and rather than chasing him away herself had called the police. Who knew? He had to keep calm, not panic.

He watched, mesmerized, as two burly officers stepped from the vehicle. One of them said something, and the other laughed. They looked relaxed and unhurried as they regrouped on the footpath. As they sauntered up the drive to Number Seven, he was sure they would see him. After all, he could almost reach out and touch them. He forced himself to breathe evenly, the way he had been taught. To block out everything except the task at hand. If he held his breath he would only have to expel it, risking detection.

The officers reached the door, and knocked. After a moment the blonde opened the door to admit them, all smiles. He wondered what was going on. Were the officers on the make? Perhaps the relationship was one of mutual benefit? He could not tell. Indeed he did not need to know. He let out a breath as the door shut, glad the policemen were safely inside.

He felt the wind pick up, and glanced skyward, watching as the banks of clouds threatened to move away. He hoped he wouldn't have to wait too much longer. If those clouds drifted the moonlight could create problems he had not foreseen.

Suddenly, the front door to Number Eight burst open, light pouring from the open fissure. There was a scuffling from just inside, and a man's voice. It was difficult to hear. Was the man saying he would be out until late?

The front door closed and the man bent over to tie his shoes, grunting with effort and muttering to himself under his breath. Then he straightened and made for his van, rattling his keys as he searched for the right one.

Within seconds the man reversed the white van out of the driveway, edged the vehicle around, and drove off with some speed down the length of Maybury Place.

In the shadows, he waited. Waited until the van disappeared from sight. He had to be sure. There could be no mistake. He then eased out of the shadows, pleased to move after his long vigil, and went up to the door.

He knocked, the old familiar knock he had learnt as a child, and waited. When the door finally opened and Maureen Haskell stood there, openmouthed, all he could do was smile, and say, "Happy Birthday, Mum."

Karen helped Roger with the dishes while Lisa put Grace to bed. It was half past eight, and Karen had thought after eight would be a safe time to call around since surely babies should long be in bed at such a time. Instead she found herself obliged to pick up a tea towel and help out.

Of course, as always these days, she was mistaken. Whatever schedule Grace adhered to seemed indeterminable to the average, semi-sane individual. No matter what time of day or night Karen chose to visit inevitably seemed the wrong one. She had begun to suspect that, where Grace was concerned, Lisa had lost the plot. Grace was taking over their lives, pure and simple.

At length the dishes were done, Grace had settled, and coffee had been made. Not for Lisa, though. There could be no risk of caffeine being passed on to the baby. Sitting in the lounge and looking at Lisa and Roger, both incredibly haggard, Karen couldn't help feeling that babies were more trouble than they were worth.

"Blimey," she said. "You two look like death warmed up."

Roger managed a small smile. "Thanks. You try being handsome and debonair after only three hours of sleep last night. And not three hours all together either, I might add."

"Bloody hell."

"It's not Grace's fault," Lisa said with a yawn.

"I don't know how you work that one out. Who else is there to blame?"

"She's got wind. It makes her tummy gripey and she can't sleep."

"So can't anything be done about it, then? Surely in this day and age a bit of excess gas could be easily dealt with. What does Leslie What's-her-name recommend?"

"She's given me some drops. Homeopathic ones. And a diet sheet."

"For you or for Grace?"

"For me, silly."

"Lucky you. How yummy."

Roger laughed. "You should see it. It's very long. No green vegetables, especially peas, no onions, no garlic, no spices, no coffee, no fizzy drink, no alcohol."

"Right, well, that settles it then. No babies for me. Ever."

"Apparently it's very common," Lisa said, as though that made everything all right.

"Let's hope for your sakes that it's very common for it to go away without delay."

After a pause Roger said, "So to what do we owe the pleasure of this visit?"

Karen snorted. "And here was me thinking I could call around for nothing in particular."

"Ah," Lisa said, "but we don't usually see you during the week unless there's something important afoot."

Karen attempted to look coy, but felt sure her actual expression was one of guilt.

"Okay, you've got me. But, I was thinking of it along the lines of public service, since neither of you have probably had the time or the inclination to put your noses outside the door all week."

"True."

"Well, where to start? I saw Sandra yesterday. She bailed me up and told me a long winded story about having enrolled Matthew at school, and how delighted she is because he's to have some teacher called Miss Humperdink, or some other equally ridiculous name, and how she is so much more preferable Mrs. Liberace. At least, she wasn't called Mrs. Liberace, but Sandra made them all sound about as attractive as seventies lounge singers."

"I know," Lisa said.

"You know?"

"Sandra calls in practically every day. She keeps having these little thoughts about things I might find useful with Grace."

"Her diet list is even longer than Leslie's," Roger added. "Almost all that's left is bread and water."

"Good grief. Why don't you tell her to mind her own business?"

"She means well."

"You say that about everyone. I, for one, don't think it's true. I know plenty of people who don't mean well at all. In fact, about half of them are my customers."

Lisa pursed her lips.

"All right, all right, so my tolerance chromosomes don't seem to work as well as yours. Who can help genetics?"

Roger and Lisa laughed.

"What else is new?" Roger asked.

"Gordon's potato plants have got mange."

"Mange? I thought cats got mange."

"Well, maybe it was blight. Anyway, for once he doesn't care. He's still on cloud nine after his victory last week. Which reminds me. Maureen came into the salon today, having a tart-up for her birthday. She said that Joan has been holed up in her house since last week, and hasn't come out at all."

"What? Not at all?" Lisa asked.

"Not once unless it's been under the cover of darkness. You haven't seen or heard from her?"

Lisa shook her head. "To tell you the truth, I was enjoying the respite. I suppose I've been so wrapped up in Grace that I hadn't given Joan a second thought."

Karen held her tongue, but managed to say, "Maureen is convinced she's there. The cat's there, and seems well fed, and Sandra has seen a light on one night, so there seems little doubt that she's hiding away."

"That doesn't sound like Joan at all. I would have thought she'd have come out fighting."

"Except there seems little doubt about the fact that the story is actually true. Everyone's speculating on why she would pretend to be married. No one can come up with a rational explanation, aside from a desire not to be seen as a spinster. Oh, and of course Gordon thinks she did it to be superior, although I don't know about that. I couldn't give a toss either way. I'm not married, and I don't let that stop me. I know I'm superior to everyone else."

"Ha ha. You do not."

Karen grinned. "Well, at least somebody likes me."

"And who might that be?" Lisa asked.

A smug look settled on Karen's face, but she said nothing.

"Don't tell me there's news?"

Karen nodded. "Yes, believe it or not, I've got a date."

"With Geoff?"

"Of course with Geoff. He came over last night and asked if I wanted to go out to dinner some time. Well, not just some time, but Friday."

"This Friday?"

"Yup. Naturally I said I had to check my diary, and lo and behold, there on Friday it said, 'Wash hair'. So, I hummed and ha-ed, but at the end of the day I am a hairdresser, and if I can't do something with my hair during the day at work, who can?"

Lisa and Roger grinned back at her, like a couple of Cheshire cat bookends.

"Go for it," Roger said. "Hope you have a great time."

The second Karen went home Roger and Lisa sprinted to their bedroom as if in a race to see who could get into bed first. Teeth were scrubbed and clothes were changed at top speed. In the end Roger won, but only by a fraction of a second.

They lay there, in the dark, waiting for sleep to claim them. Both of them were fatigued beyond measure, and yet for some reason, neither of them could relax enough to drop off. And so they lay, almost touching, their eyes slowly adjusting to the darkness of the room.

Roger's mind turned inevitably to thoughts of intimacy with Lisa, or lack thereof as was the case at the moment. Ironically, he was so tired it didn't matter nearly as much as he thought it might.

Lisa had her mind on a dozen things, one thought leading to another, tumbling over one another until she couldn't even remember where her train of thought had started.

Eventually she whispered, "Are you awake?"

"Yes."

"What are you thinking about?"

"Nothing. You?"

"Oh, this and that."

There was a pause. "What 'this and that'?" Roger asked, knowing full well that wives expected their husbands to say this.

"I was thinking about Karen. About her and Geoff. I mean can you really picture them together?"

"It's only a date. No harm done there."

"Really? Expectations seem pretty high on Karen's part."

"Surely going on a date can hardly be misconstrued," Roger said. "Dating's a bit like shopping for clothes. You see something you think would fit you to perfection. You ask to try it on. You go into one of those little cubicles where the curtains never seem wide enough to stop people looking in while you try stuff on, and you proceed to take your clothes off and change into the new gear. Sometimes you're lucky, and the fit is perfect. Sometimes you realize you must have been mad to think the thing would ever suit you."

"Maybe. You didn't answer my question, though. Can you picture them together?"

Another pause. "I suppose so. I can't see why not. Granted, on the face of it they don't seem to have an awful lot in common, but maybe they both have something the other needs."

"Like what?"

"Like Geoff could lighten up a little. He is quite serious, you have to admit. On the other hand, Karen is pretty flighty. A bit of seriousness would probably do her the world of good."

"Flighty? She'd kill you if she heard you say that."

"Well, perhaps you'd prefer another word? How about daffy?"

"I hope you don't mean that."

Roger laughed as quietly as he could. Things were considerably constrained since Grace had come along.

"Fooled you. I've been taking lessons off Karen too. No, I think what Karen needs more than anything is a sensible, stable relationship. She's been on her own so long that she's started to try too hard."

Lisa considered this. "Maybe you're right. I know she is lonely. Well, not lonely so much as tired of being alone."

"And who's to say that Geoff isn't the very man to fit the bill? After all, maybe he's been lonely too. Maybe he's tired of the relentless search for Miss Right?"

"Makes you feel pretty lucky, doesn't it?"

"Sure does."

They moved closer to one another, and lay silent for a while.

After a few minutes Lisa said, "Are you still awake?"

"Yes. But we both should be asleep. We'll pay for this later, you know."

"I know."

"So what is it now?"

"I was thinking about Joan."

"And next will it be Maureen, followed by Sandra, followed by Gordon and his mangy potatoes?"

"No, not Sandra. I'm fed up with Sandra Fleming and all her patronizing advice. And I think I can safely say that I'm not the slightest bit interested in Gordon's potatoes, mangy or otherwise. But I can't help thinking about what Karen said about Joan not having been seen for a week."

"She's probably just licking her wounds."

"For a week? What if it's not what everyone thinks? What if she's fallen and hurt herself, or is lying unconscious. For all we know, she might have died in her sleep and none of us have even noticed."

"Hardly likely."

"Why not? What happened sounded pretty shocking. How do we know she didn't have a heart attack with the stress of it?"

"What about her cat? Karen said Maureen said that it didn't seem to be going hungry."

"It's a cat. They hunt. They're resourceful. It could be stealing food out of other cats' bowls, or sucking up to some other old lady. After all, their number one motivation in life is filling their stomachs, followed closely by sleeping."

"That sounds familiar. Do you think Grace could be part feline?"

Lisa elbowed him. "I'm serious."

"And I think you're worrying unnecessarily. The chances are that Joan is just too embarrassed to show her face. I'm sure she'll come out when she's good and ready."

"But what about food? If she hasn't been out of the house for a week where will she be getting fresh bread and milk from?"

"I don't know," Roger said, with as much patience as he could muster. "The fresh bread and milk fairy? Who knows? Maybe over the past few weeks she's been loading her freezer up with as many muffins as she's given us. She could be engaged in a bake-a-thon right now, and tomorrow she'll turn up on our doorstep with fifty muffins, twelve chocolate cakes and six dozen currant buns."

Lisa made an exasperated sound. "I wish you would take me seriously. I'm really worried."

"In which case you should go over and see her tomorrow. But Lisa, I hardly have to remind you that right now you have other priorities. Don't you think you have enough on your plate as it is?"

As if to further make his point the sound of wailing came drifting down the hall. It was time to get up again without having caught a wink of sleep.

CHAPTER NINE

"I don't suppose I could talk you into going to work late, could I?" Lisa asked the following morning as they sat having an increasingly rare breakfast together.

"Lisa."

"I know, I know. It's just that I'm really worried. Couldn't you hang on five minutes while I zip across the road? I wouldn't be long."

"You're not even dressed," Roger said. "By the time you get ready and go over there, it'll be a lot longer than five minutes. Besides, what if Joan decides she's ready to bear her soul and you're the first one to come along? You could be hours."

"I wouldn't. I promise."

"You would. You've got too soft a heart. The minute she asks you in to talk, you're doomed."

Lisa examined her hands. "So are you saying I shouldn't go at all?"

"Not exactly, although let me be the first to say that I really don't see how this is our problem. Joan's a grown woman. This situation is entirely of her own making. Remember my old granny and her pearls of wisdom? Well, here's another one for you: you make your bed, you lie in it."

"Everyone's granny says that."

"Because it contains a truth."

"I still say we don't really know what's going on. I just want to make sure she's all right."

"And I want to make sure we've got bread on the table and money to feed the mortgage. I think Tempo have cut me enough slack as it is. Can you imagine what they'd say if I turned up late because my wife was having palpitations about a woman who lives across the road from us?"

"I'm not having palpitations."

Roger was skeptical. "No?"

"No."

"What about holding off until tomorrow? It's Saturday. You can go at your leisure. Or at Grace's leisure, as the case may be."

"But what if there's something wrong? I'd feel terrible if I didn't at least try going today."

"Then all I can suggest is that you get yourself ready. Put Grace in the pram, or even in her car seat capsule, and the two of you go over later in the morning. You never know, if Joan is really hiding, the thought that she could see Grace might be enough to convince her to open the door."

Lisa sighed. "All right. If you really won't hang on."

He shook his head, and stood up.

"I'd better go. Traffic's been murder lately."

He came around the table and stooped to kiss her on the top of her head.

"It's great that you care so much," he said. "I love you for that. But you have to see things from my point of view too."

Before Lisa could think up a reply, he was gone.

In the end it took Lisa almost five hours to make her way across the road. She'd cleared up after breakfast, shoved a load of washing into the machine and had been about to jump in the shower and get dressed when Grace had woken and needed feeding.

Then she'd had to change Grace, get her dressed, dress her again after she spilled all down the front of the outfit she'd just been manhandled into, change her diaper again after loud explosions heralded the arrival of a lovely little deposit, then top her up with feed because the poor little thing was starving from all of that exertion.

At last Lisa managed to settle her to sleep in her car seat so that she could carry her across the road to see Joan. She left Grace in the capsule on the floor of the hall outside the bathroom door while Lisa showered. After standing under the reviving jets of warm water Lisa went back into her bedroom to get dressed. She had to restrain herself from sinking onto the bed and going to sleep.

With both of them washed, dressed and pressed, Lisa was about to set off when she realized two things. Firstly, the load of washing she'd put in the machine had long since completed its cycle, and that if she didn't peg everything out while the going was good, Grace was in danger of having nothing to wear later that day. Lisa's mind reeled at not only how long everything took, but also how many clothes Grace went through. It was incredible.

She also realized she had precious little bread and milk for themselves let alone enough spare to take over as an offering for Joan. Lisa threw the damp clothes into the basket, rushed outside and started pegging at top speed, rushed back inside and grabbed her purse, bundled the still sleeping Grace into the car, and drove to the supermarket to buy the essentials.

On her return Lisa was all ready to go across the road but as she pulled into their driveway Grace awoke from her slumber and started to protest. So it was back inside for another feed, another diaper change, another spill, another outfit, another top up. Another hour and a half gone. And people wondered what mothers did at home all day.

Finally, standing on the front porch outside Joan's front door, Lisa felt so exhausted that she'd begun to not really care if Joan was home or not. She couldn't help feeling a bit resentful. Things would have been different if only Roger had waited this morning. It took her last remaining vestiges of willpower to muster up enough energy to lift up her arm and knock.

When she did knock the sound reverberated around the porch. She imagined it carrying down the hall of Joan's house. There seemed to be no way a person could miss such a noise though the empty silence.

Lisa waited.

No reply.

Not so much as a shuffle.

She knocked again.

Still no response.

"Joan!" she called. "It's Lisa. Are you all right?"

Silence.

"I've bought you some bread and milk."

Still nothing.

"I brought Grace over to see you."

At this, Lisa was sure she heard a creak from inside, as though Joan was sitting there listening to every word but refusing to respond. Only the mention of Grace elicited a response, just as Roger thought it might.

Lisa sighed, wondering what to do next. She'd gone to so much trouble to come over.

"Joan? Couldn't you let me in? We could talk?"

Another creak.

Grace started mewling from the car seat, tired of being confined. Lisa felt she'd been in it enough today. It was time to go home.

"I've got to go now, Joan," she said. "I'll leave the bread and milk out here for you."

Returning home, Lisa couldn't help but feel disappointed. She still didn't really know if Joan was all right. As she stood looking out of her front window, across the road at Joan's house she wondered what she should do next. Then she looked again and realized that in the time it had taken Lisa to walk across the road and lay Grace on her rug on the lounge floor for a kick around, one small thing had occurred.

The bread and milk had disappeared from where Lisa had left them.

The restaurant Geoff chose could quite safely be called middle of the road. It was not too intimate nor was it too noisy; the food was neither bland nor too spicy; the ambiance neither casual nor sophisticated. The prices were not too expensive, or offensively cheap, and it was located far enough away from Maybury Place to feel as though they'd gone somewhere else but not so far away as to make the journey arduous.

By arrangement, Karen had taken herself over to Geoff's when she was ready, and in an evening that on the outset seemed transcended by equilibrium, she was neither too early nor too late.

It was no mean feat.

She had begun agonizing over what to wear the night before. She wanted to strike just the right chord with her dress. Were trousers too masculine? Would Geoff interpret a dress as being too formal? Would the temperature be warm or cold?

In the end the outfit she had settled on in her mind felt wrong when she'd tried it on.

As had the next one.

And the next.

Exasperated, she finally chose a rose colored skirt made of some sort of swishy material, and a white long sleeved knit top with little buttons down the front that showed just the right amount of cleavage. She'd piled her hair up on top of her head, applied her war paint with a light hand and set off out the door.

They traveled to the restaurant in Geoff's four-wheel drive in near silence. Karen kept thinking of things to say but Geoff seemed intent on driving so she gave up trying. She hoped it wasn't a sign of things to come.

They entered the restaurant and were directed to their table by a young man in his twenties who tried his utmost to be felicitous in his banal banter. Karen couldn't help feeling uncomfortable. Wanting to go on a date might be one thing. Actually being on one was another thing entirely.

They got settled. Karen said, "Well, this is nice."

Geoff raised an eyebrow but said nothing.

"Have you been here before?" she asked.

"Once or twice. The food is usually very good. You?"

Karen shook her head.

She knew she should be focusing her attention on Geoff but found her eyes darting around to take in the details of her surroundings: the white table cloths, the sprig of flowers in a vase on each table, the other diners, the soft clatter of cutlery on china, the casual music playing in the background, the steady rise and fall of conversation.

Her eyes returned to look at Geoff. He regarded her but his expression was guarded and unreadable.

"So, here we are then," Karen said.

"Indeed."

"Perhaps I should tell a joke," she said.

Geoff's expression was sardonic. "Don't feel you have to."

Undaunted she said, "What happens to men's toupees after they die?"

"I can't guess."

"They get wig-a-mortis."

He rolled his eyes. "Very droll."

"I've got another."

"Oh dear."

"Why did the chicken cross the road?"

Geoff rolled his eyes again.

"Come on," she urged. "Have a guess."

"Why did the chicken cross the road? Because it saw Colonel Sanders coming?"

"No. Try again."

"It was free range and it would go where it damned well pleased?"

She laughed. "Actually your answers are better than the one I had."

He studied her for a few moments.

"Why do you do it?" he asked.

"Do what?"

"Make jokes all the time?"

"Do I?"

"You know you do."

She shrugged. "I like to make people laugh I guess."

"Really?"

She returned his gaze. She hadn't thought about it that much before.

"In truth I suppose I do it because it comes naturally. It's far easier to make a joke than pretend to make intelligent conversation."

"Because you don't think you're intelligent, or because you don't feel like what you have to say is important?"

Karen considered this. "Both I suppose. What do you think?"

"I don't really know you well enough to know why you do it. On the face of it you seem both funny and smart to me. There should be no need to cover up one at the expense of the other."

"You're not very good for my ego," she told him. She'd begun to think she must have been mad to have agreed to go out with him.

Geoff gave her a lazy smile. "Perhaps it's more your ego that's not very good."

Karen's gaze dropped. If he kept on like this she'd be in danger of bursting into tears.

Geoff leant over and took one of her hands in his.

"Please don't cry," he said softly. "I fear I have made my point very badly."

She nodded but kept her eyes firmly on the tablecloth.

"Karen," he said, his tone so firm that it made her look up, "I'm just trying to say, in my very inept way, that you don't need to feel you have to make jokes with me. I asked you to come out for dinner because I want to get to know the real you, the one I see hiding behind all the jokes and hilarity."

Karen withdrew her hand. "I'm not sure who she is," she said in a small voice. "Jokes are what I do best."

"And there's nothing wrong with humor. I'm not saying that. I guess what I am saying is that I wouldn't have asked you out unless I really was interested in getting to know you. I'm thirty-eight years old, and I'm single because in all honesty I've never found a woman I could picture spending the rest of my life with. But I am still looking. And I don't really want to waste any more time. So what I'm asking is that we both be real with one another. No games, no pretence, no beating around the bush."

Karen smiled. "What? Not even a little bit of bush beating?"

"You're doing it again."

"Sorry. Well, actually I'm only a little bit sorry. Do you want to know why?"

"Why?"

"Because while I make too many jokes you don't make enough."

He laughed. "Fair enough. As long as we understand each other."

"It's half your fault you know."

"Oh? How so?"

"You make me nervous."

He laughed again. "Me? You should take a look at yourself. Besides, it's only because you don't know me very well."

"Well get rectifying."

He coughed. "What do you want to know?"

"Everything."

"Everything? Couldn't you be a little bit more specific?"

"No. Oh, all right then. Let's start with your C.V."

"Must we?"

"Come on. Get on with it."

He smiled. "Fair enough. Right. Full name, Geoffrey Elliott Milne. Birth date, November twenty-first. Age, already stated."

"November? Mine's in October."

"What date?"

"Eleventh."

"My brother's is the twelfth."

"I didn't know you had a brother."

"Yes. David. He lives in Oxford. Has done for the past fifteen years."

"So when did you last see him?"

"Six years ago. When Dad turned seventy. David and his wife came for a visit. I think they found everything very provincial. Especially Daphne."

"You don't hanker to see him again? Or go to England?"

Geoff shook his head. "I've been. I don't really feel the need to go again. As for David, well, we were never particularly close. Truth is, we're probably too similar."

"Your parents are still alive then?"

"Yes. Yours?"

Karen grimaced. "Oh, yes. Alive and kicking." She leant forward conspiratorially. "They're control freaks, you know."

"I don't recall ever seeing them in the street. They can't be that bad if they aren't camped on your doorstep."

"That's because I usually circumvent such an event by calling in to see them. That way I can usually head them off at the pass. Luckily they think I have no life outside of cutting hair. Which, sadly, generally is true."

"I'm sure it's not that bad."

"Actually it's worse. But since we're trying to have a nice time I won't bore you with details. Where do your parents live?"

"Up north. When Dad retired I thought he and Mum would settle down to a comfortable life of not really talking to one another, Mum busy with her activities, Dad with his. It came as quite a shock when they announced they were tired of city life and wanted nothing more than to find a small plot of land overlooking the sea, take walks on the beach, plant a vegetable garden, and for Dad to go fishing."

"And is that what happened?"

"Mostly. Mum loves her garden, Dad loves his fishing, but they seem to have discovered a whole other rural life. They haven't got a neighbor in sight, but they always seem to be seeing this person and that person, as though they'd known some of these folk all their lives."

"Weird. Mind you, look at us. We're up to our eyeballs in neighbors."

Geoff smiled. "I think it's the disadvantage of living in such a small street. You can't help tripping over people as you come and go. It seems more civilized to at least be on speaking terms."

"Yes but things have gone a whole lot further that just waving a lofty hand at someone over the fence, or saying a cheery hello. We seem to have ended up knowing all kinds of things about one another."

"You mean Joan? Yes, well, even I have to admit to being surprised by all of that, even though, as I was quick to point out to Gordon when he wanted to gloat, it really is none of our business."

Karen considered this. "I know it isn't but somehow that doesn't make the whole situation any less fascinating. Why do you think she did it?"

He shrugged. "Beats me."

"They do say you should never judge a book by its cover, and where we were concerned we must have been up to at least page one hundred in the book of the life and times of Joan Davis. Maybe you can never judge at all. I suppose at least it's given everyone something to talk about other than your neighbors."

Geoff said nothing.

"What? You aren't going to champion their cause?" Karen teased.

"I wasn't aware that's what I'd been doing."

"Of course you have."

"No, in my mind what I've been doing is reminding everyone we still live in a free country and that if we aren't getting hurt we should mind our own business."

"There was the incident with Matthew."

"I know. But who knows what really was behind all that. We've made some pretty hefty assumptions about what goes on behind closed doors at Number Seven. All I've been trying to point out is the fine line between neighborly concern and downright interfering."

"Oh, I quite agree. Still, I suppose that's all at an end now. I can't see us having any more meetings, can you?"

"I'm not so sure. Anyway, at the end of the day, the meetings haven't been a total waste of time, have they?"

"I can't really see how you could say that."

Geoff smiled. "You're sitting here now, aren't you?"

To this, all Karen could do was grin.

"Roger?"

"Yes."

"Could you stop doing the dishes for a minute and look at me."

He turned with a heavy and reluctant sigh.

"Thank you. Look I'm sorry about yesterday. I know I had no right to get mad at you about not staying in the morning. It had just turned into such a nightmare of a day."

He shrugged. "We're both on edge at the moment. Not enough sleep, I suppose."

Lisa nodded. "It would be nice to not feel perpetually tired."

"Parents of New Baby Syndrome. I guess it will pass."

"I did try to warn you before Grace was born that I'd be hopeless at it."

"Rubbish. You're doing a fine job. Nobody can expect to be at their best when they're sleep deprived. It's something you can't really prepare yourself for, is it?"

"No. I never pictured things with Grace taking so long, either. Or feeling overwhelmed with being so much in demand."

Roger moved away from the sink. "Come here," he said.

Lisa stepped into his arms and rested her head on his chest.

"Why don't I take Grace out for a bit this morning?" he suggested. "After her feed. Then you could put your feet up."

"Or do the washing, or do some cleaning, or vacuum, or iron, or write some more thank you cards."

"Those things can all wait. Right now rest is far more important."

"Okay. If I must. You've twisted my arm."

He kissed her on the top of the head.

"Good. I'm glad we got that settled."

After they had gone - Roger pushing Grace off down the road in the pram for his first solo outing - Lisa endeavored to do as she'd been told.

She lay on the bed and looked at the ceiling. Then she lay on her side and looked at the far wall. She lay on her other side, toward the windows, and looked as the dust settled on the bedside cabinet, and then, despairing of ever falling asleep, she lay on her stomach with her face half buried in the pillow.

She longed for sleep. Craved it in the same way she imagined a mountaineer wants to reach the summit of some enormous peak; or the way a runner surges forward with the finish line in sight; or the way a desperate Sandra might try to be the first person to put her hand on some desirable item in a sale of designer children's wear.

Thoughts of Sandra led to thoughts of Joan. As much as Lisa tried, she couldn't get Joan out of her mind. It worried her that someone could shut themselves away like that. In spite of Roger's opposition Lisa wanted to do something more. He thought she had done enough, and although he was quite right when he said that she had other more important priorities - not the least being Roger himself - it didn't seem to matter. Someone they knew was hurting. To all intents and purposes they were standing by and letting it happen.

Knowing now that she would not sleep, Lisa did not even bother to try. Resolved to her course of action, she tidied herself up, ran a comb through her hair, and let herself out of the front door.

Lisa knocked.

"Joan?"

No answer.

Lisa knocked again.

Not a whisper.

"Joan? It's Lisa. Could you please come to the door?"

Nothing.

"I only want to talk. To know you're okay."

She waited.

"Look, Joan, this can't go on any longer. Please open the door."

Silence.

"Everyone's worried about you, Joan. We need to know that you're all right."

More silence.

"We know you're in there."

Still nothing.

"Right. Well. You're starting to leave us no choice. If you won't answer the door we'll be forced to call the police. Have them come and make sure you're all right."

At this Lisa was certain she heard a sound from inside the house.

Emboldened she said, "Look, Joan, you and I both know that I've got a lot on my plate at the moment. I haven't got time to waste worrying about whether you're hurt or unwell. So, I'm just going to sit here until you open the door. I'll let someone else worry about how Grace is, and whether she's hungry or not, or needs her mother, who won't be available because she's having to camp outside a neighbor's house who won't answer the door."

More rustling.

Lisa decided she had said quite enough and would stay as long as she could, hoping Joan would see reason and open the door. She settled herself on the porch step among the profusion of tubs and pots spilling over with asters, marigolds and forget-me-nots. She watched the breeze cause the lilac heads on Joan's late flowering jacaranda to sway back and forth and pulled her cardigan around her, crouching into its meager warmth. A thin blanket of cloud lurked in a way that suggested it had no intention of going any-where. She wished she'd given a second's thought to the weather before she'd left the house and put on something warmer.

Joan's cat appeared, seemingly grateful for some company. It wound itself around Lisa's legs and purred like a freight train. Lisa fondled its ears then wished she hadn't. Motherhood had turned her into a germ radar. Her fingers felt contaminated. She would have to remember to wash them later.

After about ten minutes Lisa grew tired of her vigil. She kept picturing her bed, considering herself mildly insane to have rejected the warmth of its comforting support in exchange for Joan's splintered porch. Right now she could be resting there, even if she did only lie staring at the ceiling. She could have read a few lines of a book. It seemed so long since she had even picked one up she wondered if she still knew how to read.

She should have realized the futility of issuing an ultimatum if she wasn't prepared to see it through. She could only hope Joan would interpret her actions as those of a person not easily deterred and give in quickly. Then she felt a bit ashamed of the truth of the matter: if anyone came along she could be easily persuaded to leave her post, after only the minimum duration.

Minutes ticked by. Lisa's backside got colder and colder. Joan's cat had tried to settle itself in her lap to sleep and in the process had succeeded in putting muddy paws on Lisa's trousers. She could only be thankful that the sky showed no sign of rain.

Suddenly, there was a noise behind Lisa. She turned to see that Joan's front door had been opened, ever so minutely.

"You'd better come in," Joan's muffled voice said from behind the door.

Lisa swallowed, rose from her spot and pushed the door open in time to catch a glimpse of Joan disappearing down the hallway and into her living room. Clearly she intended Lisa to follow her lead, so she closed the door behind her and made her way down the hall. She paused for a moment on the threshold, wondered what on earth she thought she was doing, took a deep breath, and stepped into the room.

Joan's living room had become airless during her self-imposed exile, as though it had been unoccupied for years on end, to the point where there should be spider webs strung across doorways and mold growing in a forest on the ceiling.

She found Joan sitting in an armchair, dressed in a nightie and dressing gown, and swathed, like the late Queen Mother, in a kneeful of blankets. Her face was pale. She had drawn her hair back into a plait that hung down her back like an etching Lisa had once seen of a pioneer woman. It seemed to Lisa as though Joan had aged ten years in the same amount of days.

Joan made a study of her fingernails and avoided making eye contact.

"Hello, Joan," Lisa said, taking a seat. "Thanks for letting me in."

Joan remained silent. She seemed deep in thought, as though trying to solve the mysteries of the universe.

"Everyone's been very worried about you. Are you all right?"

Joan sucked her breath in, kept her eyes on her hands, and said in a thin voice, "I'm sure not everyone shares your concern. I would imagine some people are very pleased indeed."

"Not most people," Lisa said quickly. "Most people, like Maureen, and Sandra, and Roger, and Karen, and Geoff. We've all been most concerned."

Joan looked up. "Really?"

"Of course."

Joan resumed her study of her fingers. "I'm sure you're just being kind. I'm sure everyone is having a fine old time running me down."

"Not as far as I'm aware," Lisa said.

Joan made a sound of doubt.

"I won't lie to you, Joan," Lisa continued. "There has been some talk. Of course there has been. But none of it has been malicious, as far as I know. Everyone is just curious, that's all. Curious and concerned."

"Then why have you been the only one to take any interest in how I am?" Joan asked, looking directly at Lisa now.

"Maureen's been over, and Sandra's been keeping an eye out for you. I think people haven't really known what to say or do."

Joan made a sound of despair. "Nor have I," she said. "Nor have I."

Lisa moved from where she was sitting to a spot closer.

"What is it Joan? What's going on? None of this makes any sense."

"I have my reasons," Joan choked. "Or at least I did have my reasons. Maybe they aren't important any more."

"What reasons? What possible reason could there be for pretending to have been married?"

Joan lapsed into silence.

"Look, Joan, you don't have to tell me. After all, it isn't any of my business. But whatever the reason, it seems to be eating you up. Surely it would be helpful to talk to someone? If not me, perhaps someone else."

Joan looked directly at Lisa. "I want to talk to you," she said. "I want it more than anything in the world. I always have. But some things are difficult to speak of, and some things are difficult to hear."

"I understand that. I want you to know, though, that if you do want to talk to me, I will say nothing of what you tell me to anyone. Not a living soul. Not even Roger if you don't want me to."

Joan laughed, a hollow sound that seemed as remote from humor as the sound of gunfire was to peace. "I don't think you'll be in a hurry to tell anyone."

Lisa frowned.

"So, it begins," Joan said cryptically. She took a deep breath, as though steeling herself. "But now that it does I hardly know where to start."

"Take your time, Joan," Lisa said. In truth she was beginning to feel uncomfortable. There was something about the way Joan kept looking at her which made Lisa want to get up and run.

"Very well. I suppose the best place to start would be with my childhood. Or to be more precise, with my mother." Joan's expression altered. "Oh she was a terrible woman. Mean and domineering and bossy and opinionated. She ruled my life, and my brother's, with an iron fist. She was relentless about every little thing. Always criticizing and nagging. Never ever satisfied with anything we ever did or said.

"Of course I adored Frederick. He was a good deal older than me, and probably thought me to be a nuisance, but at the same time he knew that our mother treated me harder than she ever did him. My father worked away from home much of the time, as a travelling salesman, and wasn't bothered about what went on in his absence as long as things were fine when he returned. Which they were. Otherwise we both paid for it, in spades.

"When war broke out I think Frederick was relieved. He saw it as a way out, a big adventure. He signed up as soon as he turned eighteen. Unfortunately, as you now know, it was a big adventure that cost him his life.

"When news came through in one of those terrible, impersonal letters that everyone dreaded, my mother became even more of a tyrant. It gave her a determination to see me turn out to be a success. Or at least what went for a success in her eyes.

"The news devastated my father. He withdrew into himself. After that he drifted from job to job, unable to hold any proper work down. As the years went by money became more difficult to find, prices higher and higher.

"Eventually, it became clear even to my mother that if we were going to get by there had to be a regular income coming in. Things had changed in the work force with the war and women were doing all sorts of jobs that would have been unthinkable beforehand. I became a secretary, and after training, secured a position with a large company in the typing pool. My wages went straight to my mother, with a small allowance for me for clothing and personals." She looked at Lisa. "You know the sort of thing.

"For me it was a life with no way out. So I kept working and over the years made my way up the ladder, until I ended up as the personal assistant of the managing director. Richard Blake was his name, although he's been

dead a long time now. We worked well together, and over the years became...
well...close.

"If he went away on business I would go too, and that was how it all
began. I was lonely, he handsome and charming and caring, oh, and married,
but that didn't seem to matter at all. His wife didn't understand him, he was
longing to leave her. All the usual things."

Joan laughed again, that same empty sound. "Of course, I was no babe
in the woods. I was twenty-five when it started, thirty-five when it finished.
Old enough to know better. But I was desperately lonely, and it was convenient and easy and familiar, and a release from the rest of my wretched life.
He kept telling me he would leave his wife, and part of me wanted to believe
that, but I knew he never would. Not even when I found out I was pregnant."

Lisa's eyes widened. "You had a baby?"

Joan nodded. "I lied and told my mother I was to be transferred to
another office in another city for five months, a non existent office. Richard
paid for me to have somewhere to live and I just drifted until the baby was
born. It was then that I started calling myself Mrs. Davis, making up the
story about Frederick who was conveniently away at sea. It became a habit I
never gave up. It made it easy to fend off unwanted questions and attention,
and gave me a respectability I would never have otherwise had.

"So I had the baby, adopted it out, went back home, trapped with my
mother until the day she died, then stayed with my useless father for another
five years until he passed away. Richard arranged another job for me, with an
associate of his in another firm, and that was that. I never saw him again."

"Or the baby," Lisa said softly.

"Well, that's not strictly true. In fact, it's not true at all."

"So you know where he or she ended up?"

"She. It was a girl. Yes, I know where she is."

"So where is she?"

Joan looked at Lisa. "She's here."

"Where?"

"Right here."

Lisa looked confused.

"Lisa," Joan said, "there's not an easy way to tell you this, but it's you.
I'm your mother."

<h1 style="text-align:center">CHAPTER TEN</h1>

Grace lay in the cocooned splendor of her pram and gazed up at the sky as though trying to make sense of the world. Roger walked at an even pace, taking care not to bump her around too much. The pram, he found, had more aesthetic than practical qualities. The wheels were too small to be able to easily mount curbs. If he strode out a step too far he kept banging his foot against the wheel strut.

At first he felt self-conscious about pushing a pram - not because of any perceived threat to his masculinity - but because it felt so alien and unreal to him. But as the walk progressed he began to relax and get into his stride.

The clouds that blocked out any hint of the sun had brought the air temperature down by a good few degrees, but not enough to trouble either him or Grace. While she would be too little to sit up and take notice of her surroundings for quite some time Roger still felt as though she was enjoying the different sounds and sensations as they walked along. He thought it all must be very overwhelming when you had absolutely no idea what was going on.

As he neared the local shopping centre - where he planned to buy yet more bread and milk - he found himself accosted by people he had never seen in his life, who wanted him to stop in order that they could admire his precious cargo. He couldn't help feeling immensely proud.

With the shopping completed, Roger felt they had both had enough. It was time to head for home. They were about half way there when Grace decided she'd had her fill of adventure. She closed her eyes and went to sleep. Roger spent the rest of the walk back humming to himself and feeling all to be right in the world. It seemed ironic to feel so content when parenthood had proved to be tougher assignment than either he or Lisa had anticipated.

He hadn't wanted to admit to Lisa his feelings of inadequacy. He, who kept on telling her how everything would be fine, that they would know what to do, that the mysteries of being parents would be somehow divinely transmuted into their lives, at times found himself overwhelmed by the enormity of responsibility. While he had been full of bravado beforehand - and Lisa unsure and diffident - now the tables were turned. When Grace required some hitherto unperformed ministration Roger would stand by with panic practically surging through his veins. Lisa, on the other hand, now seemed to have a feel for what to do. Feelings of guilt competed with those of thankfulness that the bulk of responsibility wasn't on his shoulders alone.

Turning into Maybury Place, his thoughts began to focus on Lisa. He sincerely hoped that she had taken advantage of the break and had a rest. Since he had proved to be such a moron with Grace, he had channeled his energy into providing support for Lisa. He saw his role as one akin to a parent at a sports game, urging little Johnnie - or in this case his wife - on to greater heights, trying to be positive rather than critical, giving useless pointers and directions. A cheering party of one on the sidelines of parenthood.

At times, though, he likened himself to one of those parents who end up in some horrible exposé on bullying. The comments go too far, there's too much pressure on little Johnnie, and the parent has to restrain themselves from running onto the field and either hitting the referee on the head with a heavy object, or shaking the child for being so entirely useless.

Not that Lisa was useless. Far from it. But the emotional roller coaster of it all took some getting used to. Whether it was from lack of sleep, stress, or the dreaded hormones, at times she seemed almost irrational. He had to remind himself that they were going through an overwhelming period of their lives, one that required calm. He had forbidden himself from even entertaining the idea of yelling at her to snap out of it.

He turned into their driveway and headed around the back of the house, parking the pram in the lee of the back porch. He let himself inside. It seemed strange that Lisa had not come rushing out to meet him, but then he realized she might very well still be asleep.

As he made his way down the hall, Roger started to catch the sound of strange noises. They were muffled, and more like an animal than a person. He quickened his pace and burst into their bedroom. There he found Lisa not asleep but rolled up in a fetal position as though in agony. She stared vacantly at the wall and rocked herself back and forth in an alarming way, tears pouring down her cheeks and periodically emitting primal sounds.

"Lisa?"

She did not even seem to notice his presence.

"Lisa? Honey? What's wrong?"

She groaned again.

He went over and sat down on the bed beside her and tried to make eye contact.

"Are you all right? Are you in pain? Should I get a doctor?"

Suddenly she seemed aware of him and let out a blood-curdling cry. Not knowing what else to do, he scooped her into his arms, hoping he would not hurt her further by doing so. Her body flopped like a rag doll.

"What is it? What's happened? Has there been an accident?"

Lisa began sobbing. "It's not true. It's not true."

"What's not true? Lisa, tell me. If you don't tell me, I can't help you."

She started to cry even harder, as though her heart had broken. Roger's distress increased by the second.

"No, no, no," she wailed. "Not Joan, oh, not Joan."

"What about Joan?" Realization dawned. "Don't tell me you were right? Don't tell me she's dead?"

Lisa groaned again. "My mother, my mother," she said.

"You want your mother?" he asked. Another realization. "Oh, please, don't let it be your mother who's dead."

When Lisa started saying, "I wish she was, I wish she was," he knew something was really wrong. And perhaps not with anyone else besides his beloved wife. He realized the urgent need to get some help.

Leslie came as quickly as she could. The intervening half an hour felt like a test of endurance to Roger. He continued to hold Lisa, who moaned and muttered incoherent words, talking about her mother and Joan, but for the most part making absolutely no sense whatsoever. His thoughts kept going to Grace, hoping and praying she still slept peacefully and wasn't being used as a pillow by a stray neighborhood cat. Every time he went to get up off the bed, Lisa adhered herself tighter to him, so that when Leslie came knocking he had to shout for her to come around the back and let herself in.

She came in carrying a still sleeping Grace. Since Leslie had already been to their house a couple of times for post-natal visits she knew the lay of the land, and quickly tucked Grace into her cot where she could come to no harm. She then turned her attention to the mother.

"What happened?" she asked, coming to stand beside the bed. Lisa gave no indication of having recognized Leslie's presence and continued to whimper.

Roger shook his head. "I don't know. I took Grace out for a walk and I left Lisa to get some rest, but evidently something must have happened. How else would she have ended up in this state? But I can't make head nor tail of what she's saying."

"And she's been fine up until now?"

"Yes. A bit overtired, but nowhere near not coping."

Leslie picked up Lisa's wrist to take her pulse, but made no comment when she lay her arm back down.

"You say she's been trying to speak? Have you been able to make out the words?"

"When she speaks the words are mostly quite clear. It's just that they aren't in any structured sentences. They come in snatches."

"Any particular theme?"

"She keeps talking about her mother, and about Joan. She lives over the road."

"Could Lisa's mother have called with some news?"

Roger said, "It's possible. Her father hasn't been the best. He hasn't bounced back as fast as everyone would like after his hip replacement surgery."

"You'd sort of think she'd then be talking about her father, and not her mother, wouldn't you?"

"I suppose."

"And where does this Joan person fit into the scheme of things?"

"Well, like I said, Joan lives across the road from us. She's a bit of a busybody, but Lisa feels sorry for her. She pops over from time to time."

"Might she have come over today?"

"I can't imagine it. It's a bit of a long story, but Joan's been shut up in her house for over a week because of something that happened between her and one of the other neighbors."

Leslie's eyebrows went skyward. "And Lisa has been worrying about her?"

"Somewhat. I told her it wasn't any of our business, but Lisa hasn't been able to get it out of her mind."

"It's possible, then, that Lisa might have gone over there? To see if this Joan was all right?"

"She's already been. Joan wouldn't open the door. Lisa's been worrying that something more serious had happened to Joan."

"She could have gone again. Tried again."

"I wouldn't put it past her," he said with a sigh.

Leslie sat down on the bed and stroked Lisa's hair with a soothing hand. Lisa continued to cling to Roger and moan softly like a baby.

"Our priority is to get Lisa settled and comfortable." She looked at Roger. "I think we're going to have to give her something to help calm her down."

"Is that necessary?"

"I think it is, yes. She needs to rest. There's Grace to think about as well."

"What do you think is wrong with her?"

"Hard to say. My initial feeling is that she has had some sort of shock or other, that's been sufficient to knock the wind out of her sails."

"But it could be something else?"

Leslie looked at Roger again, her face expressionless. "I won't lie to you," she said. "It is possible that it's something more serious. Post-natal depression, perhaps."

Roger sucked his breath in. How on earth would he cope?

"Look," Leslie said, "let's not jump to any conclusions just yet. The way I see it, we need to find out first if there has been some shock or other."

"Do you think I should call Lisa's mother?"

Leslie considered this. "Maybe not yet. After all, if it wasn't news from her, Lisa's mother is likely to be very distressed if she thinks there's something wrong with her daughter. No, I think the best course of action would be to start with Joan. Let's rule her out first. Then, if you don't have any luck there, we'll try Lisa's parents."

"Should I go now?"

Leslie nodded.

"What about Lisa? And Grace?"

"Leave them to me. Grace is asleep for now. As for Lisa, well, it'll give me the opportunity to see if I can't calm her down a bit."

Roger looked at Leslie for a long while. She looked so calm, so efficient, so precisely what he needed right now. It would be a relief to hand the worry to someone else for a while.

Roger knocked commandingly on Joan's front door. In the time it had taken him to get organized and across the road, his mood had changed from panic to anger. If Joan had upset his Lisa, he wasn't going to stand by and let the matter rest.

"Joan! It's Roger. Open this door."

No response.

He knocked again. Harder.

"Joan, if you don't answer this door, I'm afraid you leave me with no option but to break it down."

He waited, listening intently. Suddenly the door opened a fraction.

"You'd better come in," a thin voice said from the other side.

Roger pushed the door open to find Joan already in the passageway on her way to the lounge. He closed the door with an angry thud, and made his way down the hall. He found Joan huddled in her armchair under blankets, looking older and frailer than he had ever seen her. It seemed clear that she had been crying. If it wasn't for the state of wife, the sight of her might have been enough to soften his resolve.

"Joan," he began, "have you seen Lisa today?"

Joan looked up at him, surprised. "She didn't tell you?"

"No. She didn't. And do you know why? Because she's crying like a baby, making incomprehensible noises, and muttering like a mad woman, that's why."

Joan gasped. "I didn't mean...I didn't know...didn't expect..."

"So you do know what this is about?" Roger asked angrily.

"I...I..."

"Joan, if you don't tell me in the next thirty seconds what on earth went on here today, I won't be answerable for my actions, so help me."

Joan drew back, shrinking into herself. "I...I...told her something."

"Told her what? What could you possibly have to tell her that would reduce her to a quivering mess?"

A lone tear trickled down Joan's careworn face. "I told her the truth about why I'd pretended to be married."

"What? What are you talking about? Why would Lisa care about that?"

"I did it because I had a baby. Out of wedlock."

Joan's voice became quieter with each sentence. Roger had to lean forward to hear her.

"So?"

"That baby was Lisa."

Roger found himself momentarily incapable of logical thought. He felt sure he must have misheard.

"What?"

"It's true."

"How could that be?"

"You know Lisa is adopted."

"Of course I know."

"I'm her mother."

Joan could not help but keep a fragment of pride in her voice. Roger knew in an instant that it must be true. Suddenly he lacked the will to stand. He staggered back and flopped onto the couch.

"How could it be?" he said again.

Joan repeated what she had told Lisa earlier. As each sentence went by Roger could feel his facial features become more and more frozen. He could now easily see why his beloved Lisa had been so reduced. To find out so suddenly the identity of a parent she had no real wish to know about might be one thing. To find out that parent was Joan, of all people, made his mind reel.

Questions started to form as Joan spoke, and with it anger. Hot, white, molten anger. It took Roger every ounce of self-control not to leap from the chair and throttle Joan where she sat.

"But how can you be sure? Weren't adoptions closed in those days? From what Lisa has told me, there's no way you could have found her without contacting the proper authorities. They in turn would never release the details of the adoptee without first seeking permission from the child concerned."

"I had no need of such procedures."

"Why not?"

"I've always known what happened to my baby."

"But how? From the little Lisa and I have discussed it, she said that her parents had no idea about her birth mother or father."

"No doubt."

"So how could you know?"

Joan's eyes took on a far away look as she recalled the past.

"After the birth a delay occurred. Some mix up or other. I never did find out. Because I wasn't young, there didn't seem to be the same need to rush the baby away after the birth like they did with other unwed mothers. In fact, many of the staff believed what I told them about my husband being away at sea. Those that knew of the planned adoption were sympathetic and tried to make suggestions to help me keep the baby.

"So Lisa stayed with me for two days before an official came to take her away, an event I found much more difficult than anticipated." Her face creased with the memory and she shook herself. "Anyway, I had to go to the solicitor's, to sign the papers. I still remember his face. He was of the old school, but not entirely without compassion. He didn't seem to know whether to condemn me or feel sorry for me. At the very least I think he thought me to be old enough to have known better.

"He, of course, knew the truth about my marital status. I would not have been allowed to adopt my baby out without the father's permission, so I had to own the truth and to admit that the father was unknown. Not strictly true, but necessary nonetheless. A shameful process.

"Anyway, he noticed some error on the adoption papers that needed correcting before I signed them so he excused himself and went out of the office to have the mistake rectified by his secretary. I sat there, alone, feeling an overwhelming desire to cancel the whole thing, to let the stigma be damned. I even went as far as getting up from my seat and going to the door."

She paused, her expression almost dreamlike.

"What happened?" Roger asked impatiently.

Her eyes went momentarily back to his, then her gaze dropped back to studying her hands.

"The door was partially open, just a crack. I then realized I could hear every word they were saying. I heard the secretary's lack of compassion as they discussed my case. She thought me disgraceful. He kept his opinion to himself and pointed out to her that their job wasn't to judge. She said something about pitying the poor child, when I heard him say there wasn't any real need for such concern. He said he knew the adoptive parents, and that pity would not be required. They were a lovely couple unfortunate not to be blessed with children, that the child would be loved and cared for, would lack for nothing.

"This took her by surprise. Naturally, she asked who they were. He paused, only for a second, and I held my breath. I thought he would tell his secretary he could not disclose confidential information. But he didn't. He lowered his voice, and told her. Charles and Victoria Roberts, he said. I heard him coming, returned to my seat, and he never knew I had overheard him.

"Afterward, I had no problem tracing them. I found their house, went there a few days later, watched and waited. Sure enough, out came Mrs. Roberts, pushing a pram and looking proud as punch. To be sure, though, I walked for a while on the other side of the street, then crossed over. I stopped her so that I could admire her baby. Any last vestige of doubt washed away when I saw the baby's face. I asked the baby's name, was told, and we went our separate ways."

How innocent, Roger thought. It had happened to him just this morning, people wanting to look and admire. Victoria would have had no reason to be suspicious. Then the enormity of the situation sunk in and he could feel his anger growing afresh.

"You mean to say that you've been watching Lisa all these years?"

She nodded. "Not all the time. Every so often I would find myself in Wellington, and find the temptation to go and see what she looked like too much to bear."

"So you would go and see her," Roger said, unable to keep the steel out of his voice.

"It wasn't difficult. Just watching and waiting."

These revelations were decidedly unsettling, especially as he realized he too had been watched from afar all these years.

"How could you, Joan?"

She shook her head. "I couldn't help myself. Especially once Lisa made the move here. To find her practically living on my doorstep seemed like a gift. When this house came on the market it seemed like a God-given opportunity. Then, once I had moved here, I'm afraid I got swept up in the whole charade. It was easy, so very easy."

"So very dishonest, don't you mean?"

She looked up at this, angry herself now. "I wasn't doing any harm."

"Weren't you?"

"Of course not. There wasn't any reason for anyone to know. If it wasn't for Gordon Price no one would still know." She looked furious. "I could kill that man."

Roger stood up at this. "I think I've heard quite enough. You're a sick woman Joan. I think you seriously need some help. I think I hardly need say this to you, but I will anyway. You stay away from me and my family."

Joan swallowed. "I thought..."

"You thought what? That we could all play happy families now that the truth is out in the open? That we'd be inviting you to come and live with us? What?"

She said nothing.

"Right, well, as long as we understand each other. I don't know what possessed you to tell Lisa the truth but she is devastated. Absolutely devastated."

With that he turned on his heel and strode from the room without so much as a backward glance. If he had turned back he would have seen Joan crumple, falling prostrate on the floor, as though her whole world had come to an end.

Maureen walked home from Sunday morning mass feeling vaguely depressed and a little dissatisfied with life. These days she found herself looking with new eyes at people and places she had known for years - comparing them to her own lot in life - only to find her own lot wanting considerably.

Why did everyone suddenly seem to have a life and lifestyle so much more perfect than her own? Why did other people's children seemed to shine with success while one of her own had moved to another country to get away from her, and the other would only come home under the cover of darkness?

How could it be that other women's husbands had aged with dignity and aplomb, while her own seemed to be living a life so at odds with her own that she could scarcely believe they were acquainted, let alone married? How were others affording the nicer cars, the trips overseas, or even just a regular meal at a restaurant while she, Maureen, struggled to make the housekeeping money Brian doled out to her with rigid suspicion once every two weeks stretch further and further?

Why did it feel as though Father Michael spoke directly to her every Sunday in his homilies, making her feel as though she no longer lived up to the ideals she held as precious? Could it be that he owned the mirror to her soul? Where had her positive attitude gone? In fact, where had Maureen gone? All the hopes and dreams she had cherished as a young person had vanished, replaced with a cold reality she seemed no longer capable of imagining away.

Maureen neared Maybury Place. She felt her pace slow, not really wanting to go home. The street no longer seemed the same to her. Somehow, by getting to know the rest of the inhabitants a little better, they had broken down the barriers of propriety, and unleashed the monster, Familiarity, together with its offspring, Contempt.

As Maureen turned into Maybury Place she found Sandra in her front yard working with a feverish passion as she deadheaded a daisy bush with a pair of secateurs. Ian could periodically be seen behind the house in the back yard as he mowed the lawn with maniacal precision, the noise of the mower rising and falling as he paced from side to side. Matthew wheeled up and down the driveway on his now infamous trike, looking bored with proceedings.

A part of Maureen longed to simply wave and walk past but she did not want to appear unfriendly. She slowed her pace even further and came to a halt.

"Lovely day," Sandra said. "I almost feel as though I should have my hat on."

Maureen tried out a smile. "You can't be too careful these days. They practically show the burn time on the weather forecast on the TV all year round now."

"You'd have to be careful," Sandra remarked, indicating Maureen's red hair and delicate skin.

"It's a fact of life, I'm afraid."

"Been to church?"

Maureen nodded. "You don't ever go? Take the little ones to Sunday School?"

"Oh, no. Not really our kettle of fish. Besides, Rose is still having two sleeps a day and I need every moment of peace I can get. That, and the fact that Ian often only has Sundays off. It's good to have some family time together."

"Of course." It seemed to Maureen, looking back, that their family had never really had time together like that.

"Once all the chores are done, that is," Sandra added, waving the secateurs under Maureen's nose. "Have to try to keep the house and gardens in reasonable nick. Just in case we decide to put the house on the market."

"Really? You're thinking of selling?"

"Perhaps not right away," Sandra said with more than a hint of regret, "but within a year or two we will need somewhere a bit bigger."

And more grand? Maureen wondered. Something more befitting an upwardly mobile man like Ian Fleming?

"Are you thinking of having more children then?" she asked.

Sandra screwed up her nose. "I don't think so. I did picture myself with at least three, possibly even four, but the reality of Rose has killed that desire stone dead."

"You might change your mind. When Rose grows up a bit."

"Ian thinks two is plenty. Schooling costs a small fortune these days, if you do it properly. And we'd like to encourage the children into after school activities - music, sports, dance, swimming and the like. None of that comes cheap."

"I dare say it doesn't."

"Of course Ian says it's important to give the children the best start in life that we possibly can, so that they can fulfill their potential." Sandra laughed, glanced over her shoulder at Matthew, and bent forward conspiratorially. "Between you and me I think Ian sees an All Black jersey in the future for Matthew, in between a brilliant legal career. And as for Rose, she could be a concert pianist while she lectures in Fine Art, or something like that."

"Won't you have to wait and see how their natural aptitude develops?" Maureen asked, her tone waving between incredulity and horror, hardly able to believe Sandra's attitude. Could she be serious?

"I suppose, to some degree. Maybe all of us have the natural aptitude toward any number of things but simply lack the development. And certainly the environment."

Maureen could think of nothing to say to this. Clearly Ian and Sandra had the lives of their children all mapped out. It struck her as ironic that the likelihood of it all coming true stood at better than average. People like the Flemings were hardly likely to settle for second best. Not if they could help it.

"That's why we're so keen on the idea of moving," Sandra continued. "You have to admit that the tone of the neighborhood has taken a distinct turn for the worse." Not waiting for Maureen's assessment, Sandra said, "So have you seen Joan?"

Maureen shook her head. "I'm afraid not."

"Very strange," Sandra said. "We don't know what to make of it. Then, on top of that, something decidedly odd is going on over at the McLeans. I went over there this morning to give Lisa a couple of baby magazines that I'd finished with, only to be turned away by Roger. I must say his tone shocked me. He wouldn't let me in the house, barely managed a reply to my questions then practically closed the door in my face. What do you make of that?"

Maureen felt her face redden. "I'm not sure," she said her tone careful.

Sandra looked at her with skepticism. "Maybe not, but it's obvious you do know something."

Maureen hadn't been about to say a word about the matter but Sandra's penetrating stare made her feel she had little choice.

"Well...it's just that..."

"What?"

"Last night, after Brian had gone out, and after I had turned the television off because there was absolutely nothing on worth watching, I heard some very strange noises coming out of their house. You know what it's like at night. Sound seems to travel so much further than it does during the day."

"What sounds?" Sandra asked with undisguised impatience.

Maureen hesitated. She struggled against her better judgment, but said in a gush, "Screaming. It was screaming."

"The baby?"

"No, no. Not Grace. Lisa. She sounded hysterical."

"So...could you make out what it was all about?"

"Nothing coherent."

"That all sounds a bit odd," Sandra said. She pursed her lips in thought. She seemed to Maureen like a doctor intent on diagnosis, weighing up the facts. Then, as if to prove Maureen right she said, "Sounds to me like post-natal depression. I hope it isn't, but if I'm right then she's probably in a bad way. Of course, a person like Lisa probably has a predisposition to something like that, not always being entirely sure about things."

"Really? I've never thought about Lisa in those terms."

"Oh yes. I'm forever trying to shore up her confidence about a whole range of things." Sandra gave Maureen the benefit of her saccharin sweet smile. "Of course I don't mind sharing what little knowledge of parenting I've managed to glean."

"I hope she's all right."

"Yes...I might try popping back later to see if there's anything I can do to help. I'm sure Roger probably doesn't know the first thing about how to take care of little Grace. After all, she can't be organized the way one organizes business systems now, can she?"

"I suppose not. You don't think they'd prefer to be left on their own?"

"Well, Maureen, what are neighbors for?"

Maureen was beginning to wonder. Gordon was high on triumph while Joan remained closeted in her house like a hermit. It seemed clear all wasn't well at the McLean's. Geoff and Karen had begun to take a sudden neighborly interest in one another while men kept trolling up the street to Number Seven like bees to a honey pot. As for the Flemings they seemed to be living on another plane of existence altogether.

Yes, Maureen had begun to wonder what neighbors were for indeed.

Leslie parked her car in the McLean's driveway and killed the engine. Rather than leaping out straight away, she sat for a moment or two, thinking, tapping her fingers rhythmically on the steering wheel. She felt bone tired. Under normal circumstances she would have gone straight home from the hospital rather than come on here but she could not in all conscience leave Roger to cope with Lisa on his own. She had to see that things were going all right and to see if there was any measure of improvement in Lisa.

Leslie always found it difficult to know what to say in times of trauma, be it death or depression or shock. She found it never got any easier, in spite of the amount of practice she'd had over the years. People were such individuals, responded to things in such different ways. It wasn't easy to know what to say for the best.

Some people responded well to the tried and true clichés, others found comfort in the simple truths of life. Some became bitter and filled with such negative emotions as to make rational conversation a complete waste of time. Others were numbed to such a degree that they never perceived a word said to them.

And, of course, there were times when words were useless, when all you could really do was offer a shoulder to cry on, providing the benefit of being a person who - on the face of it at least - wasn't emotionally involved, whatever the situation might be. Leslie wondered what the case might be here.

She sighed. There was only one way to find out. She unbuckled her seat belt, grabbed her medical bag, and headed for the house.

She went around to the back door and knocked softly. Roger opened the door straight away. He looked very tired.

"Leslie. Come in."

He led her into the kitchen.

"Hello, Roger. Sorry I haven't been back sooner. I've been at the hospital all day with another birth. I came as soon as I could."

He smiled ever so slightly. "I don't know how you manage. The hours must be murder."

She returned his smile. "Sometimes. But it's worth it. Speaking of managing, how are things here?"

"Not too bad."

"As opposed to not too good?"

He shrugged. "I don't really know what to expect, even what to do."

"With Grace? Or with Lisa?"

Another shrug. "Both, I suppose."

"Well, let's start with Grace. Did Lisa manage to feed her?"

"No. I've kept up with the formula you left for us."

"And Grace has taken that okay?"

"She fusses a bit at first, but when she realizes that's all she's going to get she gives in and gets going with it."

"What about bathing, sleeps and changing?"

"I've tried to stick to what I think Lisa normally does but whether I'm doing it right or not, I've really no idea."

"Well, that's the beauty of babies. There really is no right or wrong. As long as they're feeding, producing wet diapers and sleeping, nothing else really matters. Besides, as you've probably already discovered, for small people, they're unusually adept at telling you when they don't like something."

Roger, again, barely managed the small smile that flitted across his tired features. "Yes, I had worked that out."

Leslie swapped her bag to the other hand. "What about Lisa, then?"

Roger's shoulders drooped imperceptibly. "She was fine until about nine thirty last night when she started to get hysterical. Luckily I managed to convince her to take some of that medication you left. Eventually she calmed down."

"And today?"

"She's...she's...it's like she's not really there."

"Oh?"

Roger ran a hand over the stubble on his face. "It's like she's in a trance. She just lies in bed staring at the ceiling."

Leslie absorbed this information. "Does she respond when you talk to her? Answer questions and so forth?"

"Sort of. You sort of have to get her attention first. Is that normal?"

"What's normal? There's no such thing in my experience."

"But she will be all right, won't she?"

Leslie smiled with unfounded confidence. "Oh yes. Without doubt. The thing is, in Lisa's case it's a matter of coping with shock. It's as though her mind can't quite deal with the information its been fed. In order to get over it her conscious self has shut down for a little while."

"But for how long?"

Leslie felt sympathy rise within her. "I'm sorry, Roger. There's no way of knowing."

He sagged some more.

"The thing is," Leslie continued, "I'm fairly certain this is an isolated incident. I very much doubt that this is a case of post-natal depression, or even post-natal distress. That being the case we should have every reason to expect Lisa to get over this sooner rather than later. We know what the cause is. We just have to be patient and try to help Lisa as much as we can until she comes to terms with what she has learnt. Is she eating? Drinking?"

Roger shook his head. "I keep offering things, but she's refused everything."

Leslie straightened. "Well, we can't have that. Her mind might be taking a little holiday, but her body certainly won't be. We can't risk her becoming dehydrated. Tell you what, why don't you make Lisa a nice cup of tea, and I'll take it in to her. Have you any dry biscuits? I'll see if I can't get her to eat some of those while I'm at it. In fact when I think about it, why don't I make the tea while you think about phoning your parents to come and give you a hand? I'm sure they would be only too pleased to help out. You've got to make sure you don't burn out yourself."

Leslie wondered if Lisa would be asleep when she took the tea in, but just as Roger had said, she lay in the centre of their bed staring into space. She displayed no visible curiosity at the sound of the bedroom door opening, did not even look around when Leslie sat down on the edge of the bed. Leslie said Lisa's name as she put the tray on the bedside table, but Lisa only looked up when Leslie lifted her arm gently so she could take Lisa's pulse. It was slow and steady.

"Hello," Leslie said gently.

"What time is it?" Lisa asked, the way a small child might.

Leslie glanced at her watch. "Half past five."

"Oh."

"How are you feeling?"

"Huh?"

"I said, how are you feeling?"

"I...I..."

"It's all right," Leslie soothed. "You don't need to know."

Lisa relaxed a little. "I...I...can't think. I...it's like...I...can't seem to focus."

"Perhaps for now it's better not to try. Roger and Grace are fine. Roger's mother is coming around to give him a hand and Grace is sound asleep. You should be very proud of that husband of yours. He's done a great job."

Lisa's face fell. "It's my job."

"Not right now it isn't," Leslie said, putting as much authority into her voice as she could. "Right now your job is to rest and to get better."

"But…"

"But nothing. Midwife's orders. You just concentrate on building up your strength, starting right now with this cup of tea and biscuits."

Lisa looked at it and grimaced. "I couldn't."

"Yes, you could."

"I don't want to."

"You have to. You owe it to Roger and Grace. We all understand that you've had a tremendous shock and you need not feel any pressure to do anything. After all, everything is under control. But you must keep eating and drinking. That is essential. It would not be fair to let yourself get seriously sick by refusing to make an effort."

Lisa considered this, reminding Leslie once again of a youngster trying to decide whether to risk getting itself into trouble by not doing as it's told. Leslie picked up the cup and held it out for Lisa to take. Lisa held on for one last moment then capitulated.

It might not exactly be one giant leap for mankind, but it was definitely one small step for Leslie. She hoped it was a sign of things to come.

CHAPTER ELEVEN

At the supermarket Karen and Geoff came to a halt in front of the ever-growing array of breakfast cereals.

"Oo," Karen said, picking up a packet of her favorite cereal, "what about these?"

Geoff frowned and took the packet out of her hands. He turned it over and read the dietary information on the reverse.

"It says here that it has more sugar per serve than the average kid's lollipop."

Karen made a face. "Probably why they're so nice. Sometimes there's nothing like a bowl of these after a hard day's work."

"You never cease to amaze me. Cereal is supposed to be for breakfast."

"Says who? Really, for someone whose job requires them to think outside the square, you aren't very adventurous are you?"

"Frankly, I think peanut butter and banana sandwiches, tamarillos on toast, and pretty much everything you've thus far suggested goes way beyond the boundaries of adventure. It's much more like madness."

"Don't knock it until you try it," she said with a lofty grin. "'*Green Eggs and Ham*', and all that stuff."

"What?"

"It's a children's book. Dr. Seuss. Don't tell me you never had a childhood either?"

Geoff smiled back at her. "Maybe. But something tells me it was nothing like yours."

Karen picked up another box. "What about these then?" she suggested, handing him the box."

He examined it with a good deal of solemnity. "Not bad. Good fiber content, not too high in fat, or in sugar."

"Tastes like cardboard," Karen added in the same assessing voice.

"Oh, ha ha. Shall we get them?"

"All right. Your trolley, or mine?"

"Mine I think. Can't have you sneaking them out of your trolley when you think I'm not looking."

Karen grinned again and then her smile faded. "Oh. Watch out. Coming our way. Fleming at four o'clock."

Geoff glanced around to see Sandra bearing down upon them. Rose sat in the kiddy seat of the trolley, swinging her pudgy legs, while Matthew had jackknifed himself into the main body of the trolley, hemmed in on every side with previously selected items.

"Hello, you two," Sandra said her expression one of coy knowingness, as though she had caught Karen and Geoff engaged in some sort of suspicious act. "Shopping together now, are we?"

"Seemed silly to not go together when we both needed to stock up a bit," Karen said without inflexion. "There's the world's resources to consider, you know."

"That's the first time I've known you to be interested in conservation," Sandra remarked, her knowing look not budging one iota.

"Nothing like new interests to keep a person stimulated. Isn't that right, Geoff?"

Geoff looked noncommittal, not wanting to pursue the train of conversation.

Realizing that she wasn't about to learn anything new, Sandra said, "I'm surprised in some ways to see you here. I felt sure you'd be helping Roger out with their little crisis?"

Karen tensed. "What crisis?"

"Don't you know? I imagined you would know all about it. Of course, I'm not privy to all the details myself, but from what I understand Lisa is very unwell."

"What?"

"Oh, yes. From what I understand, she's in a bad way."

"What kind of bad way?"

Sandra shrugged her shoulders. "It sounds to me like the classic symptoms of post-natal depression. It's more common than most people realize. And, as I was saying to Maureen only yesterday, I really think that someone with Lisa's disposition likely to be more susceptible toward it."

"Rubbish," Karen said. "I'm sure if something was seriously wrong, I would have heard about it."

Sandra looked from Geoff to Karen. "Perhaps you've been too busy," she suggested in a tone just one step away from a sneer. She lent away from the children's ears, and added, "Maureen says she's even heard screaming coming from their house. It can be a very dangerous condition. Some mothers even go so far as to harm themselves. I tell you, things are badly awry at Number Six. Just mark my words and see if they aren't."

With that she gave a little wave of her hand and pushed her trolley forward, leaving Geoff and Karen standing by gaping after her.

"I came as soon as I heard," Karen said to Roger when he answered the door. The very fact that he had Grace cradled over one shoulder gave credence to what she had been told.

Roger looked mildly surprised. "Heard what?"

"About Lisa, of course."

"What, precisely, did you hear about Lisa?"

"That she's really unwell. Practically suicidal."

"Come in and see for yourself," Roger said. "I'm sure Lisa would love to see you."

He led the way to the bedroom where Lisa lay on the bed. Karen took in the pale face, the limp hair, the fact that Lisa looked bone weary.

"Here's Karen, come to say her fond farewells as you die by your own hand."

"That's nice," Lisa said with a small voice. "However I think rumors of my imminent demise have been greatly exaggerated."

Karen breathed a sigh of relief. "Thank goodness! Mind you, you aren't exactly looking wonderful, if you don't mind me saying so."

Lisa attempted a small smile. "Since when have I ever minded anything you say?"

"Oh, practically all the time. You are all right, aren't you?"

"Yes, better now."

"So, you weren't well?"

"Let's just say it's been an interesting forty eight hours."

"I'll leave you two to talk," Roger said. "Better get this munchkin to bed."

Karen's attention went straight back to Lisa. "So, what's been happening? I nearly freaked out when I heard you might be seriously ill."

Lisa's eyebrows rose. "Who told you that?"

"Sandra Fleming."

"I might have known. She just can't keep her nose out of other people's business."

"She said you might be...you know...thinking of ending it all."

"The only thing I'm thinking of ending is ever talking to her again."

Karen smiled. "Care to tell me just what's been going on?"

Lisa sighed. "It's a bit of a long story," she said. She then proceeded to outline what had transpired when she had gone to visit Joan. Karen's eyes grew wider as the story unfolded, threatening to pop out of her head completely when Lisa told of how Joan had made her big revelation.

Karen lent back and whistled. "Bloody hell. And she's been across the road, spying on you, all this time?"

Lisa nodded.

"That's creepy."

Lisa nodded again.

"No wonder she lied about being married. Still, some things do make more sense now. I always thought she treated you much better than she did me. Of course, for myself, I always put her attitude toward me down to her jealousy over my good looks, personality and charm. That, and the fact that I never gave her any sympathy, whereas you did. Now, perhaps, I see that she probably always treated you better because of what you meant to her. With you being her daughter and all that."

"Don't!" Lisa cried. "Don't say it. She's not my mother. I'm not her daughter."

"Too right," Karen said. "I'd say that too, if I was in your shoes."

Tears started running down Lisa's cheeks. She turned her head away. "Every time I think about it, I just want to die."

Karen felt alarm rising within her. She grabbed Lisa's hand. "Don't say that. Not even for a moment."

Lisa ran her free hand over her eyes, trying to stem the flow of tears. "I'm sorry," she said. "I don't mean it. Of course I don't mean it. It's just that the prospect of being related to Joan in any way, let alone to discover I have her blood in my veins, fills me with horror. When she first told me, I just couldn't cope at all. I didn't know where to put myself or what I should do. I think...I think I flipped out for a while."

"Who could blame you?" Karen squeezed her hand. "And now?"

Lisa sighed. "I'm not exactly over it," she said, "but the initial feelings are beginning to subside. At least I'm not completely hysterical any more."

"What does Roger say?"

"We haven't really talked about it yet. I don't think he knows what to say."

"No hurry, I suppose."

Lisa frowned. "Except I think he's worrying because he's having to take more time off work."

"Stuff them. No one's indispensable." Karen looked directly at Lisa. "Except best friends, that is."

Lisa managed another small smile. "Thanks. Look, I probably don't need to say this, but please, don't tell anyone about this, will you? Not even Geoff."

"Of course not."

"It's just that if I thought anyone else knew I probably would die - of embarrassment, if nothing else."

"Right you are. Mum's the word." Karen banged herself on the forehead. "Oh God. I guess that's the wrong thing to say."

Even Lisa couldn't help giving a little laugh.

"Anyway," Karen continued, "I promise to not breathe a word to anyone. On one condition."

Lisa looked alarmed. "What condition?"

"That in return you don't tell anyone what a rotten best friend I've been, not being here when you needed me."

"Don't be silly."

"I mean it. I've been so wrapped up in myself - and in Geoff - that I've totally ignored you. It's unforgivable."

"Please, don't give it another thought."

Karen frowned. "You're too soft," she said. "Anyway, as penance, I'm determined not to tell you a thing about what's going on with Geoff until you are quite better."

Lisa couldn't help but laugh. "Truly," she said, "you're the best friend a girl ever had."

The following evening, when a knock at the door came, Roger fully expected to see Karen on the threshold. She had arranged to come over after Roger's mother had departed. Half an hour had since passed since his mother had left and Lisa kept periodically asking if Karen had arrived yet.

When he opened the door, however, he found himself looking at someone altogether different.

"Hello, Sandra," he said with as much patience as he could muster.

"Roger. How are you?"

"Very well."

This might not be strictly truthful but he wasn't about to tell Sandra how the land really lay: of his fatigue from shouldering all the responsibility Grace entailed; of his concern over the amount of work waiting for him on his desk at Tempo; of his anxiety about his wife who, although better, still seemed very fragile, and who had taken on a decidedly infantile way of looking at things. Nor, finally, would he be telling her that the whole situation had him flummoxed as to what to do or say.

"Glad to hear it," Sandra said.

"Yourself?"

"Just as you say - very well. Tired of course, kids being kids and all that."

When she did not say anything else, Roger waited momentarily for her to state her business. He felt a bit unfriendly about keeping her hanging on the doorstep but he wasn't about to invite her in. He did not intend to give her the satisfaction.

When the lull in conversation became uncomfortable Sandra coughed and said, "I just popped over to see if all's well."

"Oh?"

"Yes, er, I gathered that Lisa might not be feeling entirely well?"

"You did?"

"Yes, I...it's just that Maureen mentioned Lisa had sounded upset the other night. I...well, to be honest, you did seem a little troubled when I saw you last."

"Really? And you thought you'd do what, precisely?"

Sandra colored slightly. "I don't know, really. Just see if there was anything I could do?"

"Such as?"

"Oh, I don't know. Washing, making meals, housework, ironing? Just point me in the right direction."

"I would have thought you'd have enough of all of that sort of thing to do in your own house," Roger said, his tone bland.

Sandra tried out an experimental laugh that sounded shrill to Roger's ears.

"Well, of course, there's always housework. When isn't there? But in times like this, neighbors need to rally round, don't they?"

Roger fixed a look of confusion on his face. "Forgive me, but times like what, exactly?"

Sandra gazed lamely around. "Well, when people are ill, naturally."

"Oh, didn't I say? No, Lisa's quite fine. I'm not sure what you heard, but everything's as right as rain here."

Sandra's looked perplexed. "It is? But I thought...I heard...I understood that Lisa was suffering from post-natal depression."

"You did? That's odd. Who told you that?"

She shrugged. "I don't know now," she said. "I guess I must have got the wrong end of the stick. I had even been going to suggest a remedy Lisa might like to try. To help out, you know. St. John's Wort. Marvelous stuff, or so they say. Never needed to try it myself, of course, but some people swear by it."

Roger longed to tell her what she could do with her St. John's Wort but kept his counsel. When he said nothing, Sandra began to look curious.

"And where is Lisa?" she asked, trying to peer over Roger's shoulder.

"Just getting herself ready," he said. "Karen's coming over in a minute and I think they're planning on going out for coffee."

Picturing Lisa still lying ghost-like in their bed, Roger hoped he wouldn't burn in hell too long for all the lies he'd told in the course of one conversation. Then, thankfully, out of the darkness, Karen appeared.

"Here I am," she said cheerfully, "all ready to hit the town."

It took all of Roger's powers of self-control not to push past Sandra and hug Karen with relief. He thought he'd never been so pleased to see her in all his life.

Karen left at nine thirty. She and Lisa had been closeted in the bedroom for the entire time while Roger had sat in the lounge pretending to watch television and wondering what they were discussing. But while it was good that Lisa felt she could talk to someone about the whole debacle, a part of him that felt disappointed that Lisa should turn to Karen and not himself.

Such thoughts were ridiculous really. After all, he had no sage words to say to his wife. He wasn't even sure how to treat the whole business. He'd wavered between so many different emotions during the ensuing seventy-two hours and managed to not settle on any of them. It all came back to the fact he did not feel any sort of competency. He longed to put everything right, but could not.

After he'd seen Karen out, Roger had returned to the lounge. Lisa had not even come out of their room. Roger, tired of pretending, switched the television off and turned the main overhead light off in favor of a small table lamp, then sat back down on the couch to think.

"Fancy some company?"

Roger started at the sound of Lisa's voice.

He looked up at her standing tremulously in the doorway. He smiled and nodded. He felt afraid to speak lest she disappear, afraid to speak for fear of saying the wrong thing.

She came over and sat down beside him on the couch. She moved close to him and slipped her hand into his.

"I thought you would be asleep by now," Roger said, his voice just above a whisper.

"I suddenly felt sick of bed," she explained. "Sick of moping, sick of having it all eating away at me, sick of everything."

"That's good. Or, at least it seems good to me."

"I'm sorry I've been such a pain."

"I'm sorry I've been so incapable of making it all better for you."

"Oh, don't think that," Lisa said. "If it wasn't for you, I'd never have had the luxury of turning to jelly."

Roger lifted his free hand up and stroked the side of her face. "I didn't know what to do."

She put her hand over his, and brought it down to join the others between them. "Nonsense. You were perfect. I acted like some character out of a bad movie. Weeping and wailing and gnashing of teeth, and all that."

"You had a shock. Nobody knows how they're going to react to the unexpected. Some things can't be helped."

Lisa grimaced. "I'm obviously not made of sterner stuff."

"Don't think about it any more. No sense in feeling bad about feeling bad."

She gave a brief grin. "No, I don't suppose there is. It's just that, when I think about it now, did I overreact? I mean, I'm sure there are worse things in the world than to suddenly find out who your real mother is. Worse people, too, to have as a mother."

"That's true. But it's the suddenness of the finding out that does the damage. There's no time to prepare. And although you are quite right that there are worse people to come from, nothing can detract from the fact that

Joan lied. She came into our lives under false pretences in the most despicable way. I call that opportunism at its worst."

"I can't get past that either. All the things she's said and done over the years, and all the time she knew. She knew. How could she do that?"

"I suppose, to her, it was a form of love. She wanted to be near you, the chance arose, and she took it with both hands. But she thought only of herself. It wasn't real love. Real love is much more interested in the needs of the one you love than in self-fulfillment."

"Do you think so?"

"Of course. These weren't the actions of a real mother. You know yourself, you do things for Grace that benefit her, not you. There have already been hundreds of times in her short life where you've put Grace's needs before your own. That's what mothers do. Joan didn't. She put her need before yours. In fact, she probably never really thought about what would be good for you at all."

"Really?"

"Really. She's not your mother, Lisa. Not in any way it counts."

"But there's still a part of her in me. You can't deny that. You can't rationalize it away. I've seen those documentaries about nature versus nurture, the way people who are related can grow up with no knowledge of one another and yet still have similar traits and characteristics. Blood will out."

"Maybe. It's by no means proven. After all, there are plenty of people out there who are nothing like their parents."

"Then there are others who are exactly like their parents."

"Yes, but usually one, not both. If you're going to use that argument you could just as easily say that you're like your birth father, and not your birth mother."

Lisa withdrew her hands, and snuggled closer, nestling her head in the crook of Roger's shoulder. "We'll never know, though, will we? Joan said he's dead."

"No," Roger said softly. "We'll never know. Maybe it's just as well."

"Maybe. I suppose what I worry about most is that I'll turn into Joan. End up bossy, lonely and opinionated."

Roger laughed. "If I didn't know better I'd say you were describing Sandra Fleming, not Joan. If you ask me, you've got nothing to worry about on that score. Besides, you've got me to keep you under control. And Grace. And Karen."

Lisa smiled at this. "Yes, I can't imagine Karen letting me get anything like Joan."

"No way. Look, at the end of the day Joan is not a bad person, in spite of what she's done and how she's gone about things. You were right before when you said there were worse people to be related to. That doesn't mean we should necessarily be in a hurry to forgive her for what she's done, or even have anything to do with her. That'll be up to you to decide."

Lisa was silent for a while. "I know it's up to me. I just don't know what to think."

Roger turned his head to kiss her hair. "No rush. Perhaps you just need to go with what you do feel and know, and let the rest take care of itself."

"Hmm. Maybe you're right."

"So, then. How do you feel?"

Lisa shrugged, her shoulders thin and bony against Roger's chest. The past three days had taken their toll.

"I don't know really."

"You could always do what Leslie suggested. You know - see a therapist. Someone who's an expert in these sorts of things. Someone who'll help you know how you feel and help you know how to handle it."

"No thanks," Lisa said, shivering slightly. "I hope I never have to tell anyone the whole sorry saga ever again. No, I guess my overwhelming feeling right now is that I never want to see Joan again as long as I live."

"That's understandable. It might be a bit difficult to do, however, what with her living right over the road."

"I know." She sounded lost and forlorn.

Roger waited for a moment or two. "Do you want to consider selling up? Moving away? We could even shift cities. Go and live in Wellington. Be near your family."

"Oh, no, Roger. We couldn't do that. What about your job? And your family? And our friends? Karen would kill me."

"She'd be hard pressed to do that if we were living in Wellington. As for my job, well, there'd be another. People do start again, you know. All the time, in fact."

"Yes, but not us. Besides, why should we be the ones to move? We haven't done anything wrong."

"No, we haven't. But what other option is there? Since we've decided to ignore Joan for the rest of our lives we can hardly go over there and tell her to push off, now, can we?"

"Can't we? Couldn't you?"

"Oh, no. No way. If there's any confronting to do, I won't be the one doing it."

"Chicken."

"Yes. Probably."

"I wouldn't expect you to," Lisa said firmly. "I won't ask you."

"Thank God."

"Let's not decide now." She nestled closer. "Let's just try to get on with our lives. I'm ready for that now. Let's just stay put, and stay away from Joan. As long as we're together, nothing else matters, does it?"

"No, darling," Roger said. "Of course it doesn't."

And Roger hoped with all his heart that it was true.

The following morning saw a change in the fine weather that had lingered for the last ten days. Deep banks of grey cloud had slunk surreptitiously into town during the night and parked there, intent on staying. As dawn came they unleashed their cargo in an unrelenting stream that blanketed everything within seconds.

When Joan woke up she could hear the torrents on the roof, and could tell by the amount of light in the room that it was not about to let up any time soon. She sat up, fluffing the pillows behind her to better support her weight, and lay for some time looking around her room without really seeing a thing. She became aware of a difference in herself and recognized a change had come about. The fear, grief and indecision that had paralyzed her had been replaced by a new strength and a new clarity of mind.

"I should have known," she said, wise now with the benefit of hindsight. She spoke only to herself. These days even Jess had abandoned her in favor of goodness knows where. "I should have known not to have that man in my house. If it wasn't for him..."

At first she had been overwhelmed with the embarrassment of being exposed as a liar. She knew that the rumor mill would be straight into action, that speculation as to why she would have purported to be a married woman - when all along she was nothing more than an aging spinster - would be rife.

Over all the years she had pretended to be married she had come to feel that, in a sense, she was married. Not to any flesh and blood husband, or even to the shadowy memory of a fallen brother, but married instead to the lie itself. In her mind it was not a lie, merely an extension of her imagination, of how she wished her life had been. The more strands of fantasy that had been woven, the easier it had become. Creating a past had given the whole thing more credence. At the same time it had come to be so much more a part of the way Joan lived her life.

Joan had never seriously considered or expected that the whole house of cards she had carefully built could come so precipitately down. She had come to believe it all to such an extent that she could never have conceived of anybody ever finding out. Or even caring to find out.

But then she had not factored on the pugnacious Gordon Price, or the circumstances that led to the founding of Neighborhood Watch, or a situation in which the two might come together to engineer her downfall.

"Wretched man," Joan said again, anger rising within her.

So she had hidden in embarrassment, her mind overwhelmed with thoughts of what everyone must be saying about her. She'd wondered how she would ever be able to show her face again. How she would answer the questions that would inevitably come. How she would ever be able to look anyone squarely in the eye again and hold her head up in dignity and pride.

The more she dwelt on it, the more problems seemed to arise.

What if she could not think up a good enough story to tell everyone?

What if some legal technicality existed under which she could be prosecuted for living under false pretences?

How would she be able to survive without the good opinion of others? What if...what if the real truth came out?

This final thought above all else drove Joan further within herself. She had gone over and over it in her mind. What would happen if Lisa were to learn the truth about her parentage? Perhaps it might be better? Could this be this a God-given opportunity for her to find out? What if she, Joan, did confess and it all went terribly wrong? But what if the opposite were true?

As she examined the situation from every angle, the rest of the world seemed to fade away. She existed on the barest minimum of food, things out of the freezer that she had tucked away for emergencies, the odd cup of tea when she managed to rouse herself, a few dry biscuits now and then. Sounds of the neighbors coming and going wafted in from outside, but her mind had become so consumed as to render it incapable of taking anything else in.

And then, finally, Lisa appeared on the doorstep, threatening to stay until Joan showed herself. All at once she had made up her mind, like a light bulb coming on, or the moment when the sun's rays shine through the smallest hole in a layer of cloud. Such clarity of thought and purpose urged

Joan on. Before she knew it, the whole story had come pouring out of her, words surging over the top of the walls of secrecy behind which they had been hidden for an eternity.

Joan looked down now, at her wrinkled, aged hands folded in her lap, just as she had done that fateful morning, experiencing yet again the physical pain of rejection, the look of appalled horror that had swept over Lisa's features. That expression would stay with Joan throughout the rest of her days.

It had been a foolish, weak moment on Joan's behalf. As with hosting the meeting, she should have known better. She should have held her tongue. And if she had to have spoken it ought to have been thought through with much more care. After all, any number of things could have been better.

The timing.

The circumstances.

The preparation.

Words carefully chosen.

The scene carefully set.

But more than anything, Joan herself should have been prepared for all eventualities, and most especially the outcome which became a reality: the outcome in which Lisa made it clear that the notion of having Joan as a mother was untenable - to say the least. If Joan had not been prepared to gamble with the possibility that in speaking out she would lose everything she had worked for, then she should not have played the game.

But lost she had, even though for a couple of hours she had cherished the hope that all would be well. That Lisa would have time to think it over and come to the conclusion that it was a dream situation. A mother in Wellington and another right across the road. Someone she could truly share all her intimate thoughts and feelings with. Someone to help her raise her daughter. A grandmother and baby-sitter there on the doorstep. There could be no greater outcome for Joan. Surely Lisa would realize the gift of the situation for them all.

But then Roger had come, wearing an expression she had previously thought him incapable of. Accusations were made, points clarified, and then Joan's position made crystal clear.

She had gambled, and lost.

So once again Joan had been cast adrift on the seas of sorrow, not knowing which way to turn to swim for help. She had no one to whom she could turn for advice, no safe port in the storm. Indecision chained her down as she searched the farthest reaches of her mind for the smallest vestiges of hope

- something she could cling on to that would get her through this ordeal.

She found very little.

Now, though, she had woken with a renewed sense of purpose. All the thoughts and feelings and emotions of the past few days had eddied around inside her mind, gained momentum and swirled into a fast-moving whirlpool, leading to an epicenter of decision.

Joan knew now what she must do, the only thing she could do. She only hoped she had enough courage to see it through.

Saturday again.

Lisa had felt sufficiently restored to be left home alone so Roger had managed to go to work for the last two days of the week. By rights he should have gone back into work this very morning rather than volunteering to take Grace for a walk, but the cupboards were bare and a much needed food shop required Lisa to whizz to the grocery store. However, since the powers that be at Tempo had bestowed upon him a great deal more patience and consideration that he would have expected, he thought it prudent to ease his wife back into household chores gently and to turn his back on the mountain of work he had piled up just a little longer.

Not that Lisa had not coped. In fact, on the outside looking in, a person would probably be hard pressed to find any sign of trouble. Domestic bliss, however chaotic, had returned. Grace grew by the day and Lisa had been up and dressed and cooing over her baby. It didn't seem real that just days ago she had barely been able to cast an eye over her precious infant. All was right with the world.

Or so it seemed.

Underneath it all, Roger worried. Lisa had about her a fragility, a brittleness of spirit. Oh, she had carefully worked out stratagems in her mind for how she was going to get through each day, and what she would do if Joan called unexpectedly. Beneath the thin veneer of bravado, Roger knew in his heart that real damage had been done. It would take a lot more than a sticking plaster of a smile to put it all to rights.

Roger spent most of the walk thinking about the whole situation, wondering if he had said and done the right thing in letting Lisa set the tone of where they should go from here. Perhaps he should have insisted she seek someone who would give her proper counsel about what to do in such circumstances. Maybe he should have pressed her more when the idea about moving away had been raised. He just did not know.

He had been so engrossed in thought, so completely on automatic pilot, that he had completed the circuit he had mapped out for himself before he even realized. Grace, bless her little six-week old heart, had slept the entire way.

He found Gordon out on the footpath with a bucket of soapy water and a scrubbing brush in his hand, trying to remove graffiti that someone had sprayed all over his white picket fence.

Roger first choice would have been to creep past unnoticed but could think of no way to do it. He slowed. As soon as the pram cast a shadow over Gordon, the old man looked up.

Gordon remained kneeling on one knee, and waved the scrubbing brush angrily in mid air by way of greeting.

"Look what the bastards have done now," he growled. "You just can't have a thing these days."

"Sad but true," Roger said by way of sympathy. "When did it happen?"

"Young Sandra Fleming from across the road phoned to let me know just this morning. She noticed it while no doubt spying on activities in the street."

"How good of her."

Gordon seemed to catch something in Roger's tone, and gave him a sharp look.

"Yes, well, the world's full of nosey parkers. Always has been. What it hasn't always been full of up until now is mindless, willful and wanton destruction. Well, not down Maybury Place, at least."

Roger smiled. "Actually, if you want my opinion we've got a mixture of all three. I don't know about the destruction side of it, but we've certainly got the mindless, the willful and the wanton on the loose in the street."

Gordon guffawed. "You might have a point there." He turned his attention back to the graffiti. "Doesn't help get this travesty off my fence now, does it? This spray they use doesn't seem to want to come off for love nor money. Whoever invented the stuff should be hung, drawn and quartered in my opinion."

"I think there's a team with the local council whom you can call for advice on how to remove it," Roger said helpfully. "For all I know they come and do it for you."

"Council!" Gordon said with scorn. "Bunch of lazy good for nothings.

You pay your rates, but you don't actually seem to get value for money. And every time you turn around they're putting the cost up. How the average retired person is supposed to afford them on the pittance of a pension we get is beyond me."

"It might be worth phoning them anyway. Try to get your monies worth that way."

"S'pose." Gordon grasped one of the fence pickets and hauled himself into a standing position. He threw the scrubbing brush back into the bucket sending a plume of water over the rim then wiped his gnarled hands vigorously on his trouser legs.

He peered into the pram. "Little one's growing, then. How's your missus? Haven't seen her around for a bit."

"She's fine. These first few weeks have been a bit of a shock to the system for both of us, but especially for Lisa. It's harder work than it looks."

"Yeah. Hard to remember now, but I suppose those first couple of months are a bit of a bugger. Wasn't particularly involved, though. Not like you young chaps these days. Never changed a diaper, me, and never regretted it neither."

"I don't mind. In fact, I've been quite surprised by my capability. It's fine once you get the knack of it."

"I suppose that old busy-body from across the road has been over sticking her oar in?"

Roger felt his face grow stiff. "Who, Sandra or Joan?" he said with as little inflexion as he could manage.

Gordon grinned. "Yes, well, they are a bit alike. Meant Mrs. Davis, though. Who else?"

"Not really. She's been keeping herself to herself since...er...since the last Neighborhood Watch meeting."

"Not before time. It was a lesson she should have learnt years ago. Happy to teach it to her, I was."

"Yes, well, I think it's fair to say that she has definitely learnt the error of her ways."

"Good." Gordon scratched his head. "So that's the end of all these meetings, then?"

"I don't know. I hadn't really thought about it to be honest. Too much going on, I suppose. Things seemed to have settled down a bit, don't you think?"

At that very moment the peace was shattered, as not two, but three bikers turned into Maybury Place to roar down the road, and into the driveway at Number Seven. The noise startled Grace out of her slumber and she began to wail with fright.

"Settled down?" Gordon echoed with raised brows. "Doesn't much look like it to me."

Roger started pushing the pram backward and forward in an attempt to placate Grace. "It seems I was mistaken."

"And there's my graffiti as well," Gordon added. "More fuel to the fire."

"Yes, I suppose. Look, let me talk it over with Lisa. At this stage we need to reassess our situation, so I'll get back to you. Meanwhile, since Grace has clearly had enough, I'd better take her home and get her sorted out. See you later."

Gordon turned back to his fence with the minutest farewell wave.

As Roger neared the house he realized with a good deal of thankfulness that Lisa had already returned home. As he went to turn the pram into the driveway a very new dark blue sedan sailed almost noiselessly by, rounded the cul-de-sac smoothly and came to a halt outside of Joan's house. He wondered briefly who the visitor might be, but Grace's crying cranked up another notch or two. He could delay going inside no longer.

"I didn't really know what to say to him," Roger told Lisa later.

Grace had been pacified with a feed and now lay happily on the soft quilting of a baby mat that Roger's mother had bought. She had the play gym over the top of her, and stared at it with interest, although she had yet to learn to reach out for the creatures that looked down on her.

Roger had made tea and towed away the remnants of the shopping, and had brought a tray through to the lounge so they could watch Grace, hoping to see yet more of the smiles that she'd started to make.

Lisa, cradling her cup, sank back in her chair. "Well, I don't know either. This business with...this business has changed everything. I mean, we were organizing it together, but in reality she did most of it. Especially lately."

"Not that much to it, though, these Neighborhood Watch meetings? Just set a time and date, have a venue, and Bob's your uncle."

"Yes, but then you have people saying they can't make it, and you have to rearrange everything."

"I thought we'd settled on Wednesday nights as being the most suitable."

"We had."

"There you go then."

"There I go, what?"

"Not much to organize."

"There's supper."

"Biscuits. Out of a packet. Nobody would object."

"Sandra Fleming might. The Home Baking Queen."

"Let her bring supper, then, if she's so bothered."

"What about Grace?"

"She'll be asleep. She's into a great routine thanks to yours truly."

Lisa made a face. "My hero."

Roger held his hands up in defense. "I'm just saying. We don't have to do it at all. I could simply tell Gordon that we're not in a position to have any more involvement in the whole thing."

"It wouldn't be strictly true, though, would it?"

"So? It would be believable. Surely that counts for something."

"But as you said yourself, there still is a need to meet. Nothing has really been either resolved or decided upon."

"No. And I guess if I'm honest I wouldn't like to see us being the reason the whole thing collapses. I feel we should host at least one more meeting, even if it is just to say that we're resigning. It would then give the others a forum for deciding if they want to carry on without us."

Lisa considered this. "If we are staying I suppose one of us ought to be involved. After all, we want Grace growing up in a safe environment, don't we? I mean, neither of us would like to see the same thing happen to her as happened to Matthew."

"True. So, we are staying? Not having second thoughts?"

Lisa shook her head.

"Well, then. Any other objections?"

"Yes, one big one."

Roger's eyes a fraction. "Joan."

"Yes."

"She need not be invited."

"Won't everyone else think it strange?"

"Not really. Not after what happened at the last meeting."

Their conversation came to a halt as a sound came from the street. The sound of someone hammering. Roger got off his chair to have a look.

"No," he said. "Somehow I doubt whether anyone will object. Come and have a look at this."

Lisa joined Roger at the window, and looked out to see the surprising sight of a real estate agent putting up a "For Sale" sign outside of Number Three.

Joan, it seemed, was selling up and moving on.

205

CHAPTER TWELVE

The stereo system pumped out the classic hits of the seventies, eighties and nineties courtesy of the local radio station. The station had interspersed the music with ads for things as varied as varicose vein treatment to vehicle inspections, while the mildly crooning voice of the radio announcer tried to convince listeners about the wisdom of staying tuned.

This formed the accompaniment to the sound of blow driers and chatter, with the salon being as busy as Lisa had ever seen it. Glenda cut one lady's hair while simultaneously supervising a color of another. Karen blow-dried the hair of a matronly fifty year old while overseeing a perm on a pensioner.

Waiting for Karen to finish, Lisa let the whole cacophony wash over her, content with staring into space and thinking, like Roger often did, of nothing in particular.

At length Karen came and flopped down on the couch beside Lisa, sighing heavily as she did so.

"I'm buggered," she said, letting her head flop backward and her body go limp.

"So it would appear," Lisa said with a smile. "Why so busy?"

"I told you I was going to give Mirabelle her marching orders? Well, not only has she gone - without working out her notice - leaving Glenda and me completely in the lurch, but as a parting gesture she very kindly double booked us for three days solid. Revenge I suppose, for being given the old heave-ho, but infuriating nonetheless."

"Can't you try to put people off? Phone them and make another time?"

"We have where we could, but some people are less than impressed about being fobbed off. Others say it's all but impossible to make another time. And of course with no one to man the pumps on the front desk, we're trying to rearrange appointments and make new ones, do all the sweeping up, laundry, tea and coffee making, dishes and shampooing, in between everything else."

"You should have told me," Lisa chided. "I wouldn't have come. I wish I could help out in a more practical sense, but with Grace it's impossible. The least I could have done, though, is not come."

Karen shook her head. "I knew you were looking forward to it. I just didn't have the heart to do that to you. Not with you arranging for Roger's mum to baby-sit Grace."

"You don't think you were a bit hasty over the Mirabelle situation?"

"Certainly not. Good riddance. The expression on her face alone kept putting customers off. No, this is just a temporary hiccup. We survived yesterday. Once we get through today and tomorrow, things will calm down a bit. Then, as soon as we find a replacement for dearest Mirabelle we'll be home and hosed." Karen roused herself. "Come on then," she said, "let's get you shampooed."

Lisa trotted obediently after Karen, glad to give herself over to a bit of pampering. As the warm water cascaded over her scalp, Lisa said, "Do you think you'll have trouble finding someone else?"

Karen screwed up her nose. "Hard to say. It isn't exactly a glamour job, doing the sweeping up and stuff. It's second only to those young girls dentists employ to suction the spit when they make you keep your mouth open for too long. But there are always young people around interested in a career as a hairdresser. If you can con them into thinking of it as an entry-level position on the road to somewhere better, there are always takers. Occasionally someone even pops in on the off chance that there's a vacancy. Failing that we'll have to organize an advert in the local paper."

Karen turned off the taps and had Lisa sit up. She commenced patting the excess water off her hair with a towel.

"I even asked Maureen if she'd be interested, last time she was here," Karen said.

"Really? What did she say?"

"She said she thought she'd be useless."

"Poor Maureen. I know they sometimes talk about husbands being henpecked, but whatever the opposite is, then Maureen is it."

"Rooster pecked?" Karen suggested.

They both laughed as Karen led Lisa over to the chair, re-tucking the towel around her neck into the cape as Lisa got herself comfortable.

"Maybe you should ask her again," Lisa suggested.

"Who, Maureen?"

"Yes. After all, you are a bit desperate. You could appeal to her sense of duty, all hands to pumps in an emergency, and whatnot. It would be good for her."

Karen combed Lisa's wet locks thoughtfully. "I suppose I could. She can only say no. And we definitely need some help quickly."

"It would be great for her self esteem, to be wanted."

"Hmm. I've seen more self esteem in my kettle at home. Still, what if she is useless? It might make her feel worse."

"Could she really be any worse than Mirabelle?"

Karen laughed. "No. Decidedly no."

Lisa smiled. Changing the subject she said, "So, how's Geoff?"

A pious look crossed Karen's face. "I promised not to tell you. Remember?"

"Yes, but not telling me is supposed to be a punishment for you. The way things have turned out it's a punishment for me instead."

"Curiosity getting the better of you?"

"Yes, damn it. And stop preening like a cat. Just spit it out, will you?"

"There's nothing much to tell."

"Don't play coy with me."

Karen laughed again. "All right, all right. Actually, in all honesty, everything is going really well. Of course with us both having businesses to run there isn't a lot of time to wine and dine and moon about being romantic. Having said that, though, we practically see each other every day. We often seem to end up eating together at the end of the day. He's quite a good cook."

"You fiend. I bet you engineer him to cook as often as you can."

"Naturally. He cooks all sorts of things, makes great Italian dishes and is really knowledgeable about wine. Not just in that pretentious way either. In fact, this weekend we're going out to some winery he knows for lunch and wine tasting."

Lisa thought she would probably be lucky to get a stale sandwich and a lukewarm cup of tea. She couldn't help wondering why she and Roger had never been out to a vineyard wine tasting. They had unknowingly squandered their days before children came along.

"Sounds great," she said, hoping her voice did not betray her envy.

"He's a really good conversationalist," Karen continued. "He makes me think about all sorts of things I'd never really considered before. He challenges the way I think. It's as though I've never had an original thought in my mind up until now. I just accept the status quo without question."

"Sounds very highbrow. What will it be next? Reading Shakespeare?

Reciting Keats?"

"Oh, ha ha. Mock the poor uncultured one. Seriously, Lisa, he's really good for me. I feel like I'm seeing some things in life for the first time. He makes me feel good about myself."

"That's good to hear. What about from his point of view?"

Karen snipped happily at Lisa's hair. "Oh, I'm making him laugh, don't you worry. I suppose what I like best about the whole thing is the real honesty of it. He's so trustworthy, so dependable. There's no pretence at all. It's the first proper adult relationship I think I've ever been in."

"Blimey. That does sound serious."

"It is," Karen said her tone bordering on grave. "I've never been so serious about anything in my life."

Lisa caught Karen's free hand and squeezed it. "I'm really happy for you."

Karen squeezed her hand in return. "Thanks. You know, some days I feel so happy I could pop."

"Well, don't do that," Lisa said with a laugh. "A girl still needs her best friend."

"Right you are. Hey, interesting, isn't it, about you-know-who's house being on the market?"

"Joan's?"

"Of course."

Lisa said, "I nearly did a jig the day the 'For Sale' sign went up, but I've decided to wait until the 'Sold' sign goes up to really let my hair down. If it does."

"Yeah. Geoff said the housing market is a bit depressed at the moment. Wonder what she wants for it."

Lisa told her. "I saw it in the real estate agency window," she said by way of explanation.

"Does that seem a bit much to you?"

"Maybe. Let's hope she's negotiable, and that a willing buyer comes along."

"You'd be relieved."

"More than words can say."

"How long has it been on the market?"

"Three weeks, two days. Not that I'm counting, or anything."

"Obviously not. Is that long in selling terms?"

Lisa shrugged. "I don't think so. Someone told me the average selling period is eight weeks. Whether that's true or not, I don't know."

"Early days, then."

"Yes."

"You haven't seen her?"

"No, thank God. Every time there's a knock at the door I dread the thought that it might be her. So far, I've been lucky. Except if it turns out to be Sandra Fleming instead."

Karen made a face. "I don't know if it's my imagination, but is she getting worse?"

"Without a doubt. Roger says it's because she's caught the vibes, knows we find her annoying, and is trying to make up for that. Trouble is, all that syrupy effort is just making her more unbearable."

"You can say that again."

Karen put down her scissors and started pulling strands of hair down through her fingers on either side of Lisa's face, ensuring an even cut. Not satisfied, she picked the scissors up and made a few minor adjustments, then smiled with contentment.

"There," she said. "All done. Drying time."

Lisa sat and watched as Karen skillfully used blow drier and brush to complete the effect.

"Great," Lisa said as Karen finished. "Much tidier. I had begun to feel like nothing fit me any more, including my hair. Now I'm a new woman. Well, until I get back to reality, that is."

"Grace! I haven't even asked how she is?"

"Wonderful. Growing like a weed."

"Glad to hear it. Is she crawling yet?"

Lisa laughed. "You really haven't a clue, have you?"

Karen was nonplussed. "What? Half the animal world is ready to leave their parents by now. What's wrong with the girl?"

"Nothing that time won't fix. Lots more time."

"Oh."

"Speaking of time, you haven't forgotten about Neighborhood Watch tomorrow night, have you?"

Rolling her eyes, Karen took Lisa's credit card off her to process the transaction. "No. If I live that long, I'll be there. Geoff too."

"Excellent."

Karen handed back the card. "I wish you'd let me cut your hair for free like every other best friend."

"No," Lisa said firmly, slipping the card back into her purse. She eyed the growing crowd in the waiting area. "I'll let you get on with it. See you tomorrow night."

"If I live that long," Karen said again. "If I live that long."

Dinner had been three pork chops, a tower of mashed potatoes and some late broccoli out of his garden. Gordon had eaten it, as had become his habit, in front of the television, watching the six o'clock news and alternately heckling the presenters and gasping with indignation at the outrages perpetrated upon the modern world by its own sense of justice and injustice.

Now Gordon looked at himself in the mirror as he prepared to go to the meeting, running his hand through his hair as a token smoothing gesture. With a stab of nostalgia it made him think of Martha, how she'd spent thirty of their married years together trying to persuade his cowlick to behave itself, only to give it up in the end as a bad job.

There were times when he missed Martha so much that it hurt. She would not, he knew, have approved of the meals on his knee. On the other hand she would have been proud of him for managing his own cooking, expected the heckling, and would have been equally perturbed by the state of the world today.

And tonight, as he stood there smoothing down his hair in a vain attempt to make himself presentable, he knew with absolute certainty that Martha would have disapproved too of the grin on Gordon's face. Or more to the point, the reason for the grin being there in the first place.

He'd been out in his front yard that afternoon, tidying up the plants in the pebble garden, when he'd seen the flash car slide past. He'd seen it before, knew exactly where it was headed. He watched it pull up at the curb outside Number Three, watched as the young, money-hungry man eased himself out of the car, reaching back in to pull out a briefcase, then pressing some gizmo to alarm his car.

He'd balanced the briefcase on the bonnet of the car before clicking it open and reaching inside for something that turned out to be, to Gordon's immense joy and satisfaction, a "Sold" sticker, which he proceeded to plaster over the "For Sale" sign.

Joan Davis, it seemed, was on her way. Gordon could hardly wait to get to the meeting and gloat.

Geoff happened to be at his drawing board at the same time. He saw the agent arrive and attach the sticker on the sign, and then caught sight of Gordon lurking around the bushes. He couldn't read Gordon's expression from such a distance but Geoff didn't need binoculars to see the broad grin stretch across the old man's craggy features.

Geoff felt a moment's sorrow for the fact that Joan had practically been driven from the street, pushed out on a wave of public opinion. But Karen - an uncharacteristically reticent Karen - had said to him that there was far more to it all than met the eye, and that on balance she felt it to be a very good thing indeed.

Now, hours later, he found himself trapped in a meeting with the clients from hell, with a woman who had changed her mind about what she wanted from her new house almost a dozen times, mostly on the strength of what her various friends recommended. Her husband, sitting meekly beside her, looked as though he had spent his entire life trying to make his wife happy, without any particular success.

Geoff had to keep forcing himself to concentrate, but at the same time kept thinking of Karen. He hoped this meeting wasn't going to drag on so long that he would miss Neighborhood Watch.

Life, he concluded, was indeed very strange.

Maureen went to ease her feet out of her shoes, hoping they weren't permanently bonded there. She promised herself five minutes in which she would sit without moving, before she got up to make dinner and pretend to Brian that she had been doing nothing out of the ordinary all day.

This, however, would be a lie. A very big lie. For Maureen had spent the entire day at work, the first proper paid day of work she'd done in twenty-six years.

When Karen had come over the previous evening after Brian had departed for the pub - or wherever it was that he went these days - proposing that Maureen come and help her out of what sounded like a very big crisis, Maureen had naturally repeated her assertions that she would be useless. When Karen said that even useless would be better to her than no help at all Maureen had paused for a moment or two, given it serious consideration, and accepted.

After Karen had gone Maureen had decided against telling her husband

- whom she wouldn't see before the small hours of the morning anyway - knowing full well he would probably firstly mock her, and secondly forbid her from doing it. In consequence she resolved to keep the whole thing to herself. Including, she'd thought, any money she might earn.

Karen had picked her up at half past eight this morning and they had driven through the light rush hour traffic in near silence. Maureen did her best not to fidget with nerves. Karen, who said as much, looked as though she might still be half asleep.

In the end, though, Maureen loved the day. She loved being wanted and useful and meeting new people. As every hour progressed her courage grew, as did her skills. Although using the till or bankcard terminal remained beyond her she could make tea, do laundry, make new appointments and sweep the floor.

And, if Karen would have her, she would go back and do the same all over again tomorrow.

First though, there was dinner to cook, and a meeting to attend. She could only hope that she didn't fall asleep in the middle of either.

Lisa had called Roger straight away, breathless with euphoria.

"It's sold, it's sold," she sang down the line.

"What, pray tell?"

"Joan's house! The real estate agent came around about ten minutes ago. Sure enough, up went the 'Sold' sign. After only three weeks and three days!"

"Not that you were counting."

"Oh, no no."

"Wonder when settlement day is. I can't imagine she'll be moving out this weekend."

The euphoria evaporated. "I hope the sale isn't subject to all sorts of provisos and conditions."

Roger said, "I don't think they usually put up the 'Sold' sign unless it's sold unconditionally. Before that they just wait in case a better offer comes along."

"What about the settlement date?"

"Three, maybe four weeks away at the most? You never know, it might even be sooner if they're a cash buyer."

"Yippee."

Now, with Grace tucked up in bed for what would hopefully be the majority of the night, Roger and Lisa companionably washed and dried the dishes together before the neighbors arrived. Lisa hummed a little tune, happier than Roger had seen her in weeks.

She put the fry pan down, turned to Roger and said, "Do you think the other neighbors might find it a bit odd if I serve champagne tonight, instead of coffee?"

Matthew lay on his bed and stared at the ceiling. He'd got wind of the fact that his mother intended to go out tonight, maybe his father too, if he got home from work on time. Any moment now his Gran would arrive to baby-sit.

Matthew did not want his mother to go out. The street, which he had liked so well before Christmas, had proved to be an unsafe place. Mrs. Davis next door was mad, locked up inside for weeks at a time; Mr. Price was still very frightening; Mr. and Mrs. McLean had had the same thing happen to them as had happened in his own house after Rose was born, and went about looking like ghosts. He wasn't at all impressed with their baby. She looked all wrinkly and could do even less things than Rose.

Mrs. Haskell made him sad, although he couldn't say why. His mother had once taken him to a jumble sale at Mrs. Haskell's church, which she'd helped organize. Matthew thought that Mrs. Haskell and the jumble seemed to have quite a bit in common.

Then there was Karen. Matthew still liked her. She'd cut his hair only a couple of days ago in preparation for him starting school next week. She'd managed to give him his usual lollipop, but even she seemed different. He'd overheard his mother say to his father that she'd fallen in love. Matthew wondered if that explained why she wasn't quite so much fun. Matthew gathered she was interested in Mr. Milne, who, it must be said, did seem to smile a bit more these days. He wondered if they would get married. His friend Lucy, from kindy, had told Matthew last week that the two of them would get married. He wasn't too sure about this plan.

As far as the other residents of the street were concerned, Matthew could not even think of them without something black appearing in his head.

The more Matthew thought about it, the more he felt convinced that his mother should stay here, with him, like she was supposed to. He had to make her stay. He took a deep breath, held it for a couple of seconds then screamed with all his might.

Karen kept looking at the clock, wondering whether Geoff was going to make it back in time. She'd long since given up waiting for him to come over and cook her dinner and had made herself cheese on toast. She hadn't been paying attention to the first lot, which had burnt badly, but the second had at least been edible. Unfortunately the house still reeked of burnt toast.

She lay on the couch in her lounge, in front of the T.V with the remote control in one hand, and channel surfed, delaying going to the meeting as long as she could. If she had to go, she would much rather do so with Geoff.

As the hands of the clock eased past seven thirty, Karen decided she could delay the inevitable no longer. She hauled herself to her feet and went to find her shoes. Just as she slipped the second one on the doorbell rang. Opening the door she found, to her intense relief, Geoff standing outside in the dark. Wordlessly, she wrenched him inside, threw her arms around his neck, and, using her foot, slammed the door behind him.

"You pander to him," Ian said, as they walked across the street to the McLeans.

"I do not."

"Sandra, you do. You know you do."

"I really don't think that's true. If you're going to take that attitude I could just as easily argue that you're too hard on him. He's still only a little boy. A little boy, I might add, who went through a very traumatic experience lately."

"One that you're not doing anything to help him move on from. Giving in to him over everything and putting up with him being more of a baby than Rose is not what the boy needs."

"How do you know? And why does it have to be up to me anyway? You're just as much his parent as I am."

"But you're the mother and, as you endlessly tell me, the mother's role is the most important. Surely if that's the case, it's up to you to sort it out."

They paused by the McLean's mailbox.

"Well, what do you think I'm doing?"

Ian looked at her fixedly. "I think," he said, his tone definite, "I think you are making things worse."

"I am not!"

"You are. If you ask me, that's the only thing you appear to be good at these days."

It seemed to Lisa that something strange hung in the air, that things unknown - a strange and unexplained phenomenon - had affected everyone in the street.

Looking around the room at the assortment of characters assembled there, she couldn't help but wonder at the oddness of life and how things could change in such a small period of time. Mere weeks ago most of them had barely been on a first name basis.

Now Gordon and Maureen sat talking together like they were old friends, Maureen regaling him with what looked like the confessions of a hairdresser's assistant. Gordon himself looked on top of the world. He had the air of a man who had just won the lottery. Lisa, for one, knew exactly how he felt.

Sandra and Ian were doing their level best to avoid looking, touching or communicating with each other in any way, shape or form. Clearly there were things amiss in the Fleming household. Lisa found it very intriguing.

Ian talked at Roger, expounding with gusto his negative opinion of a computer software program that Tempo was considering purchasing. Roger had difficulty getting a word in edgeways.

Geoff and Karen had arrived at the meeting fashionably late, breathless and almost giggling. Almost. Lisa felt sure giggling lay beyond Geoff's capabilities. It had made Lisa smile though, seeing her friend so happy. They were doing their utmost to be civil to Sandra as she told them about Matthew starting school next week, but their minds were clearly on other things.

At length Lisa managed to catch Roger's eye, indicating they should get things under way.

After a bit of polite coughing, Roger said, "Well, folks, thanks for coming. I know we've all got busy lives, so we appreciate you making an effort to be here."

He looked around at everyone, and drew a breath then said, "Of course, as many of you will already know, we have lost one of our number. We believe that Joan has sold her house, and will move from Maybury Place shortly."

"In three weeks," Sandra piped up.

"Oh?"

"Yes, I saw her today. I arrived home as the real estate agent departed."

"Well, then," Roger said. "Three weeks. Of course, Joan was one of the driving forces behind the establishment of this group. It seems only right that we take stock at this point, of where we are at and where, if anywhere, we want to go from here."

"You're suggesting disbanding the group?" Geoff asked.

Roger shook his head. "Not as such. I just feel we need to re-evaluate where we're at. Do we want to continue? In what capacity? How often should we meet? Who should replace Joan as coordinator if we do continue? What, if anything, should we do about the situation at Number Seven? These are all things we need to decide as a group."

"I agree," Ian said. "It's senseless meeting just for the hell of it. As Roger said, most of us have busy lives."

"Yes, but you have to get your priorities right," Sandra countered. "The whole point of the group in the first place was to improve safety in the street. In my opinion I don't feel we have fulfilled that objective."

Ian frowned, displeased at having had his say publicly dismissed by his wife.

"That's all very well," he said, "but it's not as if we've actually achieved anything yet, is it?"

Sandra opened her mouth to argue back when Roger jumped in and said, "Perhaps, like any democratic group, we ought to put it to a vote? Get the general consensus? If the majority of you feel we ought to pack it in then we can all go home and get on with our lives. If not, then we can move on to the wider issues. In summary, do you feel safe in this street? Is there anything to be gained by meeting together?"

"Things aren't the same as they used to be," Gordon said. "In my opinion you've got to be prepared to fight for your rights. If you start letting yourself get pushed around, it's the thin edge of the wedge. I mean, what would have happened if we'd gone along with Hitler and all his nonsense?"

Roger suppressed a smirk. "Man the trenches, eh, Gordon?"

"Too right. I don't want to live in a street with a whole pile of loose women running around even if it isn't against the law, or be the victim of young hoodlums. It took me ages to get rid of that damned graffiti."

"Not to mention the dog poop," giggled Karen, who could never resist bringing that up.

"Yeah, that 'n all."

"So, who's with Gordon?" Roger asked. "A show of hands?"

Gordon, Maureen, Lisa, Sandra, Roger and Karen put their hands straight up. Geoff followed suit with decided reluctance.

Roger looked at Ian.

"Okay," he conceded. "Count me in too. Just as long as this isn't going to be a waste of time."

"I would have thought you'd be a definite, Ian," Maureen said. "After what happened to Matthew."

Ian shot a cryptic look at Sandra, but said, "You have to know when to move on. It's senseless to bash your head against a brick wall."

"Right," Roger said, largely ignoring this comment. "We've decided. Neighborhood Watch will continue for now. The next question would have to be what we want to get out of it. Suggestions?"

"The removal of those people from Number Seven," Gordon said. "There's been nothing but trouble from the moment they moved in."

"There's no harm in talking about other security matters, though," Maureen said. "We don't want to get too focused on one issue."

"Don't we?" Sandra said. "I agree with Gordon. We should keep meeting until that situation has been resolved, then decide what to do."

"And how do you propose we 'resolve' the situation," Geoff asked. "You're not suggesting more vigilante techniques, are you?"

"No," Sandra sniffed. "I can't see anything wrong with sticking to our original plan of tracking down the landlord, or landlords. Whoever's hiding behind the skirts of this GEM Trust."

"With the view of doing what?"

"Appealing to them to evict their tenants. Surely it shouldn't be too difficult to convince them. After all, what's going on over there is not at all suitable for a suburban area."

"Do you think a landlord would care?" Geoff asked. "The owners aren't the moral police, are they? In my experience they're much more concerned with the basics. Like being paid the rent on time and whether the tenants are taking care of the place or not."

"Well, there'd surely be no problem with them paying the rent," Karen said. "With the amount of customers those two seem to have, they'd be making a bloody fortune."

Everyone laughed.

Roger was just about to get the meeting back on track when a commanding knock came from the front door.

"Wonder who that could be?" Roger said.

Lisa felt herself go cold. She only hoped it wasn't Joan. Roger looked at Lisa as though he would like he to go and answer the door while he continued to chair the meeting. When he saw what was going through her mind he made excuses and went to do the job himself.

He walked down the hall, opened the door, and was stunned to find himself looking not at Joan, but at the angry face and startling cleavage of Trixie Bartlett.

"I want a word with you lot," she said, and without waiting for an invitation she pushed Roger aside and marched past him.

She looked, Lisa thought, rather like Medusa, with her long blonde hair flying around her head like out-of-control snakes, her eyes penetrating, her gaze filled with animosity. The effect she had on the small group was also very Medusa-like. Every occupant in the room had taken on the form of a statue, as though by looking at her face they had been turned into stone.

All they needed now was rescuing by Perseus. Roger, lurking in the hall behind Trixie and holding his hands out in defeat to Lisa, clearly wasn't going to be the hero of the hour.

Trixie stood at the centre of their attention, her eyes traveling around to look at each of them in turn. She appeared to be studying them as one would a strange science exhibit - with a mixture of fascination, curiosity and most of all repulsion.

"What a sorry bunch of losers," she said scathingly. "Look at you all sitting here in your sanctimonious little gathering, thinking you're better than everyone else. Oh yes, don't think we don't see you all creeping across the street to meet together and whisper about us. Don't think we don't know how you look down on us. You're pathetic, each and every one of you."

"Now hold on a minute," Ian said, springing to his feet. "Who do you think you are, barging in here like this?"

Trixie turned on him, giving him a look so quelling that he sank back down into his chair.

"I'll tell you who I am, you little weasel. I'm someone who deserves a bit of respect. I've had about all I can take of your condescending looks and disapproving faces. I've never known such a poisonous bunch of small minded bigots in all of my life."

"Don't know why you're yelling at us, lady," Gordon said, his face suffused with scarlet. "If anyone should be telling anyone off, it's us. Don't know how you could have the gall to show your face in the house of these nice people, making all kinds of accusations, when it's you in the wrong and not us. People like you and that other one you live with don't deserve respect."

"How dare you?" Trixie bellowed. "Of course we deserve respect."

Gordon kept his chin up under the onslaught. "There's nothing respectable about what you two do," he said. "In fact, it's downright shameful."

Trixie stood for a moment or two and just stared at Gordon, trying to make sense of what his comments.

"You don't know anything about us," she said at length, her voice calmer now. Somehow it wasn't a comforting sign.

"I think we know enough," Karen chimed in.

Trixie's eyes narrowed. "Oh, you do, do you? Based on what, may I ask? Based on the only two conversations we've had with any of you since we moved into the street? With you," she said, pointing accusingly at Ian, "and with that other busybody who seems to have come to her senses and be getting out of this hell-hole. Both conversations, I might add, very brief and on the day we moved in."

"Sometimes first impressions are all that's needed," Ian said.

Trixie shook her head. "You people really don't have a clue, do you? You think of nobody but yourselves, do you? I don't suppose it ever occurred to you that we might have had our own set of problems to deal with on that day. That we were not as you would normally find us. That, what with moving in and everything else we were coping with, it might not actually be the best time for us to be chatting with everyone who came knocking on the door. No. Of course not. You just made your judgment, and that was that."

"Oh, come on," Sandra said. "It wasn't as if you displayed any consideration for us. If it hadn't been for Thomas locking my Matthew in the shed, none of us would've gone near you."

"That is an unfounded allegation," Trixie snapped.

"Being unfounded doesn't make it any less true," Ian snapped back. "I think no one is in any doubt about the culprit. And whatever you say, there can be no justification for the boy to have acted the way he did by locking up a defenseless pre-schooler."

"Who, as it happens, wasn't being properly supervised," Trixie said with a sneer. "Nevertheless, there were mitigating circumstances, whether you choose to believe that or not."

"As I said, nothing could justify that sort of behavior. Unless of course you take into consideration the kind of example the boy is set to follow."

Again Trixie stood there, her eyes fixed on Ian, as though she was having problems comprehending what he'd just said.

"How dare you cast aspersions on Penny's parenting skills? You wouldn't know the first thing about how she raises her son."

Gordon snorted, causing her to look at him. "We know enough to see that she's happy to let her son be brought up in a house of ill repute."

"I beg your pardon?"

"No need to beg," Ian answered smoothly. "Although I'm sure it's probably an occupational hazard."

Trixie swung back around to look at Ian, her gaze cold with dislike. "Are you implying what I think you're implying?"

"Well, you hardly need to be a rocket scientist to figure it out," he said. "Yes, we know all about what you and your little friend Penny get up to, and you ought to be ashamed of yourselves. Sure we might meet together to talk about you, but what else are we supposed to do? None of us sitting here tonight wants to live in the same street as a brothel."

"A brothel?" Trixie choked. She laughed, but there was no humor in the sound. "You think Penny and I are running a brothel?"

"Of course you are," Gordon said. "We've seen all those men coming and going all hours of the day and night."

Trixie shook her head. She put her hands on her hips the way a mother might when surveying her recalcitrant children. She shook her head with disbelief as she eyed each one of them.

"You really are the most despicable, shallow, petty, foul-minded bunch of people I have ever encountered. You go on and on about the truth, but the reality is that none of you would know the truth if it bit you on the backside. How low can you get - thinking a neighbor to be a prostitute. You're disgusting."

"Are you saying you aren't sex workers, then?" Karen asked.

"Sex workers?" Trixie made that same humorless laugh. "Don't be ridiculous. Unless of course, that's what you call yourself. After all, I do the very same job you do."

"What?"

"That's right, Miss Know-it-All. I'm a hairdresser. In fact I used to work with your mate Glenda, back in the early nineties. These days I work for myself. At home. With solely male clients. Who come to my home. By appointment."

Lisa looked at Roger, who shrugged, not knowing what to make of it. Others in the room similarly cast their eyes about looking for confirmation as to the veracity of these claims.

"Ask her," Trixie challenged. "You ask Glenda. She'll tell you."

No one said a word. Lisa thought you could probably hear the proverbial pin drop.

"Yes, I hope you are all sitting there ashamed of yourselves," Trixie said. "And, I'll tell you the rest of the story for good measure since I know you're dying to find out. I'm tempted, of course, to let you stew in your own curiosity. But it's only fair that I set the record straight for Penny too, since she's not here to defend herself against such repulsive slander.

"My friend is hiding out from her husband, who, as it turns out, is a real psycho. He's jealous, paranoid and violent, and is just rich enough to think that he should be able to control the poor woman's entire life. She's here, in hiding, fearing for her very life, so it's little wonder that she doesn't feel up to being sociable. In my opinion - and I've told her so many times - she's mad to even put her nose outside of the door. But, life has to go on. It's hardly practical to keep Thomas locked up day and night. The boy has to go to school after all."

"I suppose that's meant to justify his behavior?" Ian asked.

Trixie flashed a look of pure scorn at him. "I hardly expect to you to understand but the poor boy is traumatized, a situation not improved by the hostility we've experienced in this street."

"And that's why the police keep calling around?" Roger asked. "Because of Penny's husband?"

Trixie nodded curtly. "There have been plenty of incidents. Threatening mail. Visits to Thomas at school. Restraining orders mean nothing to the likes of Bruce White. He's mad enough and wealthy enough to think he can have whatever he wants." She straightened. "Anyway, you'll be able to stop your ridiculous meetings now, because, like it or not, we're leaving. We're giving notice tomorrow. It's no longer safe for us to stay here. But even if that wasn't the case, I can think of no place on earth I would rather live less. I don't know how you people live with yourselves. You give the word 'neighbor' a bad name. I hope I never have the misfortune to see any of your sorry faces again."

And with that, she was gone.

"I'm not quite sure," Roger said later, when only Karen and Geoff remained, "just how we managed to be so mistaken about the situation."

"I think it's called jumping to the wrong conclusions," Geoff said.

"At least you haven't got anything to feel bad about," Lisa said. "If anyone deserves to say, 'I told you so,' it's you."

"It would give me absolutely no satisfaction," he replied grimly. "Besides, my point remains: everyone is entitled to their privacy. I wasn't defending them one way or another."

"Still."

Roger switched his attention to Karen. "So, what did Glenda say about Trixie?"

She shrugged. "Fun. Good to work with. Good to party with. Basically a pretty good hairdresser."

"And she never clicked when you told her about the Trixie giving everyone problems in our street?"

Avoiding his gaze, she admitted, "Well, actually, I never got around to mentioning her. Naturally I told her we'd started up these meetings, but I never went into much detail." She glanced at Geoff. "I guess I had my mind on other things."

"It probably wouldn't have made any difference anyway," Roger said. "There'd be no reason for her to connect the two people, even if you had've told her."

Karen didn't seem particularly comforted by this sentiment. "But it might have. After all, Trixie isn't a common name, is it? Perhaps it might have saved a lot of bother if I had said something."

Lisa laughed. "Well, that would be a first. It's usually speaking out that gets you into trouble. It would be pretty ironic if, for once, the reverse turned out to be the case."

Karen smiled half-heartedly.

"There doesn't seem to be much point in over-analyzing the situation," Geoff said, draining the last of his coffee. "It's all too late now. Pointless considering the 'what-ifs'."

Roger smirked. "What? And spoil women's third favorite pass-time?"

Geoff looked confused. "Oh? They have three? What are the first two?"

"Shopping first, followed closely by worrying. Third is considering the 'what if' scenario, and fourth, without a doubt, is gossiping."

Roger ducked as a fusillade of cushions and criticism rained down on him.

"You sexist pig," Karen told him.

"I quite agree," said Lisa. "Let's just consider men's top four favorite pass-times for a moment, shall we?"

"Like...leaving wet towels and stinky socks lying around the house."

"Hogging the remote control," added Lisa.

"Avoiding housework."

"Yeah, that's a good one. And lastly, talking about sport. Endlessly."

"I don't talk about sport," Geoff said.

"It's true," Karen agreed. "He doesn't."

"I don't much, either," Roger said.

"No," Lisa said. "Perhaps it was a bad example."

"Time for the 'what if' scenario now," Roger said conspiratorially to Geoff. "They'll need to consider which wisecrack comment they could have used instead."

"Oh, shut up," Lisa said, elbowing him.

There was a moment's lull in conversation before Karen said, "Well, I suppose the up side of tonight's fiasco of a meeting is that it will probably be our last. I can't see that anyone will be particularly keen to meet together once Trixie and Penny move out."

Roger said, "No, I suppose not."

"Don't you dare suggest arranging another meeting to find out for sure if that's what everyone wants," Lisa warned.

He shook his head. "Don't worry. Such a thought never entered my head."

"In fact, when they move out, and Joan goes too, the whole street might settle down again," Karen said.

"And not a moment too soon in my opinion," Roger added.

"I wonder what the new neighbors will be like," Lisa wondered.

"Somehow," Roger said, "I don't think anyone will be in too much of a hurry to find out."

Lisa, out walking with Grace in the pram, found herself thinking yet again about the mysteriousness of life. How the seemingly insignificant could turn out to be of vital importance; how appearances could indeed be very deceptive; and how the painful moments in a person's life made a person grow and develop the most.

Just why was that?

Or how the littlest thing could set a person off down a road they'd never intended going, while the littlest thing could turn a person back. How it could be easier to say something hurtful than to say something nice, but how one tiny thing said with encouragement could make such a positive difference in a person's life.

Such paradoxes made Lisa wonder.

In some ways Lisa wished for a simpler life, for visible signposts along the way to help a person know which way to go for the best, but then, she supposed, that would take away the gift of freedom of choice. Making decisions could be so difficult, but yet there was something intensely human in being able to choose. She could not imagine life without it.

Lisa had begun to reach the conclusion that the truly good and worthwhile things in life didn't necessarily come easily, that the things she valued most all came with some sort of price. A price she was, in the main, more than ready to pay. A person couldn't love and live without making some sort of sacrifice.

She thought about her mother's arrival tomorrow and could hardly wait to see her. It had been a long convalescence for her father, but now he was at least well enough to fend for himself for a week. Their neighbor would be keeping an eye on him. Lisa knew full well that her mother would have stocked the freezer up with everything labeled, so that her dad would have no problem knowing what to do with everything.

Lisa had missed her mother. The last ten weeks had been so full of bittersweet moments that she had longed to share with her. Naturally, Lisa had told her mother about what had occurred in the street, and more particularly, what had happened between herself and Joan. But talking on the telephone was not the same as talking face to face. In Lisa's opinion, there were still things to be said.

The fact that Joan still lived in the street troubled Lisa. She did not want there to be any risk of confrontation between Joan and her mother, for Lisa was sure her mother would not hesitate in giving Joan a piece of her mind. Surely, though, there would only be an overlap of a couple of days, since the three weeks Sandra had mentioned were up two days ago. There'd already been time enough for Penny and Trixie to have moved on, and for the house at Number Seven to be empty once more.

Lisa's thoughts had so engrossed her that she turned into Maybury Place without even glancing up. When she did look up in order to cross the road she saw, to her great surprise, a removal van sitting outside Number Three. The very same removal men that had moved Trixie and Penny were now toting Joan's possessions out from the house and stowing them in the van.

Joan stood on the footpath, supervising every move they made. The sight of her made Lisa freeze on the spot.

She saw Joan look around. The older woman hesitated, just for a moment. At the same moment Lisa perceived her chance to flee. It was now or never. If she went now Joan would be rebuffed.

But Lisa did not move. She stood stock-still, unable to move so much as a muscle. Her mind told her to run. Her body seemed unable to obey.

Lisa had thought a lot about what she would do and what she would say if Joan ever came knocking on the door. How she would tell Joan just exactly what she thought of her. Now, with Joan having crossed the road to stand right in front of her, those words did not come. Indeed, it surprised her to find that the anger had gone. She found, looking at Joan's pathetic old face, that what had come in its place was pity.

"Hello, Lisa," Joan said, her voice barely audible.

Lisa continued to stare.

"I'm sure you aren't at all pleased to see me," Joan said. "I understand that. I know I made a mistake. Well," she added, removing some invisible speck from her shirt in order to avoid Lisa's gaze, "more than one mistake, really. I'm pleased to see you though. I hoped we might have an opportunity to speak."

"I can't imagine what there is to say."

"Can't you? I would have thought there was a lot to say. On both sides." She straightened. "Now is not the time, though. I know that, if nothing else."

"What makes you think I'd be interested in anything you have to say?"

"I…I don't think that at all. Not at the moment. But things might change. You might…find you change your mind down the track. I wanted to give you my new address in case you do start to feel differently about things."

Lisa stiffened as Joan offered her a piece of paper, upon which she had written her new contact details.

"The thing is," Lisa said carefully, "I don't think I'd ever be able to trust a single word you said. There would be little point in talking to someone you don't trust, even if I was interested. Which I am not."

"But that's behind us now. Everything is out in the open. There would be no reason to lie."

"Really? I doubt that somehow. Being creative with the truth is still lying, whichever way you look at it. You've had quite a bit of practice, perhaps too much to even be able to recognize the truth."

Joan said nothing, simply offered the piece of paper to Lisa again. It hung between them like a challenge.

One piece of paper.

And yet it represented so much more. To take it implied so much more.

In spite of herself, Lisa found herself reaching out for it. She found she had no taste for cruelty or revenge.

Joan nodded her approval, but her expression was far from triumphant.

"I'll say goodbye then. You'll forgive me, I pray, if I say I hope we meet again."

Lisa watched Joan stride away, to continue supervising the removal of her possessions, then looked down at the piece of paper. Common sense said she should screw it up and throw it on the ground.

Instead, she folded it and put it in her pocket.

Karen let herself out of the front door, pausing only to lock it behind her. Darkness had descended and a wintery damp hung heavy in the air. She pulled her coat around her, glad of its warmth. Although it wasn't ever likely to snow, it was cold enough to avoid lingering outside.

She crossed Maybury Place and headed for Geoff's. Lights shone both upstairs and downstairs where half an hour before there had been only blackness. She knew he had returned home. She wondered if he would be ready.

He was not. He answered the door dressed in his thick white bathrobe, and it was clear he had recently showered.

"Sorry," he said, with a lopsided smile. He ushered her in, and kissed her briefly.

"Not that dreadful woman again?" Karen asked.

"I'm afraid so. She's the client from hell. I wish I'd never laid eyes on her."

"But think of the commission."

"I do. The trouble is, what's the point of earning a big fat check, if afterward you're so worn out you haven't got the energy to spend it."

"Don't worry," Karen said, her smile broad. "I'll help you."

Geoff made a wry expression. "Yes, I'm sure you would. Meanwhile, I had better get dressed if we're to make it in time for our dinner reservation. Make yourself at home."

"Oh, I will."

Karen went into the lounge. The massive room stretched the length of the house. It incorporated, in open plan style, both the kitchen and dining area and overlooked the rear garden.

The room had a masculine feel to it, dominated by wood: wooden floors, wooden inlaid ceiling, wooden joinery around the windows and the French doors, the latter opening out onto a deck. A large Turkish rug softened the wooden floors, wooden bookcases were crammed with mainly academic tomes, and the tan colored couches were comfortable and inviting. Karen took off her coat and flopped down.

Along one wall of the lounge sat a dresser, upon which Geoff had arranged a collection of interesting items: a pottery vase with American Indian patterns, a pot plant, some sort of Polynesian bowl with accompanying implements, and an indescribable sculpture made from bone. On one end of the dresser Geoff had hastily shoved his mail, as yet unopened and evidently collected from his post office box on the way home from his meeting with the client from hell.

In spite of needing a feminine touch the room had a warm ambience. The gas fire that Geoff had started when he'd returned further enhanced this warmth. In front of the couch where Karen lounged, sat a wooden coffee table bearing a stack of house and garden magazines. While she waited Karen picked one of them up, flicking through it without actually looking.

She did not have to wait long.

"Sorry about that," Geoff said again as he entered the room. He flopped down on the couch opposite her.

"Forget it. It's not as though we're in that big a hurry, even if we have got a booking. I don't think the restaurant will cancel it yet."

"Good day?"

"Not bad. I'm always pleased when Friday is over and done with, even if I am working tomorrow morning. You? Apart from your last meeting, that is."

"Same. Not too bad. Well, actually, there was one interesting thing."

"Oh?"

"Yes. I met the new neighbors today."

"The ones in Joan's old place?"

Geoff nodded. "Well, it isn't likely to be the new residents from Number Seven since that's still empty, is it?"

"Don't tease me, Geoff. What were they like?"

"Nice. He's called Robert, and she's Linda. He was home supervising some workmen, and they were both in the garden when I went to go out to my meeting. He's a bank manager, and she's a nurse. They sound quiet, and busy, and thoroughly untroublesome."

"Thank God."

"I said I felt terrible that they'd been there three weeks and I hadn't managed to get over to say hello, but they didn't seem too put out. I think, like me, they prefer to keep themselves to themselves."

"The perfect neighbors."

"Maybe. Bit soon to tell, wouldn't you say?"

"I'd say that I've decided to never have an opinion about another neighbor again, as long as I live," Karen said with feeling. "Except, perhaps, for you."

Geoff returned her smile. "Good," he said. "I'd be upset if you didn't have an opinion of me by now."

Karen's eyebrows rose. "Oh, I do. Don't you worry about that."

Geoff smiled, went to look at his watch, only to find it wasn't there.

"Damn," he said. "Must have left it upstairs. Won't be a minute."

Karen stood up too, picking up her coat, and throwing it around her shoulders. As she did so, the bottom of it caught the edge of the dresser, sending Geoff's mail cascading to the floor. She stooped to pick it up, stacking it back into a pile, not thinking much of it until one envelope caught her eye. Her hand froze on it, and then, as if to make sure she had read it right, she raised it slowly up to get a closer look, standing back up as she did so.

What she read made her suck in her breath. There must be some sort of mistake. But, no, there it was, as plain as day. A letter addressed to GEM Trust, same post office box number as the rest of Geoff's mail.

Suddenly, realization dawned. Geoffrey Elliott Milne. GEM. She'd heard it from the horse's mouth herself. There could be no doubt. All that time, Geoff had been the owner of Number Seven, and had never said a word. Not even to her.

She looked up when he entered the room, the smile dying from his face as he read her expression and perceived what she had discovered.

"Ah," he said, with slow deliberation. "I can explain about that."

Want to find out more about Maybury Place?
Sign up for Keitha's newsletter and receive exclusive
Behind the Scenes bonus content

www.keithasmith.co.nz

And, if you have enjoyed this book,
please consider leaving a review at Amazon.com
It would be most appreciated.